JENNIFER DAWSON was ▓▓▓▓▓▓▓▓▓▓ South London. She has publi▓▓▓▓▓▓▓▓▓▓ *Ha-Ha*, described by Susan H▓▓▓▓▓▓▓▓ unusual, so original, so accomplished ... quite simply, a perfect novel', was published in 1961, winning the James Tait Black Memorial Award. It was produced on television as well as on the Edinburgh and London stages by director Richard Eyre, and broadcast several times on BBC radio. She went on to publish six further novels, *Fowler's Snare* (1963), winner of the Cheltenham Festival Award; *The Cold Country* (1965); *Strawberry Boy* (1976); *A Field of Scarlet Poppies* (1979); *The Upstairs People* (1988); *Judasland* (1989); and a collection of short stories, *Hospital Wedding* (1978).

Jennifer Dawson has worked variously as a teacher, sub-editor and on two encyclopaedias and a dictionary. Her spell as a social worker in a huge mental hospital in the late fifties gave her the background to much of her fiction. She now lives near Oxford with her husband. Her new novel, *Troy Wharf*, will be published in 1991.

JENNIFER DAWSON

The
Upstairs People

VIRAGO

Published by VIRAGO PRESS Limited 1990
20–23 Mandela Street, Camden Town, London NW1 0HQ

First published by Virago Press Limited 1988

Copyright © Jennifer Dawson 1988

All rights reserved

*A CIP catalogue record for this book
is available from the British Library*

Typeset by Goodfellow & Egan Ltd of Cambridge
Printed in Great Britain by Cox & Wyman Ltd, Reading, Berkshire

Chapter I

Ransome Street ran off Ransome's Fields at a right angle, and when we asked Cossey, our mother, what 'Ransome' meant, she laughed and said: 'Something like this,' and jumped up and down violently on the bed and laughed and bounced more. Our mother loved violent motion. She said her parents had never given her any love when she was a child, and when a fair came to Ransome's Fields, she was always first on the Big Dipper and the Chairoplanes, and was tipped upside down laughing. She had a taste for it and was never sick as we children were. We had called her 'Cossey' at first just to annoy her. We had seen the name printed on the label of a bottle of lemonade at a picnic: 'Cossey's Lemonade' it was called, and we called her that just to annoy her and then got so annoyed when it didn't annoy her, and begged her to tell us another story about when she was a child.

She would look out of our sitting-room window and down over Ransome's Fields and take a deep breath and cry: 'The Great War was so awful. If ever there were another war . . .'

'What would we do?' we asked in a terrible whisper.

This was in 1936 when Franco's revolt had just started in Spain, and our parents would whisper as we three children sat in the deep armchair by the fire watching its embers glow and fade. I saw even then that there was something funny about our mother, as we looked out over Ransome's Fields and she called again: 'If ever there were another war . . .', then gave that pause she was so good at giving.

'The Fields', as everyone in Lambeth called them, were full of old houses, three or four storeys high, with great views over central London that we longed to see. We envied the people who lived over there. One was a girl at school and we would run up to her flat to see how Big Ben was doing and to have a drink of cold water from her tap because ours was always stuck or tepid.

We'd drink and then we'd stop to gaze out again over the busy river to central London and the Houses of Parliament and Big Ben. On Saturdays, I would walk along the Embankment with my mother for my music lesson in Battersea, and afterwards Cossey would sing, 'Oh I Had a Friend who Left Me' to the tune of whatever I had been learning that week, and we would come home and sit down together at the piano and play it as a duet, and it seemed that it was over there, across Ransome's Fields and away in central London that Cossey's 'friend' had gone.

'If ever there were another war,' she would gaze out over the street side of our flat.

'You're playing that in a terribly bloaty kind of way,' she would interrupt her thoughts, 'and you've forgotten the C sharp. "Oh I Had a Friend Who Left Me . . ." If ever there were another war . . .'

Ransome's Fields were ours, but we called Ransome Street Cossey's because when she looked out at its crumbling old houses she was reminded of her childhood and the Great War. The ships' hooters sounded endlessly on the river on foggy mornings and at nights, waiting to get into the docks, and the air reeked of cough mixture and lung tonic, and Cossey could really only play the church music she had learned in the Mission Chapel as a child, so that our duets always sounded melancholy, and I wondered who her friend had been, or whether he had been killed in the Great War, as we gazed out at the strings of lighters loaded with coke and coal and sawn, yellow timber and cement and refuse that smelt of sour tea-leaves. Once, as we walked back from the music lesson singing, 'Oh I Had a Friend Who Left Me', a barge with a red-brown sail came keeling over towards us thrashing its canvasses angrily.

'Oh dear,' said Cossey, 'you frightened us.'

'What would you do if there were another war?' I asked. Cossey had told us so often about the Great War.

There was a great black warehouse opposite us in Ransome Street and we could hear the horses come clattering out on cold frosty mornings, and over the cobbles, their masters roaring and they snorting. The worst moment was when they turned corners. The sound came so suddenly that in school the teacher would stop speaking till the dray had rumbled away, and Cossey would have to raise her voice at nights as we sat round the fire in the sitting room of our flat. She had started a story about the Great War, but then decided that she'd have to go right back to 1904 first, so that we could get the feel of the cold, angry and loveless world she had lived in and how she had raged against it.

'I was six,' she said, 'and Christmas Day began badly. I could hear the marble clock downstairs chime six and poked my toes to the bottom of the bed to see what my parents had put there. I wanted something hard and shiny. A watch, only my father couldn't afford that. Or a book. But the parcel on my toes was soft, and I sat up and tore a hole in the wrapping paper. I went into my younger brother's room though this was strictly forbidden. Only yesterday I had gone into his room and seen him naked. It was only because it was Christmas Eve that I had not been sent to bed in disgrace.

'I knocked at his door on Christmas morning. He was sitting up in bed with a farm set. My parcel was a petticoat. That was that. I almost wept.

'"You can play with my farm sometimes," he said nicely. He always behaved nicely even when I pinched him for being my mother's favourite, or whispered: "Little King," and twisted the short hairs at the nape of his neck. But as I stared at my yellow flannel petticoat on Christmas morning I was too upset to tease him. He tried to be nice about my petticoat but he was dying to play with his farm animals.

'"Let's go out and see what everything looks like." I always felt that the world ought to look different on Christmas Day.

'"Do you know *why* the world is so evil?" It was a subject my father, who was a clergyman, was always discussing.

'"Let's pretend we live there," I said to my brother as we walked past some big houses. "My house is that one with the green curtains. And I've got ten children and we go to St Andrew's Church." We were not supposed to speak to people who went to St Andrew's Church. "Papists," my father cried when I was once invited to tea with a girl who went there. He had refused to let me go, but I sneaked into her church once and it had candlesticks on a red altar and coloured statues of the saints round the walls and a smell of incense. I thought how bright and cheerful it was. "*That's* the church I'm going to when I grow up. And I'm going to be a doctor."

'"Girls can't be doctors, can they Mother?" he asked that Christmas Day.

'"Of course not, dear. Not nice women," our mother replied. I resolved to give my brother six quick pinches, but Christmas dinner was ready — steaming hot goose with apple sauce and a Christmas tree in the corner hung with chocolate camels. I hummed happily over my food.

'"Father," I asked, "what does 'abhor' mean?"

'"It means 'despise' Freda," my father answered cheerfully.

'"And what does 'Virgin' mean?"

'He answered more reluctantly: "It means an unmarried lady."

'"And what does 'womb' mean?"

'"Freda, get on with your meal in silence."

'"Yes, but 'Lo, He abhors not a Virgin's womb'. It's in the hymn we had this morning. Lo, He despises not an unmarried lady's . . ."

'"I think it means 'handbag'," my brother hummed cheerfully and ate.

'"But that doesn't make sense. Lo, He despises not an unmarried lady's handbag! It's silly."

'My father rose from his seat and came over to me. My plate of goose and apple sauce was taken away from me. I started to cry. Then to laugh: "I don't want to go to heaven if I can have nice smells like this on earth. Who would want to go to heaven when they have real roast goose on earth? And smell horses! I don't think I want to go to heaven and play a harp. God must get terribly sick of hearing all those hymns. He'd much rather hear the Welsh harpist from the hills near Cilgerran."

'Christmas Day usually ended with a beating for me.'

Cossey stopped talking and we sat round the fire with her

childhood before us like something horrible spilt there in the yard below our flat. The old houses beyond sagged and dropped off bits of themselves into the street like ancient trees.

'Didn't you hate being a girl?' we asked when Cossey had finished.

'Yes,' she replied doubtfully.

'Is that why you hate women?' Vivian asked her. Vivian was ten and older than us. She always seemed unimpressed by Cossey's stories. 'Is that why you hate ladies?' Vivian stared at our mother and asked.

'I don't hate them,' Cossey replied, then changed the subject: 'The first thing I can remember in my life was the Relief of Mafeking in 1902. I was lying there in bed and I heard this awful screaming noise in the street below . . . The Boer War was raging.'

'The first thing that *I* can remember,' Vivian interrupted, 'is when you and Dad . . .'

'The first thing *I* can remember,' Floy began, but Cossey didn't want to hear our first memories and just went on: 'The Relief of Mafeking . . . If there were another war . . .'

There was thick fog outside again in Ransome Street, and Ransome's Fields on the other side of our flats were invisible except for the ghostly green side of the wooden bandstand where Guards' bands sometimes played in the summer. The smell of pickles and gas and biscuits came from the other side of the Fields. The moan of the tugs' hooters on the river and ships trying to get into the docks hadn't stopped all day.

'My first memory,' Cossey repeated, 'is the Relief of Mafeking.'

But when we children tried to tell her what our first memories were, she wasn't interested. Our lives, she felt, had no shadow and therefore no memories. 'And my second memory', she continued, 'is the blind harpist coming down our street wheeling a huge harp on a dusty velvet frame, and we were told to give him a penny and walk quickly away because poor people were evil. But I didn't believe my parents. Ever. Oh how I loved that blind harpist and his music from the hills of Cilmery!'

'I can remember music,' Vivian tried again, but our mother

changed the subject. Our lives were ruled by good sense, and so not very interesting. She had ironed out fear. Or so she thought.

Once on a hot summer day we had run naked round Ransome's Fields and she had chased us with a wet towel, laughing and crying: 'Isn't it lovely. I always wanted to run about naked.'

Our lives were not to be leavened with fear or dread. It didn't turn out like this though, but Cossey's stories went on: 'My brother and I were never allowed to play with other children or go out,' she told us. 'The world was too evil, our parents would say. Only once did my parents allow me to accept an invitation to a children's party in a big house in Dulwich Village. It was a warm day and I wore a white frock and our hostess clapped her hands and said there was a competition in the drawing room. It was a big room with bay windows looking out on to a drive, and across it there was strung a cord tied with little white bags. In each of them there was something, and you had to smell what it was. We were given pencils and pieces of paper and as I had a very good sense of smell I quickly got nutmeg, cinnamon, arnica and paregoric. I was first in the line, and I had just got to arrowroot when a hand was placed on my shoulder: "Freda, will you come with me for a moment please."

I followed my hostess into a small room. A clergyman was standing there. He had a thick, red neck and his black suit was green with age. I could hear them all laughing next door, then a round of clapping.

'"Is your heart like this?" he showed me a picture of a golden heart. "Or is your heart like this?" and there was a picture of a black one, like rotten cheese. Then the clergyman took a chair from against the wall and placed it in front of me and started to shake: "Shall we pray?" His breath smelt of mothballs and I started to cry, longing for the Welsh harpist to come and sing about the times before there was a God, and take me away from the dreadful pictures the clergyman was showing me of impure hearts like poisoned wounds all rotting at the edges.

'"Did you enjoy the party?" my mother asked when I got in, but as she could see I was still weeping, she knew the answer. I saw she had plotted my humiliation at the party and wept again in disappointment, at my only party, and what had happened to it.

'"Perhaps those are good tears," Mother said gently. Then she took us into the parlour where the piano stood and played to us, and we stood by the piano and sang:

> Quick, sympathetic bright and kind
> She moved about at love's behest.
> And young and old and sick and sad
> Rose as she passed and called her blest.

'"But I don't want to go about doing good holy deeds," I protested, "I want to become a doctor. Or be a famous musician."

'"Freda dear," my mother kissed me. Then we continued:

> Down in the valley with my Saviour I would go
> Where the flowers are blooming and the sweet waters flow . . .
> Walking in His footsteps till the crown be won.

'After that,' Cossey ended her story sitting by the firelight in our flat before Dad came in at night, 'I never really trusted adults again or believed anything they said. They had no regard for joy.'

We often walked down Princes Road and over Lambeth Bridge to meet our father from work in the summer. Central London seemed to be a marble palace lined with polished mosaics and glazed brown tiles, with luminous ceilings and stained glass windows. It seemed such a highly-decorated palace that even the public lavatories down glittering steps were a magical underworld of brass and mahogany and glowing greens. We stood under a ceiling made of glass squares while Cossey talked to the lavatory attendant sitting by her hob in her little sitting room at the foot of the brass banisters. You could hear her kettle humming and someone banging about in the Wash-and-Brush-Up-Four-Pence and the footsteps of people thudding patiently overhead. The washbasins had tiny brass taps that scalding water came bouncing out of; I used to call them 'Ladies Slippers'. The only gloomy thing about these underground palaces seemed to be the lists of

VD clinics where all treatment would be in UTMOST SECRECY.

'Do you think *that's* why Cossey doesn't like women?' I asked my older sister Vivian as we came up the steps and walked home past the Home for Fallen Girls.

'Do you think that's why Cossey hates women?' A horrible noise came from The Home for Fallen Girls.

'I suppose so. I'm glad I'm not going to be one.'

'Aren't you?' I asked puzzled. 'Why not?'

'I'm going to be a nun. A Little Sister of In Ara Coeli.' Vivian was three years older than me and I was always slightly puzzled by her sense of outrage when Cossey looked out on the street side of our flat and talked about her childhood. We went by this time to Our Lady In Ara Coeli, a convent school on the other side of Ransome's Fields whose Gothic windows looked down on the tube trains running in and out of Lambeth station. As we chanted our times-tables at the end of the afternoon, we would drop our voices at 'Twelve twelves are one hundred and . . .' with the same gloomy finality as we chanted at the end of the Hail Mary: 'And at the Hour of Our death Amen', and the tube trains would moan and huddle under the window in heavy sympathy.

It was while we were coming home from school one afternoon when our grandparents were visiting us that Vivian added: 'Gramps hates women just as much. Cossey really should be hating men, not women. But she loves them. Look how funny she always is when Cousin Jim comes.'

But our grandparents had come over, not Cousin Jim this time, and as they sat there by the fire, our grandfather would express his shock at our Catholic upbringing. Our mother had been received into the Church soon after my brother's birth, but her father, who was a fundamentalist evangelical clergyman, continued to be shocked at her 'Papistry'. He was even more shocked when Cossey sent my sister and myself to Our Lady. I remember one Friday coming smugly home from school to announce that we mustn't eat meat for dinner and explaining to him carefully the difference between mortal and venjal sin. I remember his rage as he cried: 'Papist schools!'

Our father would agree mildly. 'The Devil and me don't agree,' was the nearest he ever got to religion. Or 'Cleanliness is next to godliness, so wash your hands, children. What about some nice cold water and pumice before you start eating? God's first gift to man was soap. Then bread. Meat is mere relish. Bread is the staff of life. But before you start packing it away, some water from the crystal spring.' But the tap water was frozen and our grandfather was still booming out 'Papistry. In *my* family! The Scarlet Woman!'

We would run out into Ransome's Fields picturing the Scarlet Papist Woman in a scarlet hat with hundreds of blazing candles for hair, and incense pouring from her mouth and nostrils. 'Which is your house?' we would ask each other as we passed the big houses on the other side.

'Mine's the one with the green front door and there's a swing in the garden.'

'I'm a doctor. In that house, and I have a brass plate on the door.'

'Or a dancer, or a famous speaker,' I would add, staring at the Jeanette Short Academy of Dancing and Elocution. Or perhaps I lived in the white plaster house with the Venetian tower where the lunatics out on parole were. We would play round the green, wooden bandstand in the middle and invent games where we 'shared out' the big houses. Vivian's was always the funny pink cottage misspelt 'Mount Veiw' and Floy, our brother's, was the South London Choir School. Cossey, though, had the huge turrety house with slit windows and fortified bedrooms, and she said she had ten children and that her husband was a brilliant surgeon at St Thomas's Hospital just by the bridge where her cousin had studied. We never asked Dad which was his house. Dad would have said his 'house' was on a ship on its way to the West Indies, or a Thames barge sailing down to the Nore.

'The Gate Ajar For Me', he would put on a deep voice and imitate our grandfather's hymn-book manner, 'is the wide and open sea.'

'Didn't you want to be married, ever?' we asked him, but Dad would press tobacco into his pipe and just go on singing a nautical song.

Chapter II

—— · ——

The Scarlet Woman appealed to me in 1936 almost as much as it had done to my mother back in 1906, and after our grandparents had been seen on to the tram home to Croydon, our mother would tell us more stories about how she escaped from her home in Ondels Grove.

We had a big basket chair by the fire. It creaked when it grew warm in the evenings, and the four of us would sit inside it. And after we had gone to bed and the fire had been bedded down, we would hear the chair still creaking and expanding and Cossey's stories still came.

'Oh, Ondels Grove was so dreary, and all the people in it, and all the *things* we were never allowed to know because they were "evil". I remember one hot day and I'd been told to bring my school form home for their embroidery lessons with my mother. It was about 1911.

'"Is it much further?" a tall fair girl, Lorna, would ask as we cycled down the hill in black skirts and white shirts and striped ties and big lace-up boots. We looked like freak men. My father was only a very poor curate then and I had been given reduced fees. In return my father taught a little Greek and my mother needlework. I found myself for the first time among middle-class girls here at Tulse Hill College, but we were too poor to live anywhere but above 'Hoare Baker and Pastry Cook'. I was so ashamed as we cycled home towards the tight, close rows of East Dulwich houses.

'"Is it very much further?" the girls asked as we cycled on and on. It was a hot day in June or July and we were pedalling through the leafy groves of Sydenham and Dulwich Village. "Is it very much further to your home?" the girls kept repeating. My mother had sprained her ankle and the Headmistress had arranged for us to have the weekly embroidery class at our home.

'"Is it this road?" the well-bred girls would ask as we passed the big double-fronted houses of West Dulwich, set in their own grounds with carriage drives up to the front doors and stables at the back. "Where are we going?" Lorna Lay asked again, puzzled as we pedalled on. "This *is* an adventure!" the girls laughed as we turned off down the hill towards our toad-coloured brick terraces with leaded panes in their front porches and no tradesmen's entrances. We were all very hot and I can still remember the smell of sweat as we cycled along, and the wax from the newly-blacked boots and the smell of our sweaty bootlaces and the heavy smell of warm blood.'

'Why blood?' we asked. 'Had you fallen off your bike?'

Our mother hesitated. 'A bike was my first bit of freedom. The first time I had an excuse to go off alone, and I had cycled round the donkey trough at Herne Hill trying to go no-handed . . . The bike meant I might be going to Cambridge to study medicine like my Cousin Jim. He was going to be a doctor, and I wanted to be a doctor too, but of course my parents thought it was unwomanly. I was spinning round the drinking trough on my bike when a horse and cart came up behind me and knocked me off and your father came and rescued me. He was doing a laundry round in a pony-and-trap.' Cossey would kick off her shoes. We stared at her warped feet as she went on: 'But that was later.'

'Oh the smell,' she repeated, 'on hot days. Boot-black and sweaty stockings and hot blood . . . You weren't supposed to play games or cycle when you weren't "well". You left your soiled napkins in a bucket in a corner of the bedroom for the maid to wash and you said "resting please" at roll-call when they drew up the lists for hockey and drill.'

Cossey went on: 'My mother had told me again and again to call out "resting please", that day.

'"Why?" I kept asking, because her gentle voice only quickened my rage and defiance.

'"You know very well why."

'"I'm perfectly well, thank you."

'"But you know you have your 'visitor'."

'"A strange sort of visitor."

'"Freda dear, I beg of you."

'And my brother would overhear and ask: "Why isn't she well? She looks very well to me," he would lisp.

'"And I am. And anyway, why isn't *he* ever unwell?"

'"Boys and men are stronger."

'"They are not! I never caught smallpox when he did. And I never caught pneumonia that time we both ran out in the snow. I can knock him down with one hand." I jeered at my puny brother.

'"Men and women have different burdens to bear in life."

'"I'll give you 'burdens'," I whispered behind clenched teeth to my brother when my mother had left the room. I went into the kitchen and filled a mustard tin with red-hot embers from the range and took it back to the parlour where my brother was humming to himself sitting astride the fire-guard.

'"Catch!" I said and threw the red-hot mustard tin at him. It hit him on the face.

'"What have you done to your face?", my mother stared at the burn down his cheek when she came back in. He was so unlike Cousin Jim as he lisped back loyally: "I fell in the grate on a red-hot cinder."

'But my father didn't believe him and I got a beating. How my father so much loved to thrash me. He never seemed to like doing it to my brother, and whenever I pictured Emmy Basset or Nina Hynde nibbling a rolled-up cucumber sandwich and talking about their brothers at Cambridge I wondered if their fathers told them to unhook their delicate voile dresses when they got home . . . and lower them. "The only sensitive part about you is below the waist," Father once said.'

'What do you think he meant?' we children asked, puzzled.

Cossey just went on: 'My parents never gave me any love. They never kissed me or hugged me or played with me,' she would hug us all, 'they thought that happiness was sinful and that too would tip you straight into the eternal hellfires. So I decided it would be better to be sinful and risk hell. I would hug my younger brother when he wasn't being too goody-goody, and hug my Cousin Jim who was always as naughty as me. I would go round hugging people and things. Oh how I hated Ondels Grove. You couldn't hug anyone there or love anything. It was all just stiff bricks up and down. Life was like a sewing machine that gets stuck and just goes on turning out the same old stitches, row after row, Ondels Grove after Ondels Grove, full of people who never ever in their lives had heard it said to them by a Welsh harpist – as I had – that Ondels Grove and their lives might never have been, and instead there might have been mountains and oceans where they stood worrying about the grate-black. Oh, I wanted to get a pair of scissors and unpick all the rows and rows of stitches that were our streets and set us all free once and for all. Just stop Ondels Grove for good. There was nothing but fear in my parents' lives. My mother was always humiliated because we were so poor, and she was always terrified of being found not to have damask napkins that our better-class neighbours had. All they cared about was things. Stupid things!' And we children would have to try and stop Cossey from throwing cups out of the window, and shoes and our school books.

'Things are lies,' she would declare when we had retrieved them.

'Ondels Grove was all lies and things. And we *were* so poor. Too poor to keep up appearances as we had to, being clergy. We were too poor for me to have my lunch at school with the other girls. Instead, my mother used to cut me sandwiches and put them in a paper bag with "P. Hoare, High-Class Baker and Pastrycook" stamped across it. I was so ashamed of being caught eating them that I used to go into the school lavatories to do it.

'Then one day I found sixpence and decided to spend it on a school pudding. "One school pudding," I rehearsed in bed. I'd save this sixpence for a ridiculous piece of pudding. We all had to queue in the assembly-hall till our turn came to drop our baskets of sandwiches on the mistress's desk and curtsey slightly and walk off to the other side of the room. This day I went up to the desk and put down my sixpence and whispered: "One pudding." I was terrified. The mistress stared. "One pudding," I whispered again.

"One what?" she shouted. "Pudding," I whispered again. "One what?" she shouted. "Pudding," I blurted back. "Pudding *please*," she shouted. The girls all tittered and called me "Pudding please" after that.

'Oh I wanted to fly away to where the Welsh harpist was playing, and singing that none of it mattered at all. But instead I was sitting in a tram and a woman with an eaten face was leaning over the cross-seat opposite and calling out to me on my way home from school: "But his wife gives 'im the brown 'orses to take him up to Sanctuary Cemetery. The last thing 'e says was it was the *black* 'orses he wanted to take him to his last rest. The blacks with all the doings. But she'd drunk the lot. The whole of the Burial. So it was the old brown 'orses he got. The ones with one eye gorn and no work in the left leg and no feel and no one following."'

Sitting in our flat by Ransome's Fields at night we were often frightened by Cossey's stories, but we let her go on. 'All the girls at school were of a better class so I'd never been allowed to invite them in. Except three awful girls called the Grippes. The whole family had TB and the three daughters went to a special school at Broadstairs. They had TB in their bones as well and they were all gnarled and knotted. But they thought this was God's will for them, and when they smiled their cheeks were very rosy and their skins very white and even their noses had TB. I couldn't bear to look at their mother's grinning snout. Their father had already died of God's will, and when they smiled their "God's will" faces were unnatural and cruel, as though they'd put rouge on, as part of His will. Like puppets.

'On my first pay-day when I was sixteen, I bought a small box of chocolates and ate them leaning over London Bridge and cursing the angry God, just experimentally to see if He would curse me back, and strike me dead. But the only thing that happened was that a nice wind came along and blew very nicely through my hair and the empty chocolate box floated away. It was after this that I saw how beautiful life could be. When I got back to Ondels Grove, the blind Welsh harpist was standing there again. He had come up from Wales every year for as long as

I could remember and his songs were like a breath of fresh air from valleys where winds blew. Even my mother relented in her war against happiness and gave me a penny to give him. I vowed never ever to do God's will, and never to become like my parents who did it, or like the people of Ondels Grove.'

We often asked Cossey what the Welsh harpist had sung about as he stood there at the end of her road. Once she replied: 'He sang about how lovely the world was *meant* to be, and how strange it was that it wasn't. He sang about how there was so much here when there might have been nothing but dead water and bare ice and slime and flies.'

We children would run into Ransome's Fields and play on the green bandstand and pretend that it was a ship ploughing through all that slime and dead ice. But we were discovering by now that Cossey, in spite of her insistence on enjoying life, was by no means perfect herself. There was a fish bar down the road called 'The Perfection Fish Caterers'. The 'n' had got knocked off the end of 'Perfection' and when we wanted to tease Cossey we would say: 'You do think you're "Perfectio", don't you?'

And she would grin and say: 'Well, it was awful for girls in those days, with no love and nothing but fear.'

We tried calling our mother 'Perfectio' for a bit, but it didn't last. It made us feel sad, so we went back to 'Cossey'.

Chapter III

'My next memory,' Cossey would begin as we sat by the fire looking out on her side of the world, 'is the death of Queen Victoria.'

But it was 1935 now, and it was King George V who had died and we queued on Lambeth Bridge to see him lying in state. Floy ran down the street in the darkness crying, 'The King is dead,' and we followed him down Smack Street and the wind caught the black hatchments hanging off houses draped in mourning and a pumping sound came out and we ran away with the trams pumping behind, too.

'My next memory . . .' Cossey would go on. We were often frightened of her stories now, but we loved her and begged her to go on as we sat by the fire with the curtains drawn to shut out our mother's dark Victorian world behind us in the yards. The asphalt yards, then Princes Road turning its shabby back on a wilderness of tottering slum streets and dereliction and behind, Bemmer Street, Deliverance Street and the tangle of crooked terraces that separated us from Waterloo.

'If ever there were another war,' our mother would repeat as the trams started and stopped, then gave a high warning cry and whined along to the Elephant. Sometimes at night in the pea-souper fogs, the tram conductor would get off and lead his tram with a flare. We were taught a lot about Purgatory at school and the tram feeling its way through a fog with only a yellow eye on its forehead made us think of the Lost Souls. But now as our mother talked about Flanders trenches and the First World War we pictured the gassed soldiers out there instead and trams leading each other across a stricken battlefield to 'Strand' and 'Temple'.

'The Great War was so awful,' Cossey would repeat. 'It needn't have happened, but everyone said the Huns would take over Europe if we didn't beat the Germans back. My father would open the crypt of his church and we'd sit down there during a raid, the whole parish, and my brother playing the piano and my father crying out, "Oh God Our Help in Ages Past". I can't hear that without hearing the satisfaction of sacrificing all those young men.

'My brother came back from the trenches and the Battle of the Somme and people were all gloating and celebrating. When I saw him standing at Victoria Station I could hardly recognize him, he kept making such gibbery movements with his mouth as though he had a ventriloquist's puppet in his lap and he was talking to it all the time. His manner was far too cheerful. Every word began with "The jolly old" and he would have to make rhymes out of everything. "Topping shopping" and "This bore the war", talking very fast and blinking his eyelids up and down very fast too, and touching his straw hat up and down. He was always asking us the time and before we told him, he would cry, "Hey ho the holly. This life is so jolly." He would say, "May I make so bold as to ask you whether you would be so good as to consent to let me do the honours with a small goblet each of Lipton's most celebrated brew in this big, bad teapot of ours?" Or, "Shall we, good sires, regale ourselves with a little more of the gracious meats that our lady mother so bounteously provides?" Then he was killed. And when they sent his possessions back, all over his writing paper was scrawled: "Thou shalt be cast into the pit where the worm dieth not."

'The Armistice was another excuse,' Cossey went on, 'for more celebrations of blood and I longed to hear my friend the Welsh harpist's comment on the War. I cycled to the end of the road and saw your father standing there instead, all fresh and new as though he had risen from the dead. And he was full of hatred like me.'

'Did Dad go and fight?' we asked.

'He was too young. But we went together to Dulwich Library and he stood on a soap box and got arrested by the police for impeding the war effort.'

These stories were always so gloomy that we felt bad standing by the Home for Fallen Girls and in the underground lavatories where your crimes were treated with the UTMOST SECRECY. The notices seemed so gloomily connected with the Great War and the dark night signals: No Entry . . . No Exit . . . No Spitting . . . No Goods This Way. So many commands. So many reminders of an anger that Cossey could not help us with. At the end of Ransome Street there were tram points where a man with only one leg stood all day banging his hands together in the winter and clinking a metal key to and fro in a lock that set the trams along the right course. He too would tell us about the War and the Zeppelins on our way home from school.

We could hear the underground whinnying under the windows of Our Lady in Ara Coeli as we chanted the 'Hail Mary' at the end of afternoon school and sang the twelve-times table to the same melancholy tune standing beside our desks while the partition creaked and we gave our sudden ominous drop in pitch at 'the hour of our death' and 'seven twelves make eighty-four' so that both seemed to belong to the same catastrophe. When we left the old tram-points man, we would run to the Fields side of our flat and look out of the windows onto the bandstand and pretend we were famous conductors and grow cheerful again, running out on to the iron fire escape that made a twangy sound when you jumped on it and rattled when women mangled their washing out there and the water rushed down through the perforated steps. We stood under it to get wet.

'It's men Cossey should be angry with.'

'If ever there were another war . . .' Cossey would repeat her warning.

'What would you do?'

'I'd just fight it,' she replied grandly, 'as I fought the Great War.'

'But you were only a girl,' we protested. 'And anyway, I didn't think girls went to fight.'

'But I fought it in my own way, and if there were ever another one, I'd go out and fight. I'm thinking of going out to Spain. Only Dad won't let me. But if there were one here . . .' We would hold our breaths.

The Spanish Civil War was what our parents talked about, and we would gaze at the harsh notices hanging above us in the sky: Keep Off . . . Commit No Nuisance . . . No Loitering . . . No Ball Games . . . Keep Out. We would run out among the instructions: Poor Man's Lawyer . . . Incinerators . . . Wash House . . . Home for Fallen Girls . . . and that final sign of the angry God beside the Waifs and Strays Society and the Ragged School, 'Ancient Lights', the worst judgement of His along the tops of the dark buildings. The trams came pumping down the road as the old points-man told us the Zeppelins used to pump. 'Ancient Lights' was stamped along the grimiest, angriest buildings, and Cossey would have to entice us home with funny stories about how she finally left Ondels Grove and ran away with Dad.

Maybe it was Cossey's talk of the Great War, or maybe it was just the horses crashing out of the South London Pantechnicon at dawn and slipping on the granite setts and screaming in the dark; or maybe it was the train collision we had heard once on the other side of Ransome's Fields behind the Baptist Chapel. Whatever it was, we knew by the time of the Spanish Civil War in 1936 that there was something terribly wrong with the world that Cossey and Dad didn't hide. And yet at the same time there was something that Cossey loved so that when we all looked out at the Ransome's Fields side of the flat we would feel cheerful again.

'Tell us about the people who live over there in the house with the shutters . . . Or tell us about the ship you took to Newcastle. Tell us about when you were a girl. And you met Dad.'

Cossey would start up again: '"Is it much further?" the girls from school asked me as we turned into Ondels Grove where we lived. I was taking them to my home for their needlework lesson. I was sixteen.

'"Is this the road?" They stopped to stare back at the big houses with the stone steps and urns and drives and panelled front doors. I was the only one who lived on the wrong side of the hill. We cycled down Ondels Grove. The trains were rumbling over the East Dulwich railway bridge.

'"How exciting," they exclaimed, "to live so near a busy railway." Until now I had always been so careful not to let them know where I lived. I always hung behind at the end of the afternoon, and at lunch-time when the baskets of lunch were handed out, I would lock myself away to eat my sandwiches, throwing away the compromising paper bag.

'"What does your father do?" the girls would ask.

'"He's a doctor only he's away most of the time." Sometimes I said he was dead, only now the girls were coming home to see for themselves. We had turned into the road of pinch-lipped yellow houses where we lived and came to the front door of the shop.

'"What are we stopping *here* for?" Emmy Basset asked. "Does someone's aged nurse live here?"

'I swallowed hard and lowered my head and took them through the shop. The apprentice was covering the dough and he shouted out as we crossed because of the draught we made. But the girls were well-bred and all commented on the nice warm smell of baking bread.

'"I do wish we had such good, fresh bread at home. And look at the flowers!"

'My mother was at the door of the stairs to greet them. They saluted her politely and filed upstairs into the little sitting room. She had done her best though, her eyes said, with flowers on the window sills and an anthology left open at Tennyson's *Maud*. She had got out the best tea service that the maid was not allowed to touch and laid it out on the table.

'We all stitched in silence.

'"The test of a lazy young woman", Emmy Basset interrupted it, " is the length of her thread, my mother always says."

'"Oh dear! Then please don't look at mine," the girls laughed. They began to ask about my brother. They talked about their brothers at Oxford and Cambridge. After tea they went and the maid brought in a basin of hot soapy water and my mother put it on the table and washed up. I dried in silence. Then I started my Latin homework. I looked at my mother and remembered when I was a child how once her cheeks had thickened and she had grown breathless quickly and, when she sat down, a ridiculous hump appeared in her stomach, sitting on top of her as though she had pinned a large bag-pudding under her dress.

'"Mother, where do children come from?" I had asked her.

'"Hush dear. Don't ask questions like that. God sends them."

'"Then I do think He should give you some warning before He sends them," I replied. The last time He had sent one, I had come in from school to find my mother lying on the cold tiled floor screaming. The maid had gone home and my father was at a Holiness meeting.

'"Fetch the doctor," she screamed, not mentioning God.

'"God wasn't very considerate last time," I reminded her. "Even with an air raid and the Boche coming over you get *some* warning. I mean they come round and blow their whistles. You'd think God would at least give several blasts on someone's air-raid whistle before He sends babies trooping down. And why does He send them *naked* when we're not supposed to be *ever* naked?"

'"Freda dear. Please go to your room."

'I went upstairs. My brother was in the bath. "And how I despise Adam," I banged on the bathroom door and shouted at him, "whining up to God and telling Him: 'It was the *woman* that thou gavest me who is to blame.'"

'My mother said nothing more but when my father came in he got the leather strap off his suitcase and practised with it on the white counterpane.

'"You can't do that to her,' my mother protested. "She's not well." He coiled up his strap again and waited three days, my mother spying on me till she could report to my father that I was "well" again. I was told to stay in bed the next morning and the curtains were drawn. I could hear my father practising with his strap against the bed in the spare room. Then he brought my mother in to be chaperone and to see that I remained decently clothed throughout. When he had finished, my mother brought me a hot water bottle to lay on my buttocks.

'"We had to do it," she tried to apologize. But I was hot with excitement though, to try it again. After that I was always doing my best to get into an argument about God with my father.'

21

There was silence. 'Is that why you hate girls?' Vivian asked Cossey, slowly and brutally.

'I don't hate them,' Cossey protested vaguely. 'It's just that it was so awful for them once.'

'And did the Welsh harpist ever come again after that?'

'It was soon after that that I met Dad. I was tearing furiously down Ondels Grove after a thrashing and skidded into the donkey's drinking trough at the bottom, and your father was coming along the road in his pony-and-cart delivering the washing his mother did. I'd hit my head on the stone trough and he helped me up and straightened my front wheel, only he didn't really get it straight enough and I had to ride home all zig-zag, but I didn't mind. It was as though I'd met the Welsh harpist down there by the water.

'I wanted to be a doctor like my Cousin Jim,' Cossey went on, 'but that wasn't considered womanly so I sat for a scholarship to Cambridge to become a teacher. I was so excited. I could see women students riding around on their bicycles. Soon I would be as free as they were. And after chapel we each took a tray with a cup of tea and a roll and butter on it and we were allowed into each other's rooms for one hour. And a girl called Emily Vassal invited me into her room and told me about Shaw and Ibsen and lent me *A Doll's House* which I read greedily all that night. And when I went down to the examination next day the first question on the paper was "To whom do you first owe service?" And I wrote a long essay saying that I owed my first duty not to God, nor to my country, nor to my family, but to *myself*!

'So I didn't get the scholarship and came home and told your father at Dulwich Library what I'd written in my essay and he said quite right too, my first duty was to myself, and had I got over my bruises? And I said no, because the bike still had funny, itchy wheels and a sort of stutter, and he said bring it along to the Labour Party meeting tonight and he'd try to mend it again, and we walked along talking, and after a bit he told me I didn't know anything about Socialism, but why didn't we go off to Newcastle together. He was applying for a job there in the docks. I said I couldn't leave my parents and he said, "I thought your first duty was to yourself?" So we went down to Limehouse to look for a boat called the *Percy Warrior* and Limehouse was full of Chinese and I was scared, so he took my arm and we walked round the docks past low, dark shops lit by candles, and stacked with tiny eggs piled up.

'The streets were narrow and damp and smelt of nutmeg and tea and butter and the wharves were steep and black and we couldn't find the *Percy Warrior* and Gilbert called over to a ship that was docked there: "Ahoy there. Show a leg abaft." And I said: "That doesn't sound quite right. That's not nautical, I don't think." But the ship was the *Percy Warrior* and its deck was littered with clucking hens and dogs in cages, and more minute eggs: "What misguided hens to lay such wretched eggs," I stared at them by the quay.

'But Gilbert had seen a lamp-lit gate and was walking ahead to the *Percy Warrior*. A few men stood round spitting, and behind them the wharves were very black and behind them the Artisans Dwellings and the other black tenements with windows covered with old rags. We stared down at the jumping water, pooh-poohed it just as I was to pooh-pooh childbirth: "I just don't believe in all that dreadful angry stuff." The *Percy Warrior* gave a sudden bounce in the water, then banged against the dockside. Smoke came from the port holes and behind them men watched us. Doors slid open. Panels were drawn back. We were led into a greasy saloon smelling of German sausage. There was a soiled leather seat in the corner and a little coal fire, and damp ferns dripped at the steamy window.

'"I ought to have brought you some nice lace," I said to the captain, "to make curtains with." We were given the only cabin and a curtain screened it off. The only room that had a proper door was the WC. It was in a cupboard at the bottom of a steep flight of stairs, and the door jammed when you tried to open it.

'"Whoops," I said and sat down on the wooden seat with a bang. There was a wheel beside me and when I touched it the whole ship rocked and Gilbert called out: "The captain respectfully requests you not to take over the steering." I pointed at the wheel. "You've already altered the ship's course twice and almost sent it up the Surrey Docks as far as Ondels Grove, and the noise has woken your parents."

'"Cooeee," I pretended to call out to them as we unmoored and started off down the river: "What would you say if you could see me now?"

'The sailors were clearing the chairs away but the room still smelt of German sausage. I stared at our bunk and at the German sailors standing round. The bunk had wooden sides, and when I touched its mattress it felt damp and slimy and unpleasant and there was an equally slimy set of cushions and a slippery leather blanket and the eyes of the sailors were all staring so that Gilbert said: "Let's go on deck and look at the stars and see the Nore as we pass out to sea."

'The bed's cushions were like old men's wet mouths so I agreed, and we spent the night on the deck with the sailors banging about inside and peering out at us. Then suddenly we were in Newcastle, but the job Gilbert was after had gone and it was raining so we came home and my parents consulted lots of clergymen about what to do, and when I told them about the slimy wet cushions they only grew more angry, and when I described how lovely it had been on deck with nothing but water and stars all round Mother cried "Hush dear. It's your wedding we're discussing."

'Gilbert took me to Goose Green, where his mother lived in East Dulwich. She had come from Holland and looked so young and spoke English so well that I was sure that she was really his wife, but I could see she didn't like me because I was patronizing and behaved like the Lady Bountiful descending on her from the Vicarage. Mrs Gerber, Dad's mother, was tall and thin with gold hair and high cheekbones and a lean, distinguished face not at all like a British washerwoman. She used to cycle to Highgate and back twice a week collecting the washing of her Dutch compatriots and they would give her German sausage and apelstroop as well. But she didn't like me. You see I'd gone to visit her in such a condescending way: "What a very nice flat you live in, Mrs Gerber," I had pronounced in my daughter-of-the-vicarage way. "What nonsense people talk when they say the working classes are feckless! And what lovely tea this is! And such a good pastry. I've got a secret too. *We* live above a pastrycook!"

'Mrs Gerber lived with Miss Lenege,' Cossey added.

'*Our* Miss Lenege?' we children asked. Miss Lenege had a room in our flat in Webbley Mansions then, in 1936.

'Yes. She came in weeping one day. She worked in Jones and Higgins in Rye Lane and the police had charged her with stealing a yellow blouse. I felt so sorry for her that I took the blouse away and ripped off the yellow buttons and stitched mauve ones on, and cut out the label in the collar, so that when she went to the police station next day, the supervisor looked at the blouse and shook her head: "That's not one of ours. It's been used too. It smells of carbolic soap." I had gone with Miss Lenege, and I kept telling her: "You musn't feel guilty, or you'll give yourself away." So she was let off and the supervisor apologized and Gilbert looked at me, and laughed.

'Soon after that Mrs Gerber was ill and I went into the Grove Vale Pharmacy for her. It sold herbal remedies and I could see Mrs Gerber was often in bad pain. We passed rows of boxes and mahogany drawers: Ipecac, Magnesium S, Borax and so on. Then came herbal cures in rows of glass jars with glass lids and labels that made me want to laugh. They were all arranged alphabetically – Abscesses, Adenoids, Bad Breath, Boils, Bad Legs.

'"Bad Dreams," I went on recklessly chanting, "Bad Behaviour . . ., Badly-dressed People like you," I pointed at the customers, "and Badly-spoken people like you, Gilbert . . ."

'I put my hand over my mouth as it came out but Gilbert only smiled and afterwards he said: "How I love you!"

'"Why do you love me?", I laughed again. I was so surprised.

'"Because you make everything you look at seem so alive and cheerful and interesting."

'There was a man standing at the corner with a hurdy-gurdy and it sounded so cheerful that I begged him for a go and made a lovely sound. The organ was much heavier than I had thought, but I could see your father standing there with a special wind blowing through his hair promising me I'd escape from Ondels Grove and Prayer Meetings and Women's Bible Fellowship. I'd never seen such a beautiful man apart from the Welsh harpist. Dad's breath smelt of cold rivers and life coming back to grass after winter, and wind creaking in the trees, and he seemed to have come from behind such a big mountain. But when I took him home! Oh that visit! My parents had left Ondels Grove then and lived in a proper Vicarage with servants, and your father went round by the tradesmen's entrance. He didn't know I wasn't a domestic. He sat with his plate on his knee munching as though he was out on a Band of Hope outing.

'"Freda dear, now we've refreshed ourselves with our tea, perhaps you'll play to us." I looked over at Dad, afraid that he would sing his flippant song about the gentry:

>   All the little pigs they grunt and how!
>   The cats meow, the dogs bow-wow
>   Everything's a perfect wow . . .

'I was cold with anticipation as I dragged my hands over the keyboard and sang my song. Gilbert was talking to my father who had just come in, offering his hand: "How-do. Not badly thanks, except that I got out of bed the wrong side this morning."

'My mother interrupted, asking Gill what he did. "Conjuring," he faltered. Then in silence he picked up a small golf ball belonging to my brother and put it at his mouth and cried: "Watch this." He pretended to swallow it, opening his mouth wide, then patting his stomach as it seemed to go down, then finally retrieving the ball from behind his back. There was a terrible silence as we took this in. The maid lowered her head and slipped out of the room and we could hear her tittering below stairs. My mother stood there beside her china cabinet. It was lined with green velvet and gave off a smell like camphor that I still associate with being genteel. That was the only time Gilbert met my parents before we ran away and got married.'

Chapter IV

―――― . ――――

'If ever there were another war,' Cossey would begin again. It was 1937, and there had been 'indiscriminate bombing' in Spain and after she had told us what this phrase meant, she would add: 'If ever there were another war. Here in England . . . If there were ever another . . .' She would pause and wait while we stared out at the tall buildings with their angry instructions: No Loitering . . . Commit No Nuisance . . . Fallen Girls.

'What would you do?' we'd ask in the silence. Floy was standing by the wall letting down the tyres of Cossey's bicycle to punish it for tipping her into a pile of horse droppings on our way to Mass on the Feast of the Beheading of St John the Baptist. Our mother's bike always stood in the kitchen beside the Imperial Boiler.

'If ever there were another war . . .' Cossey repeated that day as the air hissed out of her tyres. 'If ever there were another war . . .'

'What would you do?'

'I'd kill you all.' We could hear the trams outside thrashing down Smack Street, their hum rising to a sing-song as they cried: 'Put out your dead!' and their chains clanking out in confirmation as they got up speed.

'*How* would you kill us?' we asked in panic. Vivian sat there disdainfully.

'I'd put you all in the Imperial Boiler.' We all stared at the Imperial Boiler burning happily away in the corner of our kitchen beside Cossey's bike. Dad had once told us about the Imperial Guard in Germany and Floy started to sing a school song called 'Imperial Burden'.

'We couldn't all fit in,' he stopped singing and said incredulously, in a big voice.

'*You* wouldn't have to fit in, boyoh, boykin,' Vivian said, jeering at him. 'You're the boyoh. The Little King. Cossey wouldn't put a boyoh in a boiler and boil him along with the girls, would you, Cossey?' But Cossey went on gabbling in a low voice as though she were saying her prayers and the trams outside seemed to copy her.

'What if Dad didn't want us killed?' we asked tonelessly, as though we were simply asking, 'What if Dad didn't want to come for a walk?' Then we stood outside in the dark of Ransome's Fields. The street hoardings shouted at us: Get Younger Every Day. The pawnbrokers had a sign outside: All Goods Must Be Redeemed . . . Vivian sang a hymn about redeeming blood and the green hill far away, and when we reached the stricken houses of Paradise Street she sang, 'This Day shalt thou be with me in Paradise Street . . '.

'Cossey's only showing off,' she added as we stood there listening to the flap and swish of torn wallpaper knocking in a draught and smelt the damp that crept at us from the derelict houses. 'Cossey's only showing off.'

The moon was long and low and sagging at its bottom and like a balloon too full of water and about to burst out over the watery sky. 'I hate the moon,' Vivian went on. 'Cossey is making it all up because she wants to frighten us as she used to frighten us at Baston Square.' We hadn't seen Cossey in such a black mood since we had come to Ransome's Fields two years ago from Baston Square with Miss Lenege.

Miss Lenege was the German woman who had lived quietly in our spare room since we had moved to Webbley Mansions beside the Fields. She sat all day in her little room up two steps and smelt of paraldehyde which she got from the dispensary at the TB clinic over Ransome's Fields. She was lonely, Cossey would say. She would creep carefully out of her room at night as though the ground were made of wet mud and sit with Cossey when our father was out at a Labour Party meeting. She had a funny accent that went up and down in the wrong places and she pronounced her 'v's' like 'f's' and suddenly cried 'Ach so' at the end of a sentence of Cossey's. She too was afraid of another war.

'Would you put her in the Imperial Boiler too?' Vivian asked

Cossey when we got home. Miss Lenege looked very offended and put down the lace cottage that she was making for the church sale-of-work. Her mouth was big and stained and she pulled it open to show us she'd just had a tooth out.

There was a dentist's chair perched on one of the stalls in the Lambeth Walk and sometimes we saw a long fang being waved triumphantly about by a man in a top hat as we raced among the barrows. There was another chair on three orange boxes where the Korn King took out people's corns. Once I was handed a whole box full of shiny silver corns and callouses by the Korn King's anxious apprentice. The Korn King himself usually had a pretty fair-haired boy sitting on a seat on the top of his stall with bare feet and smiling as 'the doctor' held up a model of a huge bunion, a wart, then a corn, and cried softly: 'That corn's no longer alive, eh? No longer with us. Not alive-alive-oh, eh? Because she's sitting here with me, pretty now. Back here with me now, eh?' He would nod to himself and bang on his surgical instrument case while we longed for Miss Lenege to recognize the shiny white skin corns and climb up on to his throne on top of the stall with her dignified expression and put her foot out: 'Ach so.'

'This boy here,' the Korn King would go on softly and judiciously, 'he hasn't got them, not yet, but a lot of people hug them till they go to the grave. You love them eh, don't you lady?' He would turn back to Miss Lenege who would frown. 'Have you got an old mother that you love, or an old Dad?' We would shake our heads on behalf of Miss Lenege, because she was a German refugee, while the Korn King passed round photographs of elderly couples. 'Anyone you'd like to do a real service to, eh?'

But Miss Lenege would drag us away from the photos of Neville Chamberlain and the Queen and the Little Princesses at Windsor Castle, and we'd go back slowly to Ransome's Fields with the autumn wind blowing the leaves along the grass and on to the pavement, and the TB patients crossing to the dispensary and coughing as they lowered themselves on to the rows of benches. Then more wind would come coughing, too, and the sound of the railway below and the singing from the Baptist

Chapel at the corner that stood askew from the rest of the Fields and had notices outside about Ladies Gala Afternoons, and Recitative Leagues. We'd smell the smell of damp and rats and bed-bugs coming up from Paradise Street and run back to Webbley Mansions where Cossey would be sitting waiting with tea, and Mrs Lee, our daily cleaning-woman, would be wrapping her varicose veins in a cabbage leaf. Her legs were always bare and spread apart, and she wore gym shoes and a cotton dress, even in winter. She always wore a hat with hat-pin and carried a big bag made of coloured squares of oilcloth that made noises when she fumbled in it. She always kept this bag and its contents a secret, and she would never eat with us and never even eat our food, or any fresh food.

One day she leaned over at me as she was fumbling in her mystery bag and whispered hoarsely pointing at her newspaper: 'So she stitched her hubby up in calico from the House and dropped him in the canal and he come up bumpy and swollen and all the stitches bust, so they all knew where that calico come from, and what he had for his last dinner.'

'If ever there were another war,' Cossey began.

'You'd stitch us up in calico,' Vivian interrupted rudely, 'and drop us in the canal. Cossey's showing off again,' she turned to Floy and me. We all stared accusingly at Cossey and she never again said: 'If there were another war . . .'

In fact, as the Second World War drew nearer she grew more silent and we would beg her for more stories about the Welsh harpist and how she first met Dad. We sat at the window and the twilight crept on like a hand stretching very slowly forward to take what it needs bit by bit. Cossey would draw the curtains and shut out the street and we'd sit at the back looking over the dark of Ransome's Fields, and fog would creep slowly round the light, and we could picture the naked light bulbs of Faith Healers across the Fields, as Cossey said: 'I want you to have all the freedom I never had. Nothing matters except life. Just think! There might not be anything here except pebbles and screws, or rusty ink wells, or just damp and flies and dead ice. Or,' her voice would rise, 'there might not be any life at all. Just think. Not even flies going round in stupid circles all day, or chunks of stone, or puddles of water that wobble like fat women in the wind. Oh it was so lovely when we first got married. My parents were so horrified that they wouldn't speak to us for years. But we found two rooms in a house in Baston Square not far from the Bedlam Hospital. We would walk past thinking we could hear the sounds of the lunatics clapping, but when they came out of the asylum they looked just like you and me and we had a picnic with one in the gardens and talked about the Great War and he kept nodding and smiling: "The Sergeant Major was very kind, he was." And another soldier inmate told us he liked a plate of jelly for his tea.'

'Was Cousin Jim in the Great War?' we asked. We had been taken to Cambridge for Christmas. Cossey's uncle was a servant at St John's College and we had sat in the basement of a big house in Maids Causeway eating roast goose and hearing 'the gentlemen' moving about in the big rooms above. Then Cossey's Cousin Jim had come bouncing in. Cossey had longed to be a doctor like her cousin and leaped up when he came dancing in, shouting out how lovely it was now to be doing 'midder' and 'ENT' and 'scrape'. Cossey would forget Dad and us children when she heard her cousin calling through the letter-box or up the stairs in his peculiar voice: 'Oi-oi-oi,' as though he were the one who was saying 'Ah' as the doctor peered down his throat. 'I'm on call this week,' or 'Tommy's is on take,' he would call mysteriously, 'tonight.'

'How I loved my Cousin Jim,' Cossey would stare into the fire. 'He was five when I was twelve and I'd swing him between my legs in his sailor suit and sing:

> Nelly Bligh caught a Fly
> And tied it on a String

and he'd reply from the floor in his funny cheerful odd little voice:

> She let it out to run about
> And then she let it in.'

But now Jim had qualified as a doctor and brought a girl to see us at Webbley Mansions. She was tall and dark and wore earrings and make-up and perfume and we couldn't believe that elegant girls called Clarice who wore soft muslin dresses and carried lace gloves and parasols could possibly go in for 'midder' and 'ENT' and 'scrape' and chopping people's legs off and pushing people round and hurting them like men.

We tried to picture Cossey being a doctor instead of Clarice. She was waving some scissors in the air and vaguely snipping at things. She had been given china and silver for her wedding. Her parents and relatives, and even the parishioners, had loaded her with tea services and dinner services and little frilly things to go on cake stands. But as Cossey believed that property was theft, she had allowed most of this world to disappear. Some things she gave away and some she let us take out into the bandstand in the Fields, and now most of our crockery came from the tuppenny bazaar just round the corner in Smack Street, and when she asked us to lay the table for dinner we would tease her by laying it with a skewer and a tin-opener for her and a tea-strainer and a rolling-pin for Dad. We children would have competitions to see which of them could eat their spaghetti first, Dad frowning over his rolling-pin and breathing heavily and Cossey crying: 'Why can't I have a fish-slice and a dish mop to eat with? It would be easier than this shoe horn or whatever it is.'

'How I hate things,' she would snip, holding her scissors near the edges of Clarice's sleeve. Jim grinned as she pretended to slice it up and fry it and eat it and Clarice's cartwheel hat as well. We tried again to picture Cossey as a doctor, helping Jim hold people down while their legs were tarred.

'Could you . . . Could cousins marry in those days?'

'Yes . . . No . . . Yes . . . That is . . . I don't know.' Cossey changed the subject: 'In those days life was so hard for girls who wanted to do anything.' Our mother had just had another baby, it was another girl.

'Do you wish Samey had been a boy?' we asked her.

'No, but when I was your age, life was quite different for girls.'

Cossey would watch the TB patients with hunched shoulders crossing Ransome's Fields to the clinic run by the London Medical Mission: 'My father used to run a Mission too,' she would begin, 'down in the Surrey Docks. The Mission was one room upstairs and there was a midden at the back where old women used to pick and scream at each other at dawn. That's where our bedbugs came from, my mother used to explain. They'd drop on us from the ceilings, and once when I was looking for them, I saw great animals with waving arms instead. I screamed out and my parents held me down, but I was on a wooden bunk in the fever van. A strange lady came into the van and looked at the other person in the next bunk and then put sweet peas on me. They smelt so strong. And in the hospital I played with boys like Cousin Jim for the first time and went in to a long garden. I'd never been into a garden before, or run behind trees and hidden. There was a brick house at the end and we ran to it but they put the dead bodies there. Then a nurse took me down the garden to the house at the end, but I thought it was the house where they put the dead bodies in. A couple stood there – the woman was in a cape. They took me in their arms and I screamed and screamed and they smelt even more of death but they were my parents. They put me in a mail cart and I kicked and kicked at the flowers painted on its sides all the way home, screaming till the green and blue flowers were almost worn off. I couldn't believe these were my parents, and later I felt certain I was a foundling. I never belonged in Ondels Grove.

'Do you mean you could marry Cousin Jim then?' Cossey was silent. 'As he wasn't your cousin?'

'He was much younger,' she said at last.

Cousin Jim had just been to see us at Webbley Mansions again and with Clarice. He had dark staring eyes that we loved to watch, staring at them in the firelight, and at his sleepy cat's mouth till Cossey got a pair of scissors and brandished them over Miss Lenege's long woollen cardigan that was hanging over a chair and cried: 'Silly, silly things. A world of things I'd like to cut up into slices and fry and feed to the birds.' Jim just grinned like a cat. 'I wish I'd gone to Cambridge. Or to St Thomas's in London, like you. But the Welsh harpist . . .'

Cossey stopped sadly, then started again: 'He told me I didn't belong in Ondels Grove and that my real father was a Peruvian Jew or a Spanish Catholic peasant . . . Every time my father punished me, the Welsh harpist stood there at the end of the road promising me such good things if only I had the courage to run away.'

After Cousin Jim and Clarice had gone Cossey would continue: 'Once when I thought I heard the Welsh harpist, it was really Cousin Jim with his dark bristly hair and his funny contented smile. He wanted me to go to the medical school with him and be a doctor too.'

'So he wasn't really your cousin then, was he, if you were really a foundling and your real father was a Peruvian Jew like you said . . .' Floy began earnestly, but Cossey interrupted him: 'As you said,' she corrected his grammar, 'your grammar is foul, Floy.'

That was all she said about Cousin Jim, but she told us how he had come when she and Dad were living in Baston Square in two rooms after they had married and had Vivian.

Chapter V

You could see the stars at night in London then, and sometimes they seemed so distant that they were in the cold silence of an alien place. Sometimes, though, the same stars seemed so close that they might have been birds or flowers out there waiting to be picked, or someone waiting to sing. Then Cossey would forget her childhood and look out on the Fields and describe how the Welsh harpist had told her that loving life was the only thing that mattered. We would creep over to the street side of our flat and see the harsh warnings high up in the sky about Fallen Women, Waifs and Strays, Ancient Lights and Keep Out, and wonder which of the two sides would win.

Cossey would tell us how lovely it was being married in 1924, and free for the first time in her life. She would run out in bare feet just to prove it, and eat fish and chips sitting on the bed. Our parents lived in Baston Square then, near the Elephant and Castle, and had a cooker on the landing looking over the Bedlam Hospital. They would go for long walks when Gilbert got in on those magical spring evenings when the hard ground seemed to yield to the trees above and toss fresh air round the city as they walked. 'We're all only here on sufferance,' Cossey would exclaim. 'Why waste a moment of life worrying about whether you've got the right shoes on? Or whether there's any hope for the lemon curd?'

'Humph,' said Dad.

Their landlady wore a faded, sleeveless overall, the wrap-round kind and gave slow, faded smiles up from her basement. Their room was right at the top of the house, and the double bed filled it almost completely. The brass knobs on the bed-ends unscrewed and they spent a lot of time playing ball with them and lost one once and didn't know what to say to their landlady. So Cossey, who was pregnant, tapped her stomach and explained she'd been hungry and eaten it, and the landlady gave another slow, faded stare. Cossey loved pretending to play an imaginary piano on her stomach. 'My Cousin Jim says he'll come when it's time for doctoration. He's qualified now.'

Gilbert would buy her small things when he had a Saturday free, some blackhead soap, sherbert sweets and a wooden parrot on a stick that made Cossey laugh as he stood there making its jaw work up and down, then bow and talk Dutch, then sing: 'On Ever On, To The Land of the Free.'

'It's like you,' she would laugh. 'I mean, it says, "Take me as you find me. I'm nothing but me."' Gilbert frowned as she hugged him. His black wiry hair was perched in a bristly brush on the top of his head making his forehead seem huge.

'Perhaps our son will be a genius,' Cossey cried. Gilbert frowned again. She often seemed to be laughing at him. 'Perhaps Timothy John will be a genius,' she repeated, staring at his neutral face and broad, snub nose. They sat on the bed under the sloping roof while the gas hissed above them in the wall and tarnished the balls on the bed-ends. 'Perhaps my real father was a Peruvian Jew,' she clutched the lapels of his jacket. 'Cousin Jim at Cambridge says . . .'

'Have you been seeing your cousin again?'

'I went to his hospital for an overhaul when I knew I was pregnant.' Gilbert frowned again. They sat under the roof playing ball again with the knobs on the bed's head till one crashed on the floor and the old Lithuanian lady in the room below called out angrily: 'What is it? Come! So soon.'

As they turned the gas down the cockroaches raced round anticipating all their attacks. They rolled up newspapers when they found them in their food. They loved rice and cake, and Cossey was just chasing one furiously out of a bag of biscuits when there was a call from the narrow stairs and their landlady stood there with Cousin Jim. He stood there calling in his resonant voice that was meant for calling across gardens and high public buildings where famous people met, or across hospitals, or the Houses of Parliament.

'Child,' he called up. The smell of biscuits came from the Elephant and Castle and pickle from the factory in Fentiman Road and his strong voice made even that seem interesting and attract all the other tenants in the house. They all looked on as he stood there calling: 'Child, it's me. Little me. I've got an afternoon free for affectionate you. I want to take you out.'

Cossey hugged him and banged on her stomach and imitated the superintendent at the slipper-baths they went to in Manor Place: 'How are you doing in there, Number Six? Nearly time, ladies and gentlemen.'

Jim gave his curled-up smile in his lazy way as Cossey went on: 'We can't afford much doctoration. Do you wish the baby was really yours?' Gilbert had come in and looked at her cousin sheepishly. 'He thinks it will be a genius,' she teased Gilbert.

Cousin Jim smiled again: 'You could both come out in my car,' he said slowly.

They heard the Lithuanian lady below call: 'What is it? Come. So soon.'

'I've just bought a car,' Jim went on. 'I'm going to take you both for a spin.' The car had two seats and a dicky in the back where Cossey and Gilbert sat with the wind blowing through their hair. 'This is how life should be,' she cried when they got out at Dulwich Park.

Gilbert suggested that they should go for a row on the lake. Gilbert started to row, but jammed the boat into another one and two men shouted at them: 'Good show,' staring at Cousin Jim, 'taking the basement staff out for a brief airing?'

'How are your parents?' Cousin Jim asked quickly as they disentangled themselves and rowed away. 'Is your mother well, Freda?'

'Mother doesn't really believe in being well, I don't think. And Gill's mother's been ill all this last winter. She swears by Baldwins "For relief of all winter's ills" . . .'

When Jim had gone that night a policeman came. Gill's mother was in Dulwich Hospital and they were asked to go to her as soon as possible.

'I didn't know she was *all that* ill,' Freda protested. 'Do you remember how you proposed to me, the day we went to the Grove Vale Pharmacy to get her some of her favourite drugs? I thought she had recovered.'

'I had a letter when we were away,' Gill confessed.

'Well she'll probably pull through now we're back.'

It was a Saturday afternoon and the patients were sitting along the hospital verandahs wrapped in coloured blankets in long silent rows. Mrs Gerber was in bed though, propped up at the end of the ward. She smiled at them and tapped the metal frame of her bed with her wedding ring in a kind of sing-song way and asked Freda how she was. Freda tapped her stomach in response: 'The baby's wearing a hole in my dress. He's so anxious to come out into this lovely world.' Gill grimaced.

'I needed Gill's help to start him,' she added, grinning at her mother-in-law, 'but as soon as he's born he shall be mine and mine alone.' Mrs Gerber tapped again on the frame of her bed. 'Shall we buy you some grapes next time we come? Would you like that?'

Freda leaned over trying to peel her mother-in-law an orange. But the pith got caught on her fingers and she spent the visit trying to flick it off and only succeeded in transferring it from one finger to another then back. 'How much of your life do you spend doing things like trying to get a bit of pith from one finger to . . .' Mrs Gerber tapped the bed again and the big feeding cup frightened Freda suddenly like a big cannon laid beside her frail mother-in-law and ready to be fired.

Gilbert was saying he would bring his mother a spy-glass next time, so that she would be able to see out more, and pick out the masts of ships down the river beyond Blackfriars. The chairs on the verandah still sat in long, silent rows. 'Or you might be able to see out to One-Tree-Hill and Lewisham.'

They laughed and the metal frame of the bed tapped and the feeding cup seemed ready to fire off again.

Mrs Gerber left them enough furniture to use in a small flat after her death, and at her funeral they met Miss Lenege again, the German woman Freda had helped out, the time she shop-lifted. Freda wanted to burst out laughing when she saw her in the yellow blouse she had stitched all those mauve buttons on to disguise it. She looked so smug and satisfied in it. She was vague though about where she would live now that Mrs Gerber had died.

'If you've got any sheets with iron mould on them,' Freda teased her, 'I'd be delighted to help out there as well. I'm an expert at getting stains out.' But Miss Lenege just pressed her lips together and smiled and told them a Dutch philanthropist was helping her to find a flat.

'We want a flat too,' Freda replied. The room in Baston Square was getting cluttered up with all the small things they had bought each other: a matchbox with a tiny peg-doll inside, or a set of chocolate wasps or Japanese water flowers; the parrot that jumped up and down in a ring; but above all by Freda's new typewriter. She had bought it with money she got for a long article she had written. She had told Gill it was about the emancipation of women, but it began: 'Let's face it, every woman will always sacrifice everything to her family and children. Why? Because she's not really a rational being as her husband is . . .'

'I didn't know you thought *that*,' Gilbert stared. 'I thought when we first met . . .'

'I only wrote it to earn enough to buy this typewriter. See? Since *you* couldn't afford to buy me one. Soon we shall be needing more money than you can ever earn. I bet I can earn more than you.'

Freda and Gilbert saw a lot more of Miss Lenege after Mrs Gerber's death. She had a way of turning up at their lodgings at Baston Square on some vague mission for the old Lithuanian woman who lived below. They could hear her shuffling around and clearing her throat, and muttering gloomily when Miss Lenege tapped on her door: 'What is it? Come! So soon!' Then they could hear Miss Lenege's heavy accent as though she were always dragging something bigger behind her, asking after the old lady's health.

Sometimes when Freda and Gilbert were woken in the night by a mouse in their waste-paper basket, Gill would bang it away as though he were bursting a paper bag, 'Shoo!' then pretend he was the mouse, putting on a German accent and crying, 'Gentle Fraulein,' to Freda, 'why do you so much dislike my presence in your waste basket?' He made his voice sound so much like Miss Lenege's that Freda burst out laughing and the Lithuanian woman below cried: 'Now silence. Now please come. Silence.'

The next day Freda had brought in Bath Chaps from East Street Market and as she leaned over the pig's cheeks at supper she stared at the pig's startled mouth and sang at it:

> Take oh take those lips away
> That so sweetly were foresworn . . .

and the pig looked even more surprised till Freda cried: 'Poor innocent piggy! He doesn't know we're laughing at him. He thinks he lives at the centre of the civilized world. Let's become vegetarians.'

So for a week they lived on red cabbage but the colour came out when Freda tried to boil it and Gilbert threw it out of the window saying it tasted of washing. They could hear Miss Lenege below exclaiming about the fling of boiled cabbage that had shot past the window as it sped down to the pavement. Her protruding teeth reminded them so much of the pig on their plates last week that they both fell silent, feeling guilty. They had neglected Gilbert's mother as she lay dying and were suddenly subdued. Gilbert had accused Freda of keeping him from his duty and Freda accused Gilbert of planning to go to Russia on a TUC conference the week her baby was due to be born. They both felt guilty and when they heard Miss Lenege on the landing outside they would invite her in for a cup of tea.

'Is Miss Lenege Jewish too?' Gill asked once they were alone again.

'Roman Catholic, I think. She invited me to her church.'

'What about the little one?' Miss Lenege gave an eagle look at Freda's stomach when they next met her on the landing.

'What little one? Oh you mean Timothy Jo! In here! He says he's having a lovely time. All nice and warm in his quarters.' She tapped her stomach.

'Oughtn't you to be under the care of a medical man? I know a dear old soul under whose wise guidance . . .'

I didn't know you had had a baby? Freda thought. First stealing yellow blouses and then . . .

Aloud she said: 'Perhaps I should see a doctor. It doesn't look as though Cousin Jim . . .' She sounded sad. They set out for the surgery.

Miss Lenege gave a little skip and pulled gently at the big bell that hung beside the doctor's front door. But the old doctor wasn't there and a deep woman's voice called sharply at the gap in the letterbox: 'There's no need to ring the bell. I haven't got time to come to the front door as though you were my guests! Please go down the steps and round the back into the surgery and wait your turn like everyone else.'

They went down to a damp area full of wet leaves and in at a Servants' Entrance smelling of tom-cats and into a basement waiting room.

'It's the lady doctor,' someone said. They could see her behind the faded brown curtain moving about. Freda stared at the door, the window, then at the rows of patients opposite. A woman in a brown coat that smelt of damp held her huge stomach up, dropped it and sighed. Her eyes seemed to be only a small afterthought laid on top of her wrestling body. Freda was depressed, it was hard to believe that these people were real. They stuck to the walls like bits of stuff blown in by a storm, she would tell us later.

Most of the patients seemed to be holding their breath, counting and tapping and waiting for some terrible attention. Freda jumped when a shadow came across the curtain that ran down the room, and the shadow of the doctor's wispy grey hair was thrown across the glass of the window. The woman next to Freda sighed and whispered: 'Go on love, it's you.'

Miss Lenege had already stood up, but the woman doctor ignored them both and sat on her desk and recited: 'There was a young lady called Starkie who once fell in love with a darkie. Bashful?' she added, staring at the row of cats that had settled themselves along the basement window-sill.

Gilbert was in Russia at a trade-union congress when their baby was born. It wasn't Timothy John but a girl, and they were too poor to pay for a hospital, so Freda had had to go to her parents and lie in her mother's bed gloomily. Nothing had changed. Her own childbirth had been no different from her mother's. And her father expected her to stay in the house till she had been taken to his church to be churched and purified, hanging on the end of his stole supplicating readmission to the House of God and asking to be forgiven for having polluted it.

Then Miss Lenege came to visit her and told her she had been a teacher before she was forced to leave Germany. Freda saw that her face was the colour of blackboard chalk and wasn't surprised. Miss Lenege told her that she too was looking for a better neighbourhood to live in. Perhaps together, if they pooled their resources? . . .

'Freda must try to understand,' she said, 'why her husband had gone away just when she needed him most. Gilbert,' she said, 'had always been very close to his mother, and he felt very deeply about her death.' Once, Miss Lenege remembered, she had come into Mrs Gerber's flat late one night to find her weeping and Gilbert, a little boy of five, trying to understand why his mother was weeping, and comfort her. She was weeping, she explained, because she had been to hear Madame Patti sing. Mrs Gerber had loved music and had often been with Miss Lenege to the Queen's Hall.

After that, Freda felt even more unworthy, and wished she had got to know her mother-in-law better instead of just thinking of her as a very good class of Dutch washerwoman. Freda too knew what it was to weep for joy and be overcome when she heard the Welsh harpist and saw that where there might have been nothing but chunks of raw stone and wasps, there was love and music and a mysterious wind blowing round people and coming from afar.

Chapter VI

Cossey and Dad got to know Miss Lenege after the birth of Vivian. They would meet her on the stairs when she was visiting the Lithuanian lady below, and sometimes in the Catholic church where Cossey had taken to going to Mass. Once, though, they met her in the Empress Butcher's. Mr Byles had unhooked a ring from a pig's snout and had banged its head on to his chopping block and patted its nose: 'All pure meat,' he jerked the pig's lips back from its busy teeth.

'Oh how spiritual you look in comparison, Mr Byles,' Cossey had exclaimed. Gilbert had started to laugh and shut her up when they saw Miss Lenege tripping over the road towards them from the church opposite, then claiming the pig's head and directing the butcher how to take his iron ladle and knock the pig's teeth out one-by-one so that they clattered over the shop's floor and Miss Lenege picked them up and instructed the butcher how to sharpen his blade and scrape the pig's tongue and unlink it and let her hold it up like a trophy. 'All pure meat,' she said to Cossey.

'Some lovely fresh brain as well, Ma'am,' the butcher directed her attention to it. 'Scrub it well to get the bone-chips out, then eat it with a bit of turnip and plenty of beer.'

'Oh no,' Miss Lenege corrected him very firmly. 'Brain should be poached in a little milk and taken with wood fungus. In Germany we call them . . .' But the butcher wasn't interested in Germany and just handed over the huge half of a pig's head with a handle made from its ear so that Miss Lenege could swing it along the street like a shopping bag.

'Let's be vegetarians,' Cossey suggested again after they had left the shop. 'Poor old piggums being swung along like a handbag. How would you like it if you were . . .'

Gilbert raised his voice and frowned: 'Man is a predatory animal. He isn't meant to strike up friendly relationships with the feathered and furry beasties except in the stock pot.' He took to calling Cossey's vegetable soups 'the nobs' concoctions' and her salads 'rabbit food'. He went round to the Wash House in the Lambeth Walk once a month and said if you bathed more often you washed away the natural oils of the skin.

'You smell like a sheep,' Cossey complained.

'What's wrong with *that*?'

'You smell of sheep,' Cossey shouted again. There was a bang from the Lithuanian lady below: 'Hullo. There. Come. So soon.'

Vivian started to cry in her cot and the Lithuanian lady banged again, and they crept downstairs to breakfast apologetically next morning. The landlady had asked them to find somewhere else to live now that they had a baby, so they would creep downstairs trying not to be noticed and sit at the table in the window of the basement front-room looking up at the pavement and the tops of the trees in Baston Square.

The landlady's daughter, Verity, would come over silently from the horsehair couch where she had been set by the fire to coax the kettle to boil. She crept over towards Cossey and huddled up to her. Cossey had given her a purple spray of ragged osprey that had once been her mother's.

'Do you like my plume?' Verity asked her, holding it just behind her ears.

'It's a lovely plume.'

'What do you like about it most?'

'The purpley colour and the way it rides there like that. "I'm the Duchess of Baston Square," it says.' Verity leaned further over at her. 'Listen to my hooves going clippety-clip as I go riding away.'

The little girl stared: 'Why would I go riding away?'

Cossey replied: 'Because your lands are very big and you have to ride round each day to supervise them.'

Verity opened her eyes wider: 'What's "supervise"?'

'That's when you tell other people what's what, and they listen and agree. Instead of them always bossing you about: "Do this and do that."'

Verity's mother had come in with the breakfast crockery in a basket and stood there frowning. Verity went to Nanton Road Elementary School just round the corner. She had been told to draw a table in a drawing lesson and Cossey had said she'd help her, and had drawn a meat loaf and three balloons on the table, and her teacher had torn her work up angrily. Then Verity had been told to make a stencil so that she could embroider a picture of 'The Good Shepherd' on her work-cloth in needlework lesson, and again she had brought her work home and again Cossey had 'helped' her by adding all round the green fields where the Good Shepherd was to stand all the food that Jesus and his flock were going to eat during the year 1935, and beside it she had drawn a picture of Verity who was very thin and had no calves to her legs and was training to go into domestic service. Verity had been punished when she took her work-cloth to school stamped with Cossey's indignation. So now Mrs Cruffts discouraged her from going near Cossey and again asked the Gerbers to find somewhere else to live. Cossey would walk past the school and see Verity in her classroom chanting, and the rows of boys with shaved heads and fixed expressions sitting in grey vests down one side of the great stepped classrooms with arms folded across their chests and the girls dressed for domestic service standing down the other side of the room making arm gestures and reciting in the methodical sing-song chant of dutiful but sceptical children:

> If I Could Ride Where the Sea-Horse Plays
> And The World is Gay from the Dear Old Days.

Cossey stopped teasing Verity and was sad to see she would never be trapped into play as she unfolded her pinafore and put her sacking apron on after breakfast: 'We're going to do a wet-sweeping and dry-sweeping this week in domestic training. And hot-sweeping and cold-sweeping.'

'Oh how lovely,' Cossey would widen her eyes in mock enthusiasms, and tried to write the article Gilbert was always urging her to write about the education of girls for slavery.

'Do you know what a fossil is?' she asked Verity one day.

'No, Ma'am,' Verity gave a cautious little smile then shrank a little. Her new adult teeth were beginning to show through at the front of her mouth.

Cossey pointed at them: 'Millions of years ago, before there were any people on the earth, not to mention you and your teeth and your apron here in Baston Square . . .' Verity laughed nervously, 'before even the spiders had got out of their prisons in the rocks. When there was just nothing but black teeth everywhere, but nothing to bite them against and nothing to talk about . . .'

Verity averted her eyes and fixed them on her scrubbing brush: 'I think my mother may be looking for me.' She ran away.

'Isn't life strange,' Cossey said, as she was to repeat so often in our childhood. 'Just think of Verity growing all those white teeth just so that she can say: "Very good, Mum. I'll do the black-leading now shall I, Mum?"'

'You should write that article,' Gilbert urged her. But Cossey went on writing sentimental stories for girls' newspapers because she said they needed the money.

'We can't send our children to Nanton Road Elementary.'

'An elementary school was good enough for me,' Gilbert protested. 'I seem to have survived.'

Cossey looked sceptical, but Vivian and later, Floy, went to Nanton Road Elementary, and I could see Vivian going in at the 'Girls, Infants and Housewifery' door in the brick wall along with the big girls in their green dresses and starched caps. Under the arched entrance-door was the inscription 'LCC Service', written with a celebratory flourish, and Cossey and I, when we went to meet them at the end of the afternoon, could hear them singing 'There's Long Watch Coming' or chanting about how to mix alum and water for scrubbing door-steps. Coming home from school we would see if we could get all the way along the street without treading on the pavement. We would walk along the edges of the railings then leap across the road using a paper bag or satchel as a stepping stone while Cossey asked us bits out of the catechism: 'What did your godparents promise for you at your baptism?'

And we would chant back as we jumped: 'They did promise

and vow three things in my name. Firstly that I should renounce the devil and all his works, the pomp and vanities of this wicked world and all the sinful lusts of the flesh.'

'Verity,' Cossey would ask her as she danced along beside us, 'have you renounced all the sinful lusts of the flesh?'

'Yes Ma'am,' she would nod. For years her mother, Mrs Cruffts, had been wanting us to leave her house, and now as she heard Cossey teasing her daughter she grew even more hostile, and when she saw us all coming home playing feet-off-ground, and clinging to the railings laughing, she grew even more angry and shouted at her daughter: 'You'll end in the Bedlam over the Fields if you're not careful. I'll never find you a position.'

'Poor Verity,' Cossey would sigh. 'Women still want to drag their daughters down with them.'

'What about that talk you're going to give?' Dad asked her. Cossey had been invited to give a talk at the Hansler Hall in East Dulwich about careers for women and their equality with men. As she sat at the window in Baston Square, she could hear her children in the school nearby chanting:

> We are but little children weak
> Not used to any high degree.

She could hear our melancholy chanting and she wanted to give a rousing speech about how awful it was being a woman, and how Socialism must make things better for them: give them proper work instead of just feeding and cleaning and babies, looking after houses, and learning wet scrubbing and dry scrubbing in school.

'I needn't write my speech out,' she told Gilbert. 'Everything will sort itself out on the day. Excitement always puts me on my toes. I'm at my best when there are rows of staring, excited faces to get me stoked up and blazing forth.' Gilbert looked at her doubtfully. 'I'm never at a loss for words,' she added. They were sitting on the tram taking them up to the meeting hall. It had got stuck on 'the deads' and Cossey started to frown too.

'What are you going to talk about?' Gilbert repeated nervously, and now Cossey was nervous too. When they got to the hall it smelt of gas-lighting and bare board floors and emptiness. There were only ten old men sitting there shuffling their feet on the woodwork.

Cossey stared at them and began: 'When I was a Vicar's daughter living in a respectable suburb, I always wanted to use my drawers as a handkerchief and live among ordinary people like you.' There was an uneasy coughing as she continued to insult them. 'I want to help decent working-class people to get a bit of self-respect and learn to develop a bit of imagination instead of standing in rows and singing:

> We are but little children weak
> Not used to . . .

'I'm prepared to sacrifice my life so that your horrible little lives aren't stuck on the tram-deads . . .'

'Freda,' Gilbert begged her, 'that's rude. That's not what they need.' He got up suddenly and told the ten shuffling old men that his wife after all was not in a condition to address them that night. She had a woman's complaint.

Cossey could hear one of the old men shift with relief and say: 'She won't never deliver a speech. I can see that. If you ask me, there's only one thing a woman can deliver successful-like.' He looked at Cossey's stomach meaningfully. She was pregnant again. 'There's only one thing she can do without too much trouble to us men . . .' There was a titter of laughter. Cossey tried to shout angrily that she hadn't got to her main point yet, but the chairman was now discussing the Party outing to Sheerness next month. Then the meeting was closed and the men all went to the pub in Lordship Lane.

'Do you all despise women as much as they do?' Cossey asked on the way home. She thought she had escaped from Ondels Grove. 'You men may have had some small share in starting him off,' she tapped her stomach, 'but from the moment he's born he shall be mine and mine alone.'

'You were an old maid till I came along and took you off your shelf,' Dad retorted angrily.

'And you're so wishy-washy compared with other men . . . so boring compared with Cousin Jim.'

'It's a pity Cousin Jim is only your cousin then,' Dad shouted back, and the old Lithuanian lady below banged and called out: 'So come. So loud!' And they were silent again.

Next day was Sunday and Miss Lenege tapped on their door and suggested that they should all go out for a walk as the weather was fine.

That was the first time our parents had seen Ransome's Fields, Cossey told us later. We had walked there from Baston Square and had been drawn by the sound of the band playing there and the children crawling under the bandstand and playing games like conkers with the plane balls. Cossey had kicked off her shoes and peeled off her thick stockings and let the plane seed run between her toes and teased Gilbert's ears with the long stems of the plane balls. After that we went out often with Miss Lenege.

Once or twice at weekends we'd take a train out from Vauxhall into the country and Miss Lenege would hunt for mushrooms and puffballs that she would give German names to, and Cossey laughed because it made them sound less dirty and scruffy as they stood in bashed circles in the dusty fields. Once as we were staring at some decayed black toadstool stumps, they looked so broken and derelict that Cossey was reminded of battlefields and the Great War.

'Were you in London in the War?' she asked.

Miss Lenege's mouth was watering at the sight of the toadstools and she was licking her lips and stooping to gather them and when Cossey asked the same question a little later she saw that Miss Lenege had raw puffball in a stain round her mouth: 'Where were you in the Great War?' There was black on Miss Lenege's hands too, and she looked guilty as though she had been caught in the act of being a foreigner. There were puffballs in her handbag too, and she exclaimed to Cossey: 'I didn't want the children to get them all.' The sun was like stale egg-yolk and Cossey, who was pregnant again, was tired.

'Let's go home.'

They had called our brother 'Floy' so that if it turned out to be a girl it could be Flora and if it were a boy, it could be Francis Lloyd after Cossey's Welsh uncle. The next baby we called

Samey, so that it could be either a boy or a girl without disappointment.

Soon after we had got home from this country outing, Miss Lenege announced shyly that it was the anniversary of her happy coming into this country. She wondered if she might take our parents out to a German restaurant in Soho, for a little celebration. They sat together uneasily at a table in a draught by the restaurant's door and began a rather artificial conversation, as though they had to show that marriage was fun and that their friendship with Miss Lenege was stronger than it was. But Cossey's awkward sense of humour kept coming out and Gilbert's social awkwardness, and Cossey grew rather arch and kept trying to invent stories about the people at the tables near theirs: 'He's a famous doctor like my Cousin Jim, and over there she's a famous journalist like . . .'

'Like you,' Gilbert teased.

'Some people have never used their imaginations in their lives,' Cossey flared up. Miss Lenege cleared her throat so Cossey changed the subject and started another conversational game. She leaned over the white tablecloth and asked in a fancy voice: 'Which would you rather have, things or views or words?'

Gilbert gave his uncomfortable smile, touched his forelock, and replied: 'I'd be happy with what the ladies are happy with.'

'I'll choose words.' They sat in silence in the cold restaurant. The waiter didn't come.

'Is it a practice in this country,' Miss Lenege's slight accent seemed to become more pronounced as they waited, 'to fail to attend the theatre or the opera on a regular basis?' She looked so accusing. Once Cossey had loved her for stealing a yellow blouse and being on the run from the police. Now Cossey only wanted to get some scissors and snip off the black velvet band that kept Miss Lenege's greying hair from off her wrinkled neck like delicate ribbon tied round rope. She had admired her so much for shop-lifting and thought she had taught her not to feel guilty, but now here she was making the opera into a duty and making them both feel guilty for not going to Wagner's *Ring*. And there was Gilbert suddenly sitting in front of a big pile of sauerkraut when he should have been at a Labour Party meeting. Instead of denouncing capitalism he was holding his breath from the smell of liver sausage and garlic as Miss Lenege cried: 'We must bring music and culture to the masses.'

Gilbert's best suit creaked as he tried to agree, and Cossey remembered how it had creaked at their wedding when he tried to agree with something her father was saying.

'We must try to bring art and beauty to the populace,' Miss Lenege was repeating. Just then though, the waiter lurched forward and sent pease pudding splashing down Miss Lenege's dress. It clung to its threadbare bosom, and Gilbert said and did nothing, just stared horrified as it dripped from sequin to sequin. It was Cossey who called the waiter back. He stared contemptuously at Miss Lenege's faded dress then got a cloth and rubbed at it till the sequins spilled off and fell on to the worn carpet where Cossey tried to salvage them. There was now a white patch on the dress beside Miss Lenege's heavy brooch and the waiter and Gilbert went on wiping even more strenuously while Cossey implored them to stop. They all stared at the hole in her dress. Cossey stood up furiously as she saw the waiters laughing together standing by the sideboard.

'These foreign beasts!' she exclaimed indignantly. 'My parents always thought foreigners were utter beasts.'

But Miss Lenege only smiled ruefully: 'Perhaps they do not care too much for the British,' she said in a slow, silencing voice. 'The German and the French waiter has perhaps little respect for the . . .' She cleared her throat and said no more, but her eyes clearly reproached Gilbert and Cossey for their boorish attitudes to art and to food, and Cossey could picture her slow voice continuing: 'Perhaps they do not like such attitudes to art or to soul-matters, or to culture.'

It was as they returned to Baston Square afterwards that they heard cries coming from Mrs Cruffts' basement. Someone had tied a stocking around Verity's head and was soaking it in cold water, putting on more and more to stop her cries. Then someone took her next door because her cries grew louder and the old Lithuanian lady was getting upset. Then an ambulance arrived and took Verity to the Isolation Hospital in Liverpool Road.

Cossey and Gill leaned out of the top of the Number 33 tram as it approached the hospital next day. From its end windows they could see rows of little girls on benches in the isolation yard. They were wearing long grey calico dresses with black bows at their throats. They all seemed to have shaved heads and the long black bows and the sashes down their backs seemed to wobble like hair and mock their bald heads. Cossey waved, but she could only see the fever van outside waiting for her own children. She felt sure Vivian was inside it being packed away to some place marked only by dots and dashes and dark incinerator towers and tall fir trees and the hoot of ships away out at the Nore or hidden low down in the docks behind the South London Necropolis on foggy winter mornings — as disguised as all things had to be disguised in London, especially as far as women were concerned.

Verity had died of meningitis before they had even got off the tram on their visit. Soon afterwards Cossey found her Elementary School needlework cloth with the stencilled picture of Jesus, the Good Shepherd, beside all the food He and his disciples would eat in the year 1935. Someone had altered it to 1937. It was the year of the Coronation of King George VI and Cossey remembered how Verity had been afraid to laugh or play with the royal plume she had given to her to go 'riding round on her estates'.

'Let's move,' she begged Gilbert, seeing her own children growing up intimidated and being carried away in the fever cart like Verity. She kept dreaming of Verity. Our parents would walk down to the river when the tide was low and the smell of mud was strong and Cossey would dream that they had left Vivian and Verity behind in a window of the hospital and a nurse was leaning out waving a test-tube cheerfully and reassuring them: 'It's all right. It'll only be their singing lessons.'

'Let's move as soon as possible,' Cossey begged Gilbert.

'How can we afford it?'

'I'll write more silly stories for girls, and we'll start looking round. Miss Lenege says there are flats to let if we moved a bit further out. Maybe the river is too close for children . . . It seems as though everyone steps into the river of death as soon as they are born.' That had been the worst black mood of Cossey's that we children could remember, just before we moved to Ransome's Fields. But then things got better.

Chapter VII

At Baston Square though, Cossey still couldn't get over Verity's death. She kept seeing her being folded away among the grey calicoes in the fever van and feeling it was her child being stacked up there, and put away. She kept crying and Miss Lenege came more often to Baston Square to help her in our rooms at the top of the house, as well as to visit the old Lithuanian lady and comfort Mrs Cruffts. Cossey told us later that she couldn't bear to turn left into Nanton Road and hear us all chanting in school. She felt it was a judgement on her. Maybe the clergyman's daughter shouldn't have married the son of a woman who took in the washing. Maybe Mrs Gerber had been right before she died and Cossey was hopelessly out of her depths here in working-class Baston Square. As she walked to the school to meet us at the end of the school afternoons she could hear the ships hooting on the river and mocking the songs we were chanting as we bowed and curtseyed to each other in the big circular school where we learned our catechism and did country dancing and times-tables while the melancholy ships warned us that women and girls should lie low, shrouded by fog under the bridges or close to the wharves. 'Lie low and take cover,' the hooters reported. Cossey wanted us to go to a better school and she longed to move away from Baston Square. Once on one of our weekend walks we crossed a common and came to a ruined house overgrown with creeper. The silence made Cossey clutch Dad's hand but there was steaming horse-dropping on the drive as though the milkman had just been so we banged on its door and tore through its wrecked shrubs and confused berries.

'This,' said Cossey, 'is where you come when you have accidentally swallowed poison. This is where they brought Verity. And now us.'

'Perhaps we should move.' Gilbert started to think.

Late at night the sound of the blue night trams would come even clearer along the streets like the wounded being led across a battlefield, and when one got stuck, the shout would rise: 'On the deads again. On the deads.' Then the trams' metal chains rattled and banged again against the metal sides of the cars: 'Put out your dead.'

'Gilbert,' Cossey would repeat, 'we must move away from here.'

'You always used to say you were the one who had swallowed the poison and survived.'

'Miss Lenege says she knows of a flat for us to rent, further away from the river and the infections. At the other side of the Elephant and Castle. The mansions, she says. They're for professional people.'

'Then they wouldn't do for the likes of us.'

Cossey flared: '*I'm* professional. *I'm* a journalist.' Gilbert pulled a face. 'And I could always tell them my father is the Vicar of . . .' Gilbert pulled another face and sang: 'When Father Painted the Parlour you couldn't see Pa for Paint.'

'Gill, this is serious. Miss Lenege says . . .'

'Miss Lenege was nearly run-in for stealing yellow blouses.'

'Only because she was poor and lonely and new in this country, and couldn't get a job as a teacher. She told me her father wanted her to go to Cambridge. Just think, I might have met her there if I hadn't met you instead and been . . . Gill, with three children and another on the way and so close to the river . . . And Gill, I'm earning enough to help with the rent . . .' Gill gave a mock bow of gratitude, 'and Gill, we ought to be kinder to Miss Lenege. In Germany, Hitler has started to round Jews up, and if the same started here, it would happen to you and me too, because we're socialists and trade unionists. Gill, we're not fighting Hitlerism hard enough, and if we lived nearer Miss Lenege, she might look after the children in the evenings when we are out at public meetings about Franco in Spain . . .'

Miss Lenege had invited Cossey to go with her to an estate

agent who had a soft spot for professional women and their needs.

'If we moved there,' Miss Lenege said wistfully, 'I could have my home piano. Often I long so greatly for it,' she sighed.

'Yes, I'd like a piano too.' Cossey agreed. 'We had one when I was a child and my mother made me play "Bright Citadel of Holy Joy" when really I wanted to play', she pounded on her huge stomach, 'hip-hip-hurray for a heavenly day.'

Miss Lenege always seemed to bring out something skittish in Cossey and when she sang her fatuous songs Miss Lenege's chalk-coloured face was suddenly flushed with pleasure and her lips were wet. 'You must drink. In your condition,' she blinked her eyelids rapidly and went into the kitchen and got into the habit of making tea in the afternoons and sitting there with Cossey till we came in from school.

Our rooms in Baston Square were under the roof, and in the winter we froze and in the summer we sweltered, and all the year the pigeons clutching the roof beam clawed on the tiles above us and kept us awake at nights as though they were trying to get through to us with their horrible throat noises. We used to cook at a stove on the landing, which we shared with three other families and there was a washing-up sink and a lavatory in the yard below. Cossey used to meet us after school once a week and we went to the public slipper-baths in Manor Place and heard the life histories of the people in the next cubicles who were being advised by the bathing attendant. She stood outside by a big wheel like a ship's steering wheel and gave us all first-hand accounts of the reign of Queen Victoria in return, always beginning: 'She didn't care a thing for Prince Albert in his lifetime but once he was dead, my word. But what I say is, "What you don't do for a man in his lifetime, you can't never do after." Time's up there in Number Six. And Number Ten that's all the hot water I'm giving you.'

Miss Lenege spent a lot of time in Baston Square now, looking after us children while Cossey was typing her stories and Dad was out at meetings – Cossey always typing her stories and Dad away at meetings. Cossey tried to write serious articles about schools like Nanton Road Elementary where we did drill on the wired-in roof and stood in the round glass hall inside the classrooms with arms folded chanting about renouncing the pomps and vanities of this wicked world and all the sinful lusts of the flesh . . .

'Renouncing vanities for these poor children won't be such hard work,' Cossey would start typing at her table, but the sound of the children chanting the 'Rule of Four' or singing 'In and Out the Windows' would make her think of Verity again.

She sat at the window and stared down at the street where for centuries millions of patient feet had dragged themselves along in misery or hunger. Why had they gone on? What had they done it for, and where were they now? There wasn't even room in South London for their shadows. They were all stuck solid together, her father and her grandfather and his, in death. No room for a shadow even or a memory as they were drawn along in that stream of life and death, and no one knew where it went. It was then that Cossey was received into the Catholic Church. She started going to Confession on Fridays, and on Sundays after Mass we would go to the parks or over Lambeth Bridge to the Tate Gallery, and coming home she would repeat: 'Gilbert, let's move.'

Miss Lenege had put her head round the door one morning: 'Would you care to come with me some time to the estate agents? We might find that the two of us together?' she dropped her voice at the jaunty suggestion, 'together we might brave the worst ogres inside the estate agents' portals.' She gave her slight guffaw. Her small black eyes were bright with excitement. The block of mansions was in Ransome Street, she said, and the owners were a philanthropic Dutch family who desired to give good accommodation to professional people of German or Dutch extraction. She invited Cossey to go with her and inspect Webbley Mansions. They stood about a mile from Baston Square and looked out on Ransome's Fields which were full of big trees that cheered Cossey up. 'Big trees are like men,' she hugged one as we stood on the grass watching the park-keeper in his brown uniform picking up leaves on a spike and scowling at us and all children in general. At the side of the Fields there was a row of crumbling old houses and, in the middle, a green wooden bandstand, hexagonal and surrounded by a beaten path that seemed to be meant for acting and dancing. Ransome's Fields seemed made for us.

'That's *my* house,' Cossey pointed at a white plaster house with a tall Venetian tower. 'Which is yours?'

'Mine', said Floy pointing at the South London Choir School, 'is that one. Only you don't have to sing all the time.' Vivian's house was a pink stucco cottage with wisteria growing on it. 'You can't have that one,' Floy objected, 'if you're going to be a nun.'

'Mind your own business,' Vivian retorted. My house was the green bandstand in the middle. And we played drums and trumpets there. We asked Miss Lenege which was her house: 'Now your turn, Miss Lenege.' But she shook her head and tears came to her eyes. We turned back and went towards Webbley Mansions which stood on the corner of the Fields. The Mansions were tall and wide and solid and grand and made of polished red brick with shiny black borders. They stood on a corner of the Fields looking out on the street as well, and they smelt of roasting beef and disinfectant, and there were angels' wings all along the roof rides and great loops and bows and pots of stone geraniums extravagantly carved under the window ledges. The great oak double-doors at the foot of the stairs had twenty-four polished bells beside them and were carved with the story of Adam and Eve in a garden of Eden that looked very much like Ransome's Fields only with a smiling sickly serpent with big lips in the middle instead of the shabby green bandstand, and there was a notice pinned on Adam's carved and shiny buttocks: 'No milk today at number 16 please thank you.'

We climbed the slippery stone stairs up to the third floor and slid down the banisters to the bottom again while Cossey, who was pregnant, climbed up more slowly with Miss Lenege, followed by the caretaker shaking water out of her one good eye. Cossey started to sing, 'I don't know why I'm so happy, so happy, so happy', while Miss Lenege gave the funny watery look that she often gave when Cossey had bursts of enthusiasm about life.

On the first floor were the Stalwart Dining Rooms where the

permanent smell of roasting beef came from. Then we climbed another flight and came to a tiny flat with only two rooms facing on to an alley and a stable of horses stamping restlessly.

Cossey turned to Miss Lenege: 'You'll have a lovely view of horses' tails.' Miss Lenege stiffened. 'And from your other window,' Cossey peered out, 'you'll be able to see the Hippodrome and Mrs Hepsibah's washing.' Miss Lenege stiffened again. 'Now let's go upstairs and see *ours*.' Cossey turned and we climbed up to the third floor. 'Oh we shall be happy here,' she flung off her shoes as we all trooped into Number 18. It had a big stained-glass window that looked over the street, and an iron-work balcony decorated with big, wilting, rusty plums and rhubarb sticks. We all started to dance round the bath that stood in the kitchen beside the huge black iron Imperial Boiler. Floy pretended he was the Imperial Guard, and Vivian rooted about in the cupboard that was meant for coal and found she had come out in the sitting room by the huge windows where Cossey was already sitting in bare feet, planning her future career as a journalist. At the end of the hall there were three steps up to a fourth bedroom. It was only a boxroom and its window was high up in the wall and only looked down on to the public staircase. But up above in the ceiling was the turret and dome that gave the Mansions their important public look from the street, like a bank or a state residence or a grand cinema. We all climbed up into the turret, and Cossey leaned out of the dusty glass lantern and down over an advertisement hanging off the side of the mansions below: 'Johnnie Walker Scotch Whisky'. She laughed as she tried to reach down and touch the capital 'J' of 'Johnnie': 'I'll just get a duster,' she called to Miss Lenege, 'and sponge his trouser legs down. Then I'll get busy on his walking stick with the Mansion Polish. But first we'll go back and see what we can do for *your* flat.'

A little choking came from Miss Lenege's throat, then she moved her feet and said in her quiet way: 'Oh, I beg your pardon Mrs Gerber, but I think I've already made it clear to the landlord that my interest is in *this* flat?'

'But this is the flat for a married couple with three children!'

Cossey protested. 'We couldn't possibly live in those two pokey rooms and no lovely view of Ransome's Fields and all the lovely life going on down there on the other side of the Fields.' Vivian had run the bath and was splashing about in it, humming to herself and cleaning the taps and looking for something to dry herself on. Floy had woven some old curtain material in and out of the ironwork of the balcony and had made himself a residence and pinned up a notice on the glass windows: 'Please do not disturb or come in unless invited.' And I was staring out at the Fields and the green bandstand and the big, old houses on its other side. They looked so full of people, and beyond I could see Big Ben and Westminster Abbey and felt I was going to be something famous when I grew up. A famous actress or a musician or even an eye specialist. The Fields promised that.

But Miss Lenege stood there firmly declaring this was her flat.

'She can't want all those rooms,' we whispered angrily all the way home. 'She'd have to have six children and she looks too thin and bony for that. And she's too old.'

But when we got home Dad told Cossey he had had a large cut in his wages. The Slump and the fear of a coming war had affected the travel business badly. He was going on a half-wage, so that Webbley Mansions were quite out of the question, whichever flat it was. Our landlady had just told us that when the next child was born we'd have to leave Baston Square in any case, but Miss Lenege stood there with pursed lips in our door and we heard our parents still discussing the Mansions when we had gone to bed. It was decided that we should share Number 18 with Miss Lenege. She agreed to take the small boxroom as her bedroom and share the kitchen and living room with us and pay half the rent: 'I am a grateful guest in this country of yours,' she explained. 'You are my family now.'

We heard the Lithuanian lady in the room below clear her throat and say: 'Come! Now. So soon.'

Cossey cleared her throat: 'We shall all be very happy together and have lovely times. Bags I have the first bath at Webbley Mansions.'

'The balcony is still mine, though,' said Floy.

And so we all moved to Webbley Mansions, moored like a ship between Ransome Street and Ransome's Fields, little knowing as Cossey ran out in bare feet and hugged the trees, how it would change us all. It was here, sitting by the fire in 1936 and looking out over the gaunt grey street, that she told us about the horrors of the Great War and what she would do if there were another. And it was here looking out over the grass and the green curly benches in 1937 and over to the big houses and the Houses of Parliament that she told us how lovely life was if you let it be. She gradually forgot about Verity, and she also forgot to tell us how it was that life was both so terrible and so good. Perhaps she didn't know. All she did tell us, looking over at the green bandstand and the important houses beyond that gave on to the tube trains and the spires of central London, was that the blind Welsh harpist had come to her while she was still young and told her she was in love with life. She left it to us then, to fit the two sides of our world together as our ship, Webbley Mansions, floated sometimes in dirty black waters and sometimes on a calm blue sea. And Cossey left it to us to discover what was horribly wrong with life, though she and Dad never hesitated to warn us that something *was* horribly wrong with it, as they set out for a public meeting about Spain, or Nazism in Germany.

Chapter VIII

———   .   ———

'Oh we shall be so happy here!' Cossey would exclaim leaning over the ironwork balcony and looking down over Ransome Street. 'Ransomed, Healed, Restored, Forgiven,' she would sing her favourite hymn. The big carvings on our front doors of the story of Adam and Eve in the Garden of Eden and the serpent with the fleshy lips prancing round the tree seemed a bit like Ransome's Fields themselves. In the carved foliage of Eden we could almost see the pink stucco cottage opposite with the spelling mistake 'Mount Veiw' engraved into its stone forehead; the Venetian mansion with high railings and stone pom-poms round it where a doctor kept patients out on licence from the Bedlam asylum; then the Jeanette Short Academy of Dancing and Elocution where you could see girls' arms suddenly reaching up out of nowhere in the window frame of the big three-storeyed Georgian mansion and hear voices crying in an elocution lesson that seemed to go on at the same time as the dancing, and to consist of reciting the school's register along with the school's director, Miss Short.

Miss Short had long, thin legs and wore purple leotards and a purple tunic that didn't quite match them, and a black velvet hat with swords and spears pinned round its brim and jangling when she called out the register of school pupils for them to recite after her: 'Amy Ablewoman . . . Betty Boaster . . . Clover Cleverlegs . . .', and the pupils would all recite after her in their best elocution voices like grand dames: 'Diane Dainty . . . Elmer Eversleep . . . Francis Fancyface . . .'

'And Cossey Clevertoes,' I would hug Cossey as the voices went on and the music started up, the piano plonking up and down, up then down, then up, the tinny sound re-echoing round the ballroom as Miss Short cried: 'A nice clean *échappé* there please, Betty Baxter, and you'll never win the Derby in that third position, Jenny Jimson.'

And beyond the Fields we could see the little brick Public Baths called Lolly's Lido and see the green cotton figures inside it with green cotton bags on their heads climbing up on to the diving board, pinching their noses, then jumping off and disappearing behind the houses, then up again on to the board. Our favourite walk was still along the Embankment and over Lambeth Bridge to the Tate Gallery to see the people bursting out of their graves in Stanley Spencer's 'Resurrection'.

'I do feel just like that,' Cossey would cry, and on the way home she would point at the swimmers in their green cotton robes with bags over their eyes in Lolly's Lido, then the tube train would rattle and stop behind the Fields and big cages would open and people would come leaping out of the train's doors just as they had done in the 'Resurrection'. Even further beyond we could imagine the Sisters of Our Lady in Ara Coeli chasing their dog among the bushes of the little yard between the high buildings and Ancient Lights of our school. Cossey was earning enough now to take us away from Nanton Road Elementary School. Dad protested that schools that had been good enough for him were good enough for us, but Cossey insisted: 'I want our daughters to do proper things when they grow up, not serve in sweet shops, or the post office.'

She started to write a story about a girl who won a scholarship to the university and wanted to become a surgeon. But her editor ordered her to make wiser counsels prevail and the heroine became a nurse and married the surgeon instead. It was this kind of story that paid for Vivian and me to go to Our Lady in Ara Coeli and for Floy to go to the grammar school at Kennington Oval.

Dad had bought a gramophone on the never-never with a black handle to wind it, and Miss Lenege would stand in the door of her cubby-hole up three steps and stare wistfully down as our parents danced round and round to 'Speak to Me of Love'. Sometimes they would feel guilty as they saw her standing there with her lips slightly parted, and they would wait till she had gone down and out across Ransome's Fields to the clinic where she worked on its other side before putting a new record on and fox-trotting round to 'Singing in the Rain'.

'Would you like a chocolate?' Dad asked Cossey, carefully opening a bag of Maltesers when the music clicked off.

'No thank you. If I had one, I'd want four more.'

'You're greedy,' Dad objected. 'How funny it is that I never want four,' he teased her.

'You're righteous,' Cossey laughed back. 'You think you're so righteous just because . . .'

'Talking of righteousness,' Dad looked at us as we sat there in our convent black dresses with blue silk collars and rosaries hanging off our wrists . . . But we liked it at Our Lady. The chapel was right on the top of the school with the tube trains running just underneath and as you knelt on its tall kneelers at prayer you could hear them whinnying away to central London and hear the Sisters below giving violin lessons and tapping with their feet and calling 'One two.' We kept our coats in a cupboard in the corridor and a girl once locked me inside just before we were to climb the four flights of stairs for Friday Mass. When the class came down afterwards, the girl released me and Sister Cuthbert smiled at me and said: 'You see, Our Lord really was *with us* in His Real Presence. On the altar, as I said He would be, wasn't He?' She looked at me and waited for me to agree, and I stared at the way the hard white of her starched collar nearly touched the soft white lobe of her ear. I waited for war to start. Instead she told me that the alabaster stoup of holy water for good behaviour this term had been won by Rosina Bosz, the girl who had locked me in the cupboard. Yes, I liked school and I intended to become a famous musician or a dancer.

One day when I got home from school Miss Short came grimly out of her dancing academy's front door and down the steps followed by all her pupils. We could hear her crying furiously: 'Soon I'm going to start getting really angry.' She was telling her pupils to do improvisation and 'free dancing' inside the green bandstand in a very generous voice as though she were giving things away right and left. We could see the girls and one priggish-looking boy sitting there inside the bandstand with their comics as she made out their termly bills inside her ballroom. Then she came out and stuck a notice on her front door and on the trunks and branches of the trees in the Fields:

Look! JUST LOOK! TWO DANCING LESSONS
FOR THE PRICE OF THREE.

'She's got that the wrong way round,' Dad objected. However when Miss Short came out again and grimly set the notice right: 'Three dancing lessons for the price of two', Dad lit his pipe and read it again and again remarked: 'What about a bit of cut-price education for our children? Do you think', he suggested, 'we could ask the nuns to give them three rounds of "The Battle of Hastings" for the price of two? And you've been doing some cut-price washing-up,' he added, peering at some forks we had just washed up and tipped out on the draining board. 'And I can see a food fragment adhering to that cup that was previously adhering to your person, and your upper lip. And now it's transferred itself to . . .'

Just then he saw Miss Lenege coming back across Ransome's Fields from the shabby TB clinic beside the tube-train tracks. Her face was whiter than ever and there would be pink circles on her cheeks when she got in. She had a slow creeping walk and would slip into the flat in silence. She worked in the clinic, she said, distributing medicines from the small dispensary at its side. She would glide into the flat and sit down making heavy breathing noises and Cossey and Dad would switch the gramophone off and have rather unnatural and stage-managed conversations to protect themselves from her stare.

'How are you feeling?' Cossey would ask Dad in the artificial voice she kept for these times.

'My feelings aren't all that different from other people's,' he would reply in an equally unfamiliar voice. 'Feelings came very late in man's history, and they're still only a luxury, and mainly for women.'

'And what for men then?' Cossey would reply stagily.

'For men, life is just a battle to obey the fixed and unalterable laws of nature.'

'My chief battle,' said Cossey, 'is *against* the laws of nature. Take for example the Laws of Gravity and the way these stupid cups and saucers keep seeking the ground.'

'If battle is *against* nature,' Dad went on, 'please could you address yourself to those two furry black flies which seem part of nature's laws as they attack our meat over there in the meat-safe.' They would both gaze at the broken latch of the meat-safe. Dad had tried several times to mend it but it always squeaked open again as if to say, 'See,' as soon as his back was turned. We were always having to boil water and pour it over the sticks of white blow-flies eggs we found in the corners of our Sunday joint before we ate. Just as our parents were about to try out another rather arch dialogue, the pony with his milkfloat would come clipping along under the windows and Miss Lenege's voice would interrupt, unimpressed.

'Freda, have you taken your milk today? Nature requires.' Cossey was feeding Samey then and would rush to the window and call down to the milkman and lower a jug to the pavement tied on a dressing gown cord. But afterwards when they were alone, she would complain to Dad: 'I wish she wouldn't stare so and breathe so.'

'Well, we couldn't manage without her. She pays most of the rent.'

'She needs us just as much.'

Miss Lenege would stare fascinated as Cossey fed Samey, and Cossey would remember how they went into the country and she had dark puff-ball smears round her mouth. Miss Lenege had a spinning wheel in her little room up the three stairs at the back of the flat, and it would make strange noises at night. And her breath always smelt. 'She must be taking secret sips of the paraldehyde and veronal she dispenses from the TB clinic on the other side of the Fields.'

'I like to be of some service in this country in which I am such a grateful guest,' Miss Lenege would explain her trips over to the clinic.

We were surprised to find Cossey imitating her, standing on a chair in the kitchen, once when she was eight months pregnant and sloshing paint on to the wall above the bath, wiping splashes off the taps and adding to Dad: 'Still, it's very useful having someone in the flat when you and I are both out at meetings. But she's much older than she seems. Most of her life was lived before the Great War. And though she goes to Mass, she's really a Jew. There's a great carved chest in her room and funny melancholy dishes and candlesticks like trees spreading round her table.'

Dad was angry: 'You sound like Hitler.'

But Cossey assured him she wasn't anti-Semitic: 'It's not the fact that she's a Jew that I'm afraid of. It's the fact she's hiding something. She's much older than she pretends to be and she's been away somewhere for a very long time. In prison. Or in a hospital . . .?'

'You'd been "away" for a very long time when I first met you. You'd been hiding in a Vicarage for nearly ten years. What were *you* doing all that time?'

'Mother wouldn't let me do anything except Scripture Union and Dorcas and Ladies' Sewing Guild. They wanted me to marry a Vicar, or no one. But Miss Lenege,' Cossey went back to her irritation, 'never actually tells us what she does when she goes over Ransome's Fields every day.'

Dad had taken Cossey to Gamages to buy a mattress, and as they watched the lady assistants, they saw that one of them was wearing a wig. She was dragging the chipped enamel cans of water up the stairs to the staff dormitories, and they could hear the thuds as the jugs went up after her a step at a time, the banging matching the thud of cloth bolts on the drapery counters. Cossey could have sworn that she saw Miss Lenege in a wig slipping away upstairs. 'She's much older than we think and she was on the German side in the Great War, and she never actually tells us what she does when she goes over Ransome's Fields.'

'You weren't so mean when I first met you. I didn't know you had such trivial dislikes,' Dad cleared out his pipe.

'I don't dislike her. It's just that I can't get on with my stories when she's always sitting there with her Parish magazine breathing heavily over Father Piggot's weekly ho-ho. And she seems to belong to the past that we want to forget.'

'You're always reminding us of the past, yourself.' But Cossey had stopped talking about the Great War now that Franco was winning in Spain. She never said now: 'If ever there were another war I'd . . .' Instead she would sigh as she heard Miss Lenege's spinning wheel creaking and rattling in her little boxroom: 'Miss Lenege is like a leech. Or she's like a stone that you can't get out of your shoe.'

And yet both Dad and Cossey were glad of Miss Lenege when they went out at nights or when Cossey was busy with an article. And we went on making Sunday expeditions together, Dad striding ahead with his pipe in his mouth and us children following behind.

During the week we would play in Ransome's Fields and people the green bandstand with singers and dancers and actors and flags. We decided we were going on the stage and would make up plays to perform to Cossey out there, sweeping back the leaves from the paths and letting her sit there with bare feet toeing the dust and the plane-seed and crying: 'You naughty children! You haven't rehearsed. I want my money back, not just this tepid cocoa you've made me. I want to see the play begin.'

And if Dad were there he would nod: 'Quite right,' and play an overture on an imaginary banjo as we went behind some bushes to the Public Conveniences we regarded as our dressing rooms. When we came back, Dad had gone and there was Cousin Jim sitting on the bench beside Cossey and laughing with her. The plane trees stood round them like leopards in their spotted bark jackets. Suddenly everything seemed turned away from the noises of the London streets. Behind our green bandstand theatre we could still see the women in green swimming dresses with green bags on their heads jumping off the Lido's diving board, and down behind the Perfectio Fish Bar and the Leopard Dining Rooms. Everything suddenly seemed so inviting. The Public Baths. The big houses in the Fields. The home for lunatics when they were getting better. The Chapel askew. The TB clinic. 'Mount Veiw' spelt wrongly – as though the people there were too happy to care about a bit of 'i-before-e', and, at the end of the Fields, the singing and playing coming out of the Jeanette Short Academy of Dancing and Elocution, the plonking up and down of the piano to the burly shouts of the elocution class:

> Half past two. Mend your shoe.
> Half past three. Time for tea.

The sounds went bonking to-and-fro to the piano's accompaniment as though a whole world lay behind waiting for us.

And there, as the piano and voices went up and down, up and down, to-and-fro, stood Cousin Jim again. The voices and the piano stopped. Cousin Jim was waiting with his new car to take us out for a drive. Jim and Cossey were laughing and the Welsh harpist sent a wind from behind the mountains that drove us slowly round London standing on the running boards of his car with the wind in our hair until we saw Miss Lenege plodding slowly home. She smiled at us and held out her big hand to Jim and took a deep breath.

Cossey put on her most cheerful voice and cried: 'Miss Lenege, don't you ever want to run about with your bare toes, or run naked round and round bandstands with the wind between your legs?'

Miss Lenege thought and Jim laughed, and after that we thought that things would go on getting better and better because of the Fields and Cossey's love of running over them and hugging the trees and shouting 'Hurrah'. Perhaps there wouldn't be another war after all. Perhaps Franco wouldn't win in Spain and Hitler wouldn't dare to invade this country. Perhaps the winters would stop being foggy and the girls at school would stop jabbing pen nibs into my neck when they sat in the desks behind mine or locking me in cupboards. Everything seemed to be running along so well like the swimmers in the Lido going down, then up, then down, then up, and the piano in the dancing school going down, then up, then down. Everything seemed to be getting better and better. Cossey's black moods seemed to have gone, and I was having music lessons and Vivian was still dead-set on being a nun, and Floy wanted to be a 'total engineer' though he would get cagey when we asked him why he wanted to be a 'total' one and not a 'pink' one or a 'Thursdays' one.

It was the anniversary of Cossey and Dad's running away on the *Percy Warrior* to Northumberland and we were all going out to a restaurant to celebrate. Dad wanted to take us to a Lyons Corner House, but Cossey's magazine boss had once taken her to a French restaurant and she wanted to take us there too, and point out all the famous people she had known and still knew, she maintained.

'This place isn't for the hoi-polloi,' Dad objected. 'It's not for the hordes and the masses.' The waiters seemed to think this too as they brushed past us flipping their starched napkins as though to fan us away. Eventually one took us to a table at the back of the restaurant beside a screen where the underground trains rattled past. We could hear taps being turned on and off in the kitchens through a thin door and the blasphemings of the kitchen staff.

Cossey tried to cheer us up: 'Writers and Members of Parliament and famous specialists and all sorts of celebrities are all coming out of the Underground now and walking past just on the other side of that wall. Just listen!'

'I'm hungry,' we replied, ignoring the sounds of the trains.

'Just think of all the famous people walking along just the other side of you, Floy . . .'

'We must all get under the table then,' said Dad, 'till they've got past in case they give us a bellyful.'

'When are they going to give us something to eat?' we moaned.

'Just think,' Cossey went on talking to Dad, 'if I hadn't met you, I'd still be over there with them.' She stared at some journalists.

'No you wouldn't. You'd be sitting in your mother's drawing room making clothes for Sales of Work, and handing out soup tickets to the deserving poor.' Cossey opened her mouth, but just then the waiter came over and dumped someone else's white dish of *haricots verts* on the edge of our table beside Cossey's elbow. She tried to ignore it but it steamed in her face.

'Do you remember,' she said, 'how when you first came to the Vicarage you came round to the servants' entrance and we thought you were the new gardener's boy?' The dish of steaming beans shifted a little nearer the edge of the table. 'Whoops,' she called, and the waiter took it away and we sat in splendid isolation again at a white tablecloth with only an ash tray and two wine stains on it.

'I'm hungry.'

'When are we going to get something to eat?'

Behind the dirty frosted glass screen at our side we could hear another train coming in and its doors slowly opening and a whiny voice calling, 'Mind the Step,' and 'Stand Clear of the Doors.' Dad made several more attempts to summon a waiter. Cossey grew angry and tried to summon a different one herself. Finally a third waiter came up and deposited a huge pile of dirty plates. A piece of paper fluttered down on to Cossey's sleeve from nowhere. 'Stir the contents slowly,' she read. Dad doffed an imaginary cap and added: 'And whistle thrice.'

The people at the next table looked over at us and laughed. Cossey felt sure they were from her magazine. She looked at Dad in the creaky pin-striped navy suit he had bought for his wedding twelve years ago. The only sound was the stiff suit creaking, and the rattle of the tube trains on the other side of the glass wall. We had waited nearly an hour now for our dinner, but only another stack of dirty plates reached our table. We went behind the gritty frosted glass and into the Ladies. In the cubicle standing on the lavatory seat, we could peer down on to the tube station below and see the trains full of distinguished-looking people, surgeons and judges and MPs all going along the platform and through special doors for Whitehall, the House of Commons and St Thomas's Hospital.

Cossey looked very depressed again as she watched them disappearing and the platform empty and silent once more. We went back to the restaurant, and saw that Dad had barely noticed our disappearance. He was standing by the table where more of other people's food and plates had been stacked.

'What are we doing feeding our faces here when the Spanish Republic is on its knees,' he asked, 'and trade unionists in Germany are being flung into prison right and left? Let's go.' We marched out of the restaurant hungrily and over to the tram stop in silence.

'I'm off to Germany tomorrow,' Dad went on. 'We've decided to stop all trade union visits to Germany, so I'll be out of the country.'

'You're always out of the country. That's your second name.'

'Socialists who've escaped from Germany to Switzerland have been telling us terrible stories about being rounded up by Hitler. We should be warning everyone, but instead we're just . . .'

But we three children were crying, and the tram didn't come. So Cossey bought us fish-and-chips and we walked home eating and trying to forget that something was badly wrong. Cossey looked scrawny like a screwed-up piece of paper and Dad was accusing her: 'You made me neglect my mother in her hour of need, when she was dying,' he said in a jerky voice, 'and now you . . .'

'Your hair looks sealed on,' Cossey taunted back, 'as though your mother had stuck it on there when she glued on your shirt collar and tie, and best suit.'

'You caused my mother's death so now I beg you to refrain from undermining my work for the Labour cause and our Socialist brothers . . . in Germany and Spain.'

'Give them my love and tell them that after the Revolution we'll have green trams instead of red, and water our geraniums three times a day. We're not owed anything in this life.'

'I didn't know you despised us so much,' Dad replied slowly, jerking his chin up and down. 'I knew you despised *me*, but . . .'

As we passed a pub, in Lambeth Bridge Road, Dad said casually: 'My father lived up there when he was a young man. The pub sign used to creak in the wind and keep him awake at nights. He decided to become a cabbie and bought a horse and cab to ply for hire. But he'd been sold a dud. His horse was a lady's horse and stopped at every house in the street as though my lady were just waiting up there for her horse to arrive.' Dad gave a little bow. 'Her ladyship's horse. That's me.' He doffed an imaginary cap: 'Her ladyship's horse.'

But Cossey interrupted: 'How funny to think that while your

father was trying to drag his old nag down the street without stopping at ladies' houses, my father was standing in his pulpit preaching about Moses and the bulrushes. Your father and my father. Funny if they could have met. Perhaps if they had, you and I would never have done.'

'And you would have found a different coat-hanger to hang your children on,' Dad replied quickly.

Cossey said nothing more and we walked home feeling light-headed at near escape from non-existence. It felt like a gas escape.

'What happened to your Dad?' we asked Dad later.

'He went out to the West Indies and was never heard of again.' Dad sucked at his pipe although it wasn't lit. 'I'm thinking of going to the West Indies too.' He spoke lightly as though he were making some plans for an outing or a birthday.

Cossey repeated as we walked along: 'Do you remember how you always came to the tradesmen's entrance at the Vicarage, Gill?' We were passing some big houses: 'Look at those lovely houses. Which is *yours*? Mine is the tall, thin one with the stripey curtains and that middle room with the big windows is our music room because my husband's a famous pianist.' Her Cousin Jim, Cossey said, had just moved to a house like this and started up his first practice. 'Which is your house, Gill?' she turned back to Dad.

Dad screwed his face up into an angelic smile: 'My house is the tradesmen's entrance round the back. Or the shop where they keep the hat racks and the clothes-horses and coat-hangers.' He put on a simple-minded smile as we got home and added: 'I'm surprised you don't still send me round by the tradesmen's door as you did at your Vicarage.' Just then we saw that Dad must have sat on something in the restaurant because the back of his best suit had a big patch of potato on it. He put his hands behind his back and pretended to be simple-minded again and we all wanted to cry again as he said, clearing his throat: 'I knew you despised me, but I didn't know the children did too. I didn't know the exact specifications and dimensions.' He waved his arms up and down and round as though he were outlining the shape and size of a carton. After this he spoke more and more often to us in jest, or ironically, or answered remarks with a quip or a fatuous retort like something out of a cracker. Cossey told us afterwards that after the birth of Samey she felt empty and depressed as though she had gone through all that pain and humiliation in order for someone else to have the child. It felt as though Samey wasn't hers, she would say. She'd just been selected as the whipping-boy for some more exalted woman's confinement, the wife of a lawyer or a doctor.

Dad had been away at the time of Samey's birth and all Cossey received from him was a picture postcard from Munich: 'Am visiting a German *Beerkeller*. Very worrying. But German Socialists seem to take their country and their nation very seriously indeed. I hope you are keeping well. Love Gill.'

He had forgotten she was having another baby and when he got home he was puzzled to hear a baby's cries.

Cossey got more depressed from then on and planned more outings at weekends to cheer herself up. Dad was becoming more and more neutral all the time now too.

It was 1937 and King George VI had just come to the throne and when Cossey said: 'I know, let's all go on an anti-coronation picnic,' Dad just raised his hand to his forehead and touched an imaginary forelock and said: 'Very good, Your Royal Highness. It shall be just as you desire.'

Miss Lenege nodded too, and we looked up the times of Green Line buses, and Cossey made a galantine in an old fish-kettle and shaped it like a working-man's boot.

Chapter IX

The morning of the Coronation we took the Green Line bus out to Hertfordshire. Miss Lenege had pronounced that there was a very fine cathedral at St Albans. Dad pretended to swoon at the thought of 'a very fine cathedral', so Cossey, who never liked to be thought a barbarian by Miss Lenege, pretended to be very knowledgeable about ecclesiastical architecture. But as she and Miss Lenege were talking earnestly about transepts and rose windows and ambulatories, our bus passed a watermill. Dad spied its big wheel rattling round and we all leaped off the bus and sat by the tumbling water. We wandered into some woods and sat down under a tree and tried to fight off the ants and the wasps while Cossey undid the galantine she had shaped like a man's boot and pulled chunks of bread out of a damp tea-towel and cried: 'Here's to the end of all coronations.' Dad raised his glass of cider and Miss Lenege nibbled at a piece of the heel of the meat boot and the woods smelt lovely and green and cool after the hot-clothes smell and the hot upholstery of the bus.

'Look at that bull,' Dad pointed over into a field. 'It reminds me of a grand piano with its lid up and waiting to break forth in: "God Be With Us Till We Meet Again".' We all started to sing and Miss Lenege lowered her head over her food and examined wild flowers and asked their English names.

Then we went back to the pub where Dad had got the cider and he brought out more to the wooden bench where we sat and Miss Lenege spied black mushrooms, then rejected them: 'They are not lively enough!' The sizes of British trees were wrong too, she seemed to suggest, and the shapes of its hills and the spires of its churches.

'What about the expression on the sheeps' faces?' Cossey teased her. 'Is there something wrong with that too?' But Miss Lenege had gone darting into some woods and when we caught up with her she was hastily gathering more mushrooms into her skirt and her face was smeared and she was whispering to herself about gathering them in before the boys got them.

A horse and cart went past. There was a notice along the side of the cart: 'White Horse Waste'. Dad looked at some steaming horse droppings that suddenly appeared on the scene: 'As if the colour of the horse made any difference!' he exclaimed. Cossey laughed loudly and Miss Lenege looked puzzled and we went with her back into the woods where she tried, as she often did, to teach us some German.

A small bird limped across our path: 'Eine Vogel,' we all cried.

'That is correct,' Miss Lenege cried back looking pleased, and scooped it up and pressed it against her side. It gave a click and she said: 'There was something badly wrong with its limbs,' and deftly tucked it away in her handbag.

'There wasn't, until you seized it,' Vivian said rudely. The bird fidgeted and Miss Lenege gave it a little nudge. Her bag now seemed full of birds and nuts and fungi. We got back to where Cossey was feeding Samey under a huge oak tree. Miss Lenege sat down heavily on a tree trunk breathing loudly in and out. Finally she said to us: 'It's surprising that you children have turned out as well as you have. Considering all things.'

'What things?' We thought of the strange spinning wheel that stood in our flat just by the door of Miss Lenege's boxroom. Once when our father touched it accidentally it creaked and collapsed and Miss Lenege came out of her room and called angrily: 'So!'

'What things?' we asked her. 'Considering what?'

'The English have no idea of joy or sorrow. That has all died with Shakespeare,' she sighed. 'Your Reformation and your Protestantism killed all joy and all we humans think of as our souls . . .'

We were all very subdued. Dad said slowly: 'I'm afraid it's true. The British have no respect for foreigners.'

We sat in guilty silence till Cossey lifted her glass of cider and cried: 'Here's to all the anti-coronations in the world!'

Dad doffed an imaginary cap and called: 'Yes, Your Majesty. Hear. Hear.'

'What's an anti-coronation?' we asked.

'It's when you don't believe in Kings and Queens and dairy maids all in a row in the Public Baths,' Cossey began, but just then there was the sound of a car's hooter. Cossey turned and got up and went away and came back with her Cousin Jim. We all hugged him and raised our glasses again.

'He said he might come and he did,' Cossey cried. 'So here's to Jim and the Welsh harpist and all the other people like us who want to know why some people have all the money and stage big expensive coronations for their measly relatives while others have to go to the Lazarus delousing centre and the Judas soup kitchen.'

'Look who's talking,' Dad retorted. 'Just having anti-coronation picnics, or feeling sorry for the unemployed doesn't help.' Cossey was silent. Dad went on: 'We're doing nothing to help fight Hitler. You're a journalist, but you only write girls' stories that you know are silly and tell girls their real place is in the home.'

'You're all very glad of the money my stories bring in,' Cossey defended herself. 'How are you, Cousin Jim?' She turned to her cousin who laughed and hugged us all in turn. He smelt of soap and salt and the patch of skin where his neck met his starched white collar was warm. He gave the funny dark secret cat-like smile that he gave whenever he did anything authoritative.

'Where's Clarice?' we asked him. For a moment his smile was fixed, then he paused and shrugged, then hugged us all again.

'I've got all of you instead.'

Cossey lifted her glass of cider to him: 'How strange it all is, and us just sitting here not seeing that nothing might have been here at all. Nothing everywhere. Jim, do you remember that time I came to St Thomas's when you were a houseman there and the matron banged on the wooden pews with her bunch of keys and called at me: "Mother, you must wait your turn for Doctor like everyone else." And you came along in your white coat with the stethoscope swinging from your pocket and we looked out of the window and there, beyond the buckets of blood and sputum, was a sort of incinerator chimney smoking away. Wasn't it funny to think of all those people in the hospital being born and dying while the chimney just went on puffing as though it could never have seen enough. Just like Gilbert,' she looked at Dad who had lain down under a tree and was puffing at his pipe. 'Dad has never seen how funny life is.'

'It's very serious,' he replied. 'Herr Hitler in Germany is planning to take over the whole world, while we just sit here saying, "How funny it all is."'

'I don't mean it's funny ha-ha,' said Cossey. 'I mean it's unexpected. I never thought when I lived inside that row of false teeth called Ondels Grove that one day I'd be sitting here with . . .' she looked at her cousin Jim. There was another horrible silence.

'I try to write serious things,' Cossey defended herself. 'Suppose we hadn't run away on the *Percy Warrior* . . . Dad and I . . .'

'You would have found some other driver for your cab,' Dad puffed at his pipe evenly. 'You would have found another clothes-horse to hang your . . .'

'Gilbert, shut-up!' Cossey cried. Dad gave his china-dog smile.

Cossey's face was red now and Dad looked jokier than ever. For a moment he reminded us of Cossey's description of her brother who was killed in the Great War and kept grinning and lifting his hat and crying mechanically, 'Hey ho the holly, this life is so jolly.' And how, after he had gone, a horse slipped on the cobbles and lay on the ground screaming, his knees were so hopelessly bent. And Dad's knees seemed bent too when Cossey asked him to cut us some more meat. Instead he got one thin slice of galantine and cut it in two, then reluctantly into four and then eight. While he served it out he cried: 'Bread is the staff of life. Meat and galantine are mere relish.'

He said it in such a jesting voice that Cossey shouted at him angrily: 'You look like an out-of-work dustman.'

Dad replied calmly with the same angelic smile on his face: 'Dustmen are never out of work. What with all the food fragments and waste matter that children fling around.' He started to pick up the remains of our picnic. A smile hovered on his face as he saw

The Oxford Book of English Verse that Cousin Jim had given Cossey. He said in the same even cheerful voice: 'That ought to be called "The Oxford Book of Adultery".'

When I asked Cossey what a book of adultery was, she said, throwing her head back in the wind: 'It's when the Welsh harpist comes and tells you that if you turn your back on life or turn away from anything, then not only will you be turned to salt, but everyone else will too. And everything else. Into a sort of gritty Ondels Grove, all dry, like aspirins.' The wind blew in her hair and she still smelt of delight. Dad stood there looking, then he seemed to go away again, like a child who has finished playing with another child and is called home. He put his hands behind his back and went away.

Cossey watched him go and said to Jim: 'I feel as though I had climbed up on to the moon and seen what it was all like from up there and got scorched by all the ice.'

'There's no ice on the moon,' Jim grinned.

'Everything is ice where there's no love,' Cossey choked. 'Let's go and explore those woods.'

We all watched as Cossey and Jim climbed a hedge and went into the woods. Miss Lenege perched on a stile staring after them. Her boots had eyelets that bound their sides grimly together. She stood upright again and pursed her lips, criticizing the trees Jim and Cossey had just walked away through. The huge trees seemed like great black mouths opening and leading from day into night. Vivian started hugging them as Cossey used to do in Ransome's Fields. We waited for Cossey to come back from behind their dark spotted night, or for Dad to have changed his mind. Then Vivian went into the woods after them, and Miss Lenege went back to the fields to pick more fungi, and Floy and I were left alone. The trees suddenly seemed to come tumbling down in black fountains round us as though that way were for us, and we wanted to be back in Ransome's Fields.

We waited for the adults till the darkness came but none of them came back except Miss Lenege. 'Perhaps Cossey got kidnapped by the lepers of Zanzibar,' we suggested, trying to make it sound funny. 'Or perhaps Dad went to preach cleanliness to the heathen.' But we only said it to cheer us up as we rode home with Miss Lenege in the Green Line bus to our empty flat.

Our parents had gone away before, it was true. Once when we had teased Patty Rattray. She had lived in the flat opposite ours with her mother and had been a dancer at the Lambeth Palace of Varieties until she had grown too fat and then she had become a dresser there and came back home with bits of kapok stuck in her hair and her lips pressed tightly together from holding too many pins. Her mother, Mrs Rattray, had one huge eye in the middle of her head and always sat at her window looking out and trying to get us to invite Uncle Neary down from the flat above theirs.

Uncle Neary had been blinded in the First World War and lost an arm. Sometimes he would let us press his stump and ask him if it hurt. Then he would always pretend to cry and then break into a thick bagpipes lament which made us want to cry. Sometimes we used to go into Ransome's Fields with him and he would run round and round and we would race after him crying, 'Uncle Neary, right, to your *right* or you'll bump into the seat . . . Uncle Neary there's a pram on your left . . .', then he would pretend to bump into them. He always beat us, though, in the races even though he was blind.

Once we had jeered at Patty about being so fat and being keen on Uncle Neary. Our parents had gone to a Labour Party Conference and Patty had kindly agreed to keep an eye on us that weekend and we had pretended to be very nice and had invited her to show us her fatness, then grew cruel and said that we'd never use the same public baths as she used in case it all fell out onto us, and that her flat smelt so bad that Mrs Rattray must have used her fat for cooking in. Patty went home weeping and we were horrified when we saw Mrs Rattray move from the chair she always sat in at the window looking out with her one good eye. We'd never seen her move before or her one good eye not looking out at the street like a magnifying glass. We felt very guilty and went up to Uncle Neary who lived above, but he, too, stared contemptuously out of his blind eyes as though he saw too much. He just said, 'Uhu,' and didn't tell us, as he normally did, to put his glass eye on the window sill so that it would tell him what the weather was doing.

He just stared through us and we crept away, feeling we had done something we didn't want our parents to know.

That time our parents had gone away we thought of going to the Labour Party Conference to explain to them what had happened before they came home and found out for themselves. We thought of finding Patty and begging her to come back. Patty sometimes took us backstage at the Lambeth Palace and I had decided that if I didn't become a pianist I'd become a sempstress there, or an actress. We went there that Saturday afternoon to look for her. The stage door at the side was open and we peered in. There was a huge, sad bear on the stage with a horrible sore patch on its fur and a pair of men's pants hanging out of its mouth. A man was smoking and shouting at the sad bear which struck us as being a stupid thing to do since if it was a real bear it couldn't understand and if it was a human inside there was no point in shouting. Then the bear started to shout back: 'If Moses Supposes His Toeses are Roses', which was almost as sad because we were still looking for Patty. It made us depressed to see only the bear with sticking-out nipples dancing up and down as though we had done this too.

But although we didn't find Patty that afternoon our parents did come back that time, and we felt even worse because we could tell by their happy faces that they hadn't met Patty or Mrs Rattray and had had a marvellous weekend and had brought surprise parcels for all of us for having been so good. We could hear Patty and Mrs Rattray banging about with the sewing machine in their flat opposite ours and saw that they hadn't told on us and felt we didn't deserve the foreign chocolates that Cossey and Dad brought. But this time, after the anti-coronation picnic, our parents seemed to have gone for good, and we saw how Miss Lenege must have felt when she arrived in this country.

It was dark when we got back to London after the picnic, and the trams were whining along to Newington Butts and clanking their chains and chanting nasally as they droned along smelling of Kutflem and dirty bodies. Cossey and Dad had often told us there was something badly wrong with the world, but now it seemed as mysterious as it was bad. We stared at the harsh notices high above us in the dark streets: No Spitting . . . No Nuisance . . . No

Entrance . . . Unmarried Mothers . . . Fallen Girls . . . Waifs and Strays . . . Utmost Secrecy . . . Keep Out . . . And the most awesome of them all high up among the dark rows of chimney pots: 'Ancient Lights', shining away into the darkness as though it told of a secret joy in the middle of cities when adults had gone away.

But now the stern instructions hanging high up in the streets seemed less angry and more sad. Instead of telling us to 'Get Younger' or stop spitting or fouling, they said regretfully: By Subscription Only . . . Trustees Only . . . Night Refuge Only . . . Use a Canning Respirator . . . Try Bates Balm for All Wounds and Sores . . . We wanted to be nice to Patty Rattray and Miss Lenege.

Cossey and Dad were still not there when we went into our parents' bedroom next morning, so in case Miss Lenege should come in and tell us to wash our teeth we wrote a notice and pinned it on our bedroom door:

PLEASE DO NO DISTURB BECAUSE NO ONE IS IN

Then we went back to bed and played muddlefeet under the sheets while Vivian teased Floy for having a string of meat between his legs that might break like his bootlaces did. But none of us felt cheerful enough for teasing. We played 'good' games like Snap and Happy Families and pretended to be enjoying it when Miss Lenege suggested I Spy, only in German.

We waited for Cossey to come prancing home from behind the big plane trees in Ransome's Fields calling: 'Hullo, lovies. I just went down to pay the milkman, and then I met a friend,' and we would sit down at the piano together and play 'Oh I Had a Friend Who Left Me' with Cossey's sad, church hymnal chords in the bass.

But Cossey didn't come back and Dad didn't come plodding across the Fields after her pressing the bowl of his pipe and saying, 'Cleanliness is next to Godliness.' We felt we had committed some terrible crime by being girls, Vivian and I. This was why our parents had gone away.

The big, dark sheaves of leaves hung wet on the trees, shuffling themselves between the branches in the wind. A small circus had come and pitched on Ransome's Fields, a donkey and a llama and a thin man who stooped over his feet and tied things on his ears. A smell of singeing and scorching came from the tent and we wanted to seek Cossey out in the big Georgian mansions on the other side where the tube trains rattled and music came from the Jeanette Short Academy, plonk-plonking up, then down, then up, and the swimmers in Lolly's Lido behind, climbing up onto the diving board then down then up again as though nothing had appeared to put them off.

We saw Cossey and Dad over there with them in the swimming pool as music from the Academy started up. Cossey and Dad were always going up down, up down like the music and the swimmers in the Lido and we supposed we'd just have to get used to it and wait till they came bouncing up again: 'Hullo lovies! Did you have a lovely time here all on your own while we were away? Did you play lovely games when you had the flat all to yourselves?' Perhaps that was what 'Ancient Lights' meant, always expecting that eventually, and after years and years, things would be bright again. We could hear Miss Short's voice from her Academy: 'Now where are your three pliées, girls? Amy Abley, Betty Betts and Cory Cleareyes, where are those three nice pliées?'

Hot-air balloons floated over, shining in the evening light. The streets were deserted. The circus and fair ground were deserted. All the awnings were out but the covers were drawn over the stalls and a few people were leaning down from the houses above as the midget and the two-faced monster took a breather on the empty Fields and Miss Lenege patiently crossed over to help out at her clinic on the other side. It was like that when Cossey and Dad went away.

There was no anti-Munich picnic in 1938. Our parents were both still away and, in any case, Hitler had invaded Czechoslovakia so Munich was no laughing matter as the Coronation had been. We lived with Miss Lenege and when she annoyed us we ran out in bare feet into the Fields and pretended that the sky above was our Ancient Lights, and were surprised to see the apple tree in the garden of 'Mount Veiw' bearing clusters of apples as though everything were normal.

Chapter X

We lived now with Miss Lenege at Webbley Mansions and the days and the hours seemed marked out only by the splash of the divers and jumpers into the swimming pool of Lolly's Lido on the other side of the Fields. We were very good and tried to learn German and played 'good' games like making dolls' clothes and washing the rubber tyres on Floy's Dinky Toys. No one ever said now as war crept across Europe: 'If ever there were another war' . . ., and we didn't discuss it with Miss Lenege.

She had stopped spinning and had bought herself a typewriter and we could hear her typing letters right into the night and we'd take them to the Post Office with her the next day. She always looked very worried now and unhappy and we tried to cheer her up by making fudge and playing quiet games on our parents' bed, spreading coloured tram tickets over their bedspread and talking about the glorious places stamped in lists of Destinations and Fare Stages down the tram tickets' sides: 'Chalk Farm and King's Cross, Purley Oaks, Temple and Black Wall Tunnel.' We'd pretend we were going there or to Strand or Borough, then we'd feel more cheerful and look out at the swimming pool over the Fields in case Cossey was lurking there on the top diving board above the carpet factory and the Baptist Chapel and the Leopard Dining Rooms, and, like all the other swimmers and dancers, unwilling to be put off course, and defiant of the harsh London notices: No Entry . . . No Exit . . . No Spitting . . . No Loitering . . . No Hawkers and Circulars . . . Whoever Wins Workers Lose. So many reminders of an anger Cossey couldn't help with.

But the dancers in the Academy went on dancing to the tinkly piano, up and down, as we played for what seemed years in the

Fields round the green bandstand or in the green wooden shelter where old men and women shuffled their feet about blinking in the sun, and the bad-tempered park-keepers, haters of children, scowled.

Floy dressed up in our school clothes, put on my Our Lady convent-brown serge tunic. We put on his black, grammar-school trousers and Eton collar and tie and crossed the Fields and invaded the almost empty ballroom of the Academy, dancing over its polished lino and gazing in its blistered mirrors, singing: 'Lucky You – Kissable Me,' as the music echoed round the big ballroom. Miss Short looked surprised but she didn't say anything like the bossy notices all around us, Alight Here . . . Commit No Nuisance . . . Get Younger Every Day . . . No Goods This Way . . . There were more enticing notices now: To the Slipper-Baths. To The Stage Door . . . Gallery . . . Entrance This Way. Hadn't Cossey said there might not be anything at all? And instead there was so much. We ran back to our parents' bedroom where the tram tickets were still spread over the bed inviting us to a world the Welsh harpist had promised.

We never knew whether it was our father or our mother who was ill. Or both. Miss Lenege just said they had gone away. Our father was often abroad and Cossey had disappeared before when she was annoyed with us or with Dad. Once when we had been teasing her about a striped footballer's sweater she had laboriously knitted herself, she had climbed into the swing-boats at a fair in Peckham Rye Park and hung in them upside down while we were waiting to go home to tea. Once she had disappeared on a day trip to Bognor Regis. It had rained all day and we had grown bored and she had made us sit in a churchyard while she went to buy herself a copy of the *Daily Worker*, and we had grown cross and wandered away and accidentally found her reading her paper in an ice-cream parlour.

'Perhaps she's been press-ganged by the Salvation Army,' Floy suggested. 'Or perhaps she's eloped with that man from the Labour Party who kept making that piece of plaster on his glasses wobble as he said, "Hitler wouldn't dare." And there was a slug sitting on his salad and an invertebrate adhering . . .'

'Adhering,' we screamed with laughter. 'Miss Lenege,' we tried not to tease her but we did, 'do you like animals that adhere? And do you like people that adhere?'

Miss Lenege had a friend called Frau Pfeiffer who often came now that our parents were away. We decided that they adhered to each other more than Cossey and Miss Lenege had done.

But now our parents had both gone, and the only sound outside was the old roadman scraping the paths of the Fields with his besom and the tube-train doors sliding and the trains rattling peacefully on and making Miss Lenege's heavy china ornaments shudder and the spinning wheel in her room creak.

We didn't ask where our parents had gone and Miss Lenege didn't tell us. But she took us to a hospital on the other side of Camden Town, and through a gate in a high wall where a woman in a black uniform conducted us up to a tunnel and in at an entrance hall where we expected to see Cossey or Dad. But the only person there was a fat and cheerful woman in a man's trousers and a man's jacket and cap who twiddled a toasting fork with crusts of bread on it at a big fire burning in the middle of the room and smiled and told us we were very welcome. She gave us a short history of 'her museum' as she called it, and all the exhibits she had collected in the Far East including valuable china which was not on display now she explained, directing us up a broad flight of stairs to a statue at the top.

We could hear music coming from a long room full of beds side-by-side and end-to-end, and at the far end a young man was playing 'Sun of My Soul' on the piano and trying to get the patients to join in. No one noticed us come in or go and no one recognized us, and we sensed that neither Cossey nor Dad were here and that Miss Lenege had come here on some errand to do with her being a refugee in an alien country. We went sadly down the stairs again and a man with big lips asked us if we would like to see his game, but Miss Lenege hurried us away and we stood on the open staircase of the bus and let the wind blow through our hair and imitated the cheerful woman with the toasting fork in 'her museum' and peered down at Miss Lenege who was sitting downstairs in the bus, saying prayers out of her Missal.

At Camden Town she took us to a Lyons tea room and gave us lemonade and a bun and we hoped it wasn't Cossey Lemonade because it made us feel sick at what we must have done to send her and Dad away. But we soon forgot the hospital and Miss Lenege's sad visit there and started to tease her again: 'Miss Lenege,' we would begin, 'do you like summer best? Or do you prefer winter?' We wanted to make her pronounce 'winter' with a German 'w' as she sometimes did off her guard. If she did it twice in succession, then she was a German spy we decided.

We sat on the cross-seats of the tram again coming home. We went on teasing Miss Lenege. 'Were you in London during the Great War?' we asked her, knowing that she was not and that then she'd been an enemy. We watched her face stiff as a racehorse's. The tram sang out between the Stops and Stands like a tennis ball being shot to and fro between two rackets. It would start and stop so suddenly that I kept being jerked over on to her and feeling her rosary being poked in my ribs as Floy eyed me and we kept up the taunt: 'Were you afraid when the Huns came over, Miss Lenege?' We knew Dad would have been angry with us but we went on. We knew she had left Germany later but we were remorseless: 'Weren't you afraid of the Huns and the baby-eaters? Or *where* were you . . .?' The German lady Frau Pfeiffer, who was sitting beside Miss Lenege, gave us some chocolates to shut us up. Floy took them to his room when we got in.

Frau Pfeiffer took to dropping in and we used to ask her cunningly, hearing her German accent: 'Do you know what comes after autumn?' If she said 'vinter' with a German 'w' then she too was a German spy. I had been for an audition and got a job in a pantomime chorus rehearsing for 'Puss in Boots' for Christmas at the Camberwell Palace. But my real theatre was Webbley Mansions and watching Miss Lenege and Frau Pfeiffer on the small stage we had cruelly created for them now that neither Cossey nor Dad were here and we were alone.

Frau Pfeiffer had also bought a strange plant in a pot. It had dozens of flat, green leaves like plates and every third one had been stamped with a secret pink diamond, a bit off-centre, as though another plant, a jealous one, had crept up unawares to touch it up and improve it with a bit of its own superior pink diamond self.

We started to laugh every time we saw this staring exotic plant as though it were Miss Lenege, and the jealous secret diamond one who cast its pink shadow was Frau Pfeiffer.

'Which do you like best, Frau Pfeiffer?' we would start giggling.

Miss Lenege grew angry. But we would go on: 'Miss Lenege, what was Shakespeare's first name?' The others would all watch as I widened my eyes in anticipation.

'You are foul,' Vivian would say as Miss Lenege consulted her memory and replied: 'Villiam, I think. Yes?'

Then she clapped her hands and called out cheerfully: 'Floy, my child, where are the chocolates that Frau Pfeiffer has so kindly brought for us? Bring them here to the sitting room and we will have one of them each.'

Floy fidgeted and went to his room and came back with the box and we saw that only one or two were left. Miss Lenege looked puzzled, so Floy exclaimed conscientiously: 'I had to throw the others away. You see they were all bad and had burst out of their cases and were all going "pop". So I threw them away.'

We all stared furiously at Floy as Miss Lenege asked him: 'So. Where did you throw them?'

'Out of the window. I just had to.'

'Which window?'

'Out of *that* one. No, *that* one. No, *that* one. At least I forget which one.' Miss Lenege dodged between the windows peering out, searching at the back and the front for the missing chocolates as if they could reply: 'Ho Ho. So we are here.'

We giggled as Miss Lenege peered out at the feeding pigeons and planned how to have our revenge on Floy. But as Miss Lenege searched and searched whom should we see dancing over the Fields but Cossey. She was bouncing back home, running up the stone steps to our flat three at a time in a pair of Spanish raffia slippers, breathless with the excitement of seeing us all again, her gold hair flickering like candle flames as she cried: 'Hullo lovies. Have you had a marvellous time in Ransome's Fields while we were away? When I was your age I was never allowed to be by myself for one moment.'

She stood there with a necklace made of marzipan for Floy, some nougat and a straw hat for me and, for Samey, a tiny banana the size of a pencil. Cossey smelt of garlic and European tobacco and delight. She took us to the fair on Ransome's Fields and rode round on a white china horse with a chipped, foaming mouth called 'Grace', and sat upside down again on the Chairoplanes crying, 'Isn't life extraordinary. Maybe we are all upside down, *all the time*, and we just don't happen to know it. Maybe, when God looks down on us, he thinks how absurd they all are to get cross about the pink of the cushion covers or whether we should abstain from eating tomatoes on a Wednesday.' She came down from the Chairoplanes and while we were all being sick on the ground below, she cried: 'I wanted you all to be free and have a lovely time as I never did when I was your age. So how was Webbley Mansions while we were away?'

Vivian smiled too: 'Where's Cousin Jim now?' she asked. 'Where's your trouserman?' We looked down the street.

We crossed back to the other side of our flat and looked out over our part of London across the Fields to Lambeth Bridge and the West End. Hitler had invaded Poland and Cossey never now said: 'If ever there were another war . . .' She stared at some tiny bits of haslet that Dad, also back again, had chopped up and laid on our plates with a fixed grin. 'We're not rationed yet,' Cossey cried, 'so I'm not going to eat tiny rectangles of haslet until we really have to. I want fish and chips and things with lots and lots of love.' So we went round to the Perfectio Fish Caterers and remembered how we had once tried to call Cossey 'Perfectio' and then had lapsed back to Cossey.

Now as we ate our skate and chips we started to shout at her: 'Now there's going to be another war, will you . . . are you . . . do you still mean to put us in the Imperial Boiler?'

The late night trams came whining past like the wounded on a battlefield crawling out of the trenches. The boiler stood there black and smoking and on duty too. We went to Our Lady In Ara Coeli carrying gas masks, and stood in long rows in the school classroom and with our hands folded across our chests chanting in time to the piano: 'When Farmers Dream of Barley Sheaves', making dreaming gestures with our hands at the appropriate moments and shaping barley sheaves with them when that was required. A teacher in a white dress came down the classroom as we were chanting: 'To join our hands and dance and sing,' still making the joining and the dancing gestures till she changed it to 'Oh God Our Help in Ages Past'. We roared the hymn and the pupils on the other side of the glass screen that divided the great stepped classrooms leaned against it and made it rock till the great partition was roaring too and they drew it back and we sang again, 'Oh God Our Help in Ages Past', and another horse slipped on the granite setts outside in Imperial Street and started helplessly to scream and we came home and Cossey was still there with our father, and the Mansions still smelt of roasting beef from the Stalwart Dining Rooms as they had done the day we came, in spite of the fact that war had just been declared.

At first Cossey just said that Miss Lenege had been called back to Germany. She had left us the plant in the pot with strange pink diamond spots on its leaves as though someone had painted every third one and then gone away. Cossey added, pointing at the fussily-decorated leaves, 'Doesn't nature waste her time doing *that*, when she could be cleaning our flat up for us! What a waste of time putting pink diamonds on the leaves of flowers when you could be . . .' and Dad interrupted, staring at the plant: 'Never laugh at dumb nature. It can't answer back.'

But we all felt too sad to laugh and Vivian said: 'Miss Lenege can't have been called back to Germany because that's where she *escaped* from. So where is she?'

'She had to go for an investigation,' Dad said. It was only later that Cossey admitted that she had told the police about Miss Lenege's journeys across Ransome's Fields and the way she kept typing letters at night. 'You see she's an enemy alien. And some of them may be helping the Nazis. But she'll come back, I'm sure. Once they've checked up on her past in Germany. Once they realize she's not a spy.' But Cossey's voice trembled and we knew she'd done something terrible just as our voices admitted we had too. Miss Lenege had clung to us children those last few days before they rounded her up and took her away. It was as though our teasing had driven her away and we cried when we saw her little bedroom up three stairs under the turret that had such a marvellous view. The little room was stacked with papers and her spinning wheel looked so perilous as though, if you breathed near it, it would snap and fall down with an accusing clatter. And over the road the cry of another horse came from the South London Pantechnicon. He had slipped and fallen on the cobbles and the waggon behind had tipped and the furniture was clattering out too. But the old man who had stood in Ransome's Fields for as long as we could remember beside a tall model of a medieval castle made entirely of corks, was still standing there with his fortress and his placard:

> Perseverance, cork and glue
> Eighteen-hundred and eighty-two.

It was as though the declaration of war on 3 September 1939 had in its way tuned the harsh noises of the streets, had even sorted and spun their random sorrow and anger into the genuine music of a grief we too were involved in.

Chapter XI

But it didn't last long, this solemn chapter of 1939. After war had been declared, we expected to see Ransome's Fields swallowed up in black fire from Europe. But instead, Cossey was hiring bikes for us as she had often done before. We were all to go hop-picking for our war-work, she explained. It would be lovely in Kent, and weren't we all lucky? We stared down the Lambeth streets expecting to see the familiar brewers' drays turned into gun-carriages or hearses, but instead there was just the normal rumble of the wheels over the cobbles, and the same advertisements along the walls telling you that your pick-me-up was Oxo.

Dad went cheerfully to the Army recruitment centre, but otherwise London seemed so unmoved that Vivian remarked: 'I thought you said war was so terrible that only our Imperial Boiler could do justice to it.'

The tugs on the river were silent. The houses on the other side of Ransome's Fields were silent. The parks were silent and at twilight no sour park-keepers in brown flannel coats and hats shook their handbells in children's ears and banged them at loiterers. Even Lolly's Lido was silent. The TB patients stopped crossing the Fields to their clinic. It was as though they had been rounded up with Miss Lenege and taken to a place more secret even than the ones evacuees standing at the street corners were off to.

Cossey looked at Vivian and changed her mind about hop-picking, and sent us instead to the Oddfellows Hall where evacuees went to be medically examined before being despatched to Paddington. We stood half naked in a long silent queue in front of a trestle table where elderly doctors sat. We stood in more long queues to have our heads examined for nits, then were hung with bags of food and labels, names and numbers, but no destinations. When Cossey saw us sitting there in long rows at Paddington singing: 'When you're browned off just say it's Tickety-Boo', she changed her mind about evacuation: 'We're middle class.' She stared at the emaciated children with secret eyes; children she had always tried to make us avoid in the streets. 'We're middle class and I've found us a marvellous place in Hampshire for when you've finished your fruit-picking.'

She had answered an advertisement in the *Tablet*. An elderly invalid lady living in a big house near the sea was looking for someone to be a companion and lady's maid to her. Cossey went down there with Samey. We were to follow on bicycles, but very slowly, going via Paddock Wood where they already had too many hop-pickers.

The fields reminded us of Miss Lenege's food hunting activities and her sudden departure. We cycled in silence. Dad tried to explain again why she had been taken away: 'They would have arrested her in any case,' he defended Cossey. She hadn't been able to vouch to the police for her political past. She was Jewish, but that alone didn't give her a safe conduct since she was an enemy alien. Cossey had heard her typing at nights in her room.

'But it was only a book about German culture,' Vivian protested. But Miss Lenege's white unaired body and her rueful red eyelids and her heavy sentence on the British seemed to be the final evidence against her. She was not one of us. We felt guilty again as we pictured her being led away from Ransome's Fields, somehow on runners and unprotestingly; being wheeled out of our lives. We stared at the old carved furniture that had furnished our flat as though it were even more hers now; the legs of the table heavy and squat and carved into parrots' heads with thick sharp beaks and ugly squinting eyes; the feet of the chairs carved into snakes and fish; and the knobs on her desk like horny fingers. Such a lot of her remained, even the ashes of her mother and a few bones in the great Chinese vase in her small room up three stairs that she had claimed as her home.

'It wasn't just that she had TB,' Cossey confessed. 'I suppose we both hated being so dependent on her.'

'I'm the upstairs lady,' Miss Lenege had tried to joke with us, and we had pretended to think she had made a hilarious joke. But when her back was turned, Floy had tried on her black feather hat and cried:

> Twinkle twinkle little hat
> How your feathers smell of fat.

'Oh you baddy!' Cossey had laughed, and Floy had gone on imitating Miss Lenege: 'I have just put in two suppositories and I am listening to Bach on my radio, so please do not disturb me.'

Floy and I had giggled and Cossey had cried again: 'Oh you two little horrors!'

'Where is Miss Lenege then?' Vivian was still asking harshly.

Cossey interrupted her: 'Aren't you children lucky to be having another baby!' She showed us the baby's gas mask in the corner, like a small rubber coffin but with a pump, and stuck by our big brown ones smelling of vanilla. Cossey tapped her stomach and laughed again: 'When we're all reunited at Apslet House we shall have such lovely fun!'

In the meantime she was making herself a maternity dress out of the kitchen curtains: 'You always wanted another baby, didn't you?' She laughed again. 'Aren't you lucky children,' she tried again later, packing our clothes, 'going fruit-picking while Dad has to stay in London fighting old Jerry.'

But Dad came back from the Army recruiting centre shaking his head: 'The Army's not what it was,' he sighed.

'Why?' Cossey asked sceptically. 'What happened? Rejected?'

Dad nodded: 'Teeth too prominent. Too easy for Jerry to identify.'

So Dad fixed a small engine to the back wheel of his bicycle. 'Mount and follow,' he instructed Vivian and Floy and me. 'You've all had too much childhood as it is. Now for serious food-gathering and money-spinning.' We were to make a fortune picking hops, then perhaps we'd be evacuated to America.

Cossey had decided that her background and schooling

qualified her for the job as a lady's companion. But she felt that her family ought not to arrive at Apslet House until she had paved the way for a husband and four children and a fifth on the way. She and Samey set off.

'I have a feeling that Apslet House may be calling us,' Dad clenched his chin in his fist and thought. He saw we weren't earning enough in the hop-fields even to pay for our corrugated iron hut and the straw for our palliasses.

'But Dad, we're supposed to stay away at least four weeks.'

'What is a little arithmetic when you're hungry?' he replied. 'What's holding you up?' he would stop the engine on his bike and call back to us as we pedalled hard to keep up with his mechanical propulsion. When he saw us battling with the wind, he would call back: 'Character formation! What's holding you back?'

'We've just seen a striped bird.'

'What do you want with striped birds when you've got a good BSA bicycle under you? Once we get to Apslet House, I hope', he looked at our streaming noses, 'that you'll all remember the Principle of the Simple Cotton Handkerchief.' We had stopped by a small deserted graveyard. 'I'll give you sixpence for going in and gaining a sermon from stones.'

'What did you learn?' he asked when he came back from the Dragon down the road.

'They'd all died of fever.'

'Ah,' Dad nodded and thought. 'Disease. Cholera! In that case your sixpences will have to go for hygienic purposes. Soap and water and simple wholesome food.' He got out some bread and some raw spinach he had plundered from a field. We sat down and squeezed the contents of a small pasty on to our dry bread and munched bitter spinach.

'Ah! Bread!' Dad chewed happily. 'The staff of life for the proletariat. Meat is mere relish for those on the upward ladder of life.'

'Those cows are coming towards us, Dad.'

'No man worthy of his salt is afraid of quadrupeds. Man is their natural overlord.' Nevertheless Dad had a stone gripped in both hands as we retreated backwards from the field to our bikes. Then he gave me a bottle and asked me to go to the nearby farm and get some milk.

'And if she tries to charge you, tell her your father once lived there.'

'Well, if *you* lived there,' I objected, 'why don't *you* go and get the milk?'

'Hmmm. I'll tell you why when you get back with the milk.'

When I got back with the empty bottle, Dad confessed: 'I didn't actually *live* there. I walked there one summer when I was your age. No vehicular transport for God's little ones then. None of these two-wheeled inventions that are making our journey to Apslet House a mere flight of the bumble bees. So count your blessings.' He frowned as he noticed a puncture in the back tyre of my bike. 'Still,' he cheered up, 'feet were made before wheels, so put your best foot forward. Press on.'

We forgot Miss Lenege as we pushed our bikes down autumn lanes and plunged into the wet leaves. Everything seemed plain sailing. We had left London behind, and its fogs and threatening murmurs about women. Everything seemed fine until we reached Apslet House. Cossey was sitting in the drawing room as we arrived at the back entrance. She had picked hips and haws for jelly, and laid down eggs, had weighed evacuees, and had dug the lawn for potatoes. But she still hadn't got round to telling Mrs Rackham, the invalid lady she was now a companion to, that more of her family was to follow. There she was, sitting in her new maternity-dress. 'Before the war,' she was saying, 'before Old Jerry, we were never nanny people. Or car people. We just didn't care for cars and nannies.'

Then the maid announced that there were evacuees in the kitchen, and we stood there in the drawing room in dripping macintoshes clasping gas-masks and cycle-pumps and padlocks. Water fell on the Afghan carpet. Cossey had told Mrs Rackham that her husband was in awfully hush-hush work. Now she watched the water dripping off her children while Dad appraised the Tudor drawing room: 'A bit pokey,' he shook hands with Mrs Rackham, 'but still, there's no place like home, so they say.'

'How do you do,' Mrs Rackham replied. Her voice was deep.

'I'm doing fine,' Dad went on, 'though last night I had a nasty scare. I was couched in a hay-loft, and took a Pontefract cake and when I woke in the morning, the first thing my waking lids clapped open on was a great big clot of black blood on my palliasse. I thought my number was up, but when I looked more closely, it had the word "Pontefract" stamped on it. So I'm fine, thank you, Ma'am. How are you?'

'I hope you are as well as I am,' Dad went on in the silence, 'and that most of your summer photographs have come out reasonably well.' There was a pause. Mrs Rackham stared.

Cossey cleared her throat and tried to make sense of this remark. 'When we lived in central London . . .' she began quickly.

'Ah yes, those slipper-baths in the Lambeth Walk. Those were the days. What's the German for hiccups?' Dad went on manfully. Then he covered his mouth.

Cossey fidgeted and began again: 'When we lived in London Town . . .'

Dad lowered himself on to the Sheraton sofa, shook out his Easie-Grip cycle-mitts, dropped them into a Tang Dynasty vase and got out his pipe.

The house was a large Tudor one with diamond-paned windows, barley-sugar chimneys and high, topiaried box hedges. Dad looked out and said he'd have the trees down if Mrs Rackham so desired. 'And the old windows out too. You'd get more light. And I'll even-out that box-hedge for you.' He fiddled with some garden shears.

Cossey protested: 'That's topiary. It's meant to be all peaky.'

'There's certainly something wrong with it,' Dad went on fiddling.

'We've always adored old houses,' Cossey interrupted hastily. 'When we lived in Ransome's Fields . . .'

'That chair looks a bit rickety too,' Dad interrupted, gazing at a great mahogany carver. 'Ah well, capitalism contains the seeds of its own destruction, as you are no doubt aware, Madam. Forward with the masses.'

Mrs Rackham summed us up grimly, then she picked up her crutches and hobbled out of the room.

'You look like a tramp,' Cossey almost wept. 'We just aren't working-class.'

'We are the evolution of the masses,' Dad replied firmly, 'the survival of the fittest.' He still had the gardening shears and was clipping perilously near the hem of the velvet curtains. He lopped the heads off the flowers absent-mindedly and made a movement towards some coatsleeves: 'Science says clip back the unproductive species.'

'You're dragging us down,' Cossey was in tears. 'Why must you drag us down?'

'Mrs Rackham says would you like to see the cottage?' A maid as severe and starched as a Matron came in. Cossey was delighted. She could never be angry with life for long and always somehow managed not to 'Let the sun go down on her anger', or on her disappointment or on her defeat. But for us it seemed that our halcyon days on the road were over as Dad appraised Apslet House: 'We shall have to make the place ship-shape later.'

Just then the maid came in again and announced that Mrs Rackham wondered whether we would like to see whether we found the stockman's cottage suitable. He had been called up and his tied cottage was vacant, beyond the servants' quarters and outdoor workers' yards. Cossey was cheerful and Dad triumphantly stoical.

The 'cottage' was a disused gun-emplacement from the First World War, built into the hillside, with a corrugated-iron roof that sloped down to the hill's face. On one side were woods, and on the other a waste of scrub and bramble which Mrs Rackham said we could dig for victory. In addition, Cossey was to go up to the big house every day and do light cleaning in place of the servants who had left for the munitions factories.

'They only want to work where there are money and men.' Mrs Rackham stood at the door of our new house on her crutches, while Cossey explored and exclaimed: 'Aren't you lucky children to be living in a cottage overlooking the sea. In central London, you always wanted a country cottage didn't you?'

Autumn came and we were sent to the village school. Winter came and our well froze and we didn't wash for weeks. Winter came again after Christmas and the wind blew the corrugated iron roof of the cottage up and down.

'You aren't local children,' Cossey would say when we came home using four-letter words and sniggering. 'You're not cottage children,' Mrs Rackham would say when she came down to inspect her property. She would stand in the doorway swinging between her sticks. 'You must say "must", not "mid" . . . "yours" not "yourn". Isn't the boy old enough for his public school yet?'

'He was just off there,' Cossey explained, 'when the war came.'

'Which?'

Cossey paused and then said: 'Oh Winchester. Of course. My father was an old Winchester man and an Oxonian.' We all giggled, but it wasn't really very funny the way it went on. Snow fell and the cattle would come pounding and crashing over our sloping corrugated roof for warmth. Their thundering kept us awake all night.

'Tap gently,' Dad would say as Cossey confronted the frozen door of the Elsan lavatory in the mornings. 'Science is the secret weapon. Exploit the laws of inertia.'

'No! Violence!' Cossey would fling her weight against the door.

'No, just understand expansion and contraction,' Dad would wave his *Wonder World of Modern Science*. 'Use Science.'

'There isn't time, if you want to go somewhere as much as I do.'

'Go where God meant you to, behind my lady's bushes.'

'No, that's the auricula I planted last month' Cossey would cry indignantly. We children heard their morning manoeuvres as we sat over a fire of twigs and rag and potato peelings and dried tea-leaves.

Europe began to crumble and we sat in an icy wind. Snow and sleet skewed in while we ate in our coats. The cold drove the mice in. Samey would pull mouse-droppings from her porridge and lay them side-by-side in her Dinky-Toy lorry: 'Eeny-meeny-mina-mo.'

The kitchen was a lean-to outside the gun-emplacement and we took turns to put on two coats and race round to the back and bring back a pan of Victory stew which we put on a piece of newspaper and took turns to spoon from. 'Eeny-meeny-mina-mo,' Vivian sang as we picked out more droppings.

'Not very *comme il faut*,' Cossey would shake them from the spoons and the cups. 'Not very *faut*,' she would gaze at a packet of biscuits which the mice had tunnelled right through so that it collapsed in her hands. 'But still, when the summer comes . . .' Holiday-makers would come and she would hear children with good accents inviting hers to learn tennis or ride with them on the cliffs.

It was Christmas and Mrs Rackham had given us children a book token and we sat round the fire of potato peelings and discussed what to buy with it. Dad took out a toothbrush as we talked and absentmindedly started to brush his teeth, then he slipped out quietly while we still debated, and went into Winchester and bought himself a thick second-hand volume with our token. It was called *Designs of the Deep* and he sat there brushing his teeth and reading over Christmas and ignoring our outrage.

Cossey glared at Dad: 'I'm my father's daughter at any rate. My father was a varsity man and taught himself Greek and Latin and won a scholarship to Cambridge. I could have gone to Cambridge too and discussed Plato and lectured in the university like my father. He was consulted by professors and bishops and we had maids who called me "Miss Freda". My father tried his hardest to keep me from ruining myself.'

As Europe collapsed it seemed as though our parents had never cared about politics. It seemed as though they had never worried about Fascism in Spain and Nazism in Germany. Instead, they fought over the land. Mice ate a hole right through *Designs of the Deep*, ate our bedclothes and our mattresses. They ate the curtains and Dad borrowed a sample-book from a draper in Winchester and Cossey chopped out all the samples and made patch-work curtains of them while Dad took the empty pattern book back to the shop and explained about mice loving samples.

The snow melted. A child's bootee hung on a wooden fence. The holiday-makers would come back. The summer girls would let us ride their ponies and invite us over for tennis. Cossey put on her best dress made of sample-patterns and we went to a Flower Fete called 'Women in History'. She watched the ladies eating rolled cucumber-sandwiches in white gloves on Mrs Rackham's lawns: 'Now *we* are all wanting to know who *they* are. But soon they'll be wanting to know who *we* are,' she decided cheerfully. 'I shall soon be out there with the best of them, teaching them Greek and Latin, and discussing philosophy with the clergy. And there will be parties for children while the adults discuss ideas. No, we never were boarding-school or nanny people. Socialists aren't. Look, I'm going to make you new dresses and one for the baby. What lucky children you are!'

Then we walked down to the beach, down a steep path, followed by Dad. Hampshire was a Defence Area now and the Army had laid rolls of barbed wire along the beach. The sea came up and smashed right through them. The sea went back. The sea moved forward again impervious to the barbed wire. The wire rose stiffly impervious to the sadly seeking sea.

'Guess what,' Cossey said to me one day, 'I've found you a job, in a ballroom in Winchester. The teacher's going to pay you three-and-sixpence a week for sweeping out the ballroom of her dancing academy and feeding her goldfish.'

As the war progressed Cossey and Dad grew even more apart in their attempts to relate to each other. Life became like trying to add sixpence to sunshine, or divide war by ice-cream or any other of those tricks the mind plays when you are nearly asleep. Miss Lenege had had a way of uniting Cossey and Dad, but now that she had gone, their quarrels seemed, as Germany invaded the Low Countries, as meaningless to us as trying to connect might to liquorice allsorts, or send July to the King, as Germany invaded France.

I can still see Cossey's triumphant expression as the pom-pom guns thumped along the beaches and the headland, and the sea sucked at the shingle and dragged it down the beach. Cossey had just had another daughter without Dad noticing it. Our parents seemed like the sea and the barbed wire's imperviousness to each other. Mrs Rackham had asked Cossey to go and live at the big house so that she could give her employer more attention. She wanted to send us all away to school now that France had fallen. Cossey was to wear a dark dress and Dad was to work in the cellars. We could hear Cossey shouting about Cambridge and why she never deigned to be a student there and why she wanted us to go to schools Mrs Rackham was going to pay for in Winchester. We could hear her repeating, 'We *are* middle class. At least I am, and I want my children to be. I want Alma to have music lessons and Floy to go to a Public School. Your accents leave a lot to be desired of.'

She told us in her Apslet voice that Dad was being called away on awfully hush-hush work. But we were sceptical because we had heard them quarrelling again: 'This is no place for a Socialist,' Dad had said, holding up his green baize apron, and Cossey had replied: 'Socialism is fun until your children have to go to the village school and come back with sloppy accents and play with cottage children. My father would turn in his grave. He taught me Greek and the Higher Criticism. Not just how to gape like a cow and say "yourn" instead of "yours".'

Then Dad just faced Cossey and drew himself up and gave her a formal salute; clicked his heels to attention and said in the stilted voice that had been his ever since Cousin Jim had gone away with Cossey, 'Fair Madam, fare well. And fare well, all ye pretty little ones and the ever growing childer.' We giggled as Dad ended stagily: 'I no longer have the intention of being my fair lady's step-ladder to higher things and other suchlike sundries of the gentry. But do not let this parting grieve thee and remember that the best of friends must part.'

He sang the last bit in his tea-room tenor, and it was only later that we realized it was final, as he cycled away with dignity down the rough path that led to the outer world. Dad had cheated Cossey. She could not even generously grant him his freedom. He had simply gone, like that, without any show of feeling. Our parents' separation might have been the last scene in a charade where the audience tries to guess: 'waistcoat', 'suitcase' or 'chestnut'. The rest of us were going to live up at the big house now with Mrs Rackham.

'Dad and I always meant to buy one of those big Georgian houses on the other side of the Fields,' Cossey told us as we packed to move away from the gun-emplacement. 'But the war stopped all that. Just as it stopped my journalism. We always seem to live upstairs,' she smiled as we settled down in the rooms above Mrs Rackham's quarters. 'First we lived upstairs at Baston Square. Then at Webbley Mansions. And now here.' But we weren't at the top of the house, Floy pointed out.

'No, the Lasts live up there,' Cossey explained. 'They've been evacuated from some rather slummy part of London. They remind me a bit of the Cruffts at Baston Square and poor Verity who died.'

We could hear Mrs Last shouting at her daughter and her deaf mother up one flight from our rooms. 'Give over, Carole,' Mrs Last always seemed to end, and Floy would glance upstairs and then at Cossey as though they both knew something that the rest of us didn't.

Floy's voice was breaking and sometimes he would give such a funny smile that I was slightly unnerved. It was as though Vivian and I weren't there, or had gone away with Dad and Miss Lenege. Floy would watch Cossey feeding her new baby with the smile we didn't like. He was a choirboy at the local church and came home with his white surplice for Cossey to starch. I tried it on once and he was furious and made Cossey wash it again and restarch it. Then he stood guard over it till Sunday came and he could restore it to the church vestry where only males went. He started washing his hands a lot and giving Cossey that funny little smile that she seemed to understand. Once he even got out of his chair at lunch and cried up at the Last family upstairs: 'What have I to do with thee, oh women?'

Cossey laughed. That was all; then added, looking at Floy: 'Oh you little horror!'

Chapter XII

'Such amusing children,' Mrs Rackham's friends would beam at us and say to each other when they came to her house. They would see us Gerbers on the staircase and in the hall and out in the gardens playing round the elms or in the topiary. 'Such a happy, united family.'

They would catch sight of me digging for dead dogs in the vegetable gardens, or Vivian making us all a residence behind the holly; or Floy standing by the great gates, or calling up the shallow oak staircase exclaiming: 'Francis – ' Francis was his real name. ' – Francis,' he would groan and beat his breast. 'My most unfavourite saint. Give me a slap on the belly with a wet fish any day rather than be called . . .'

'Stop showing off,' Vivian would call in an unfamiliar new drawl.

But Floy would be discussing Keats with Mrs Rackham's grown-up sons: 'Personally, I think he would have just petered out if he had gone on writing much longer.'

Vivian would call from the top of the polished stairs where she was standing in Cossey's court shoes: 'Floy, no one wants your views on Keats, so stop showing off.'

'But I like showing off. I refuse to have my ego thwarted. And anyway, bags I not wash or dry after supper tonight.'

'You know you can't "bags" till half an hour before supper. And anyway, bags I supervise.' The guests would laugh as our charades became even more accomplished. No one at Ransome's Fields had ever properly appreciated us; or so we thought.

'Bags I put away,' the ritual would wind on.

'Bags I scrape . . .'

Vivian would stand over the unfortunate one who had to wash

and dry after Mrs Rackham's guests had gone. We had to sing for our supper now that Dad had gone. But we enjoyed our new role as entertainers.

'Such amusing children'; we would pretend not to hear and to be unbiased by self-consciousness as we went on.

'Now Scragg,' Vivian would put on a lady-of-the-manor voice, 'sponge the plates down before you begin. And remove all stubborn food fragments and egg soil. That's always the golden rule in the house of hygiene, isn't it, Scragg?'

'Yes Mum,' the one of us appointed as Scragg would reply.

'And "Madame" isn't such a long hard word, is it Cragg?'

'Scragg. Not Cragg,' Floy would protest, correcting her.

'And I hope you weren't thinking of going out tonight, Scragg?'

'I was going to the Blessed Heart Club, Mum.'

'Ah no. Because that plate in your hand still has a fish tail adhering to it, and if I am not greatly mistaken it's the identical fish tail that adhered to His Lordship's front tooth at dinner tonight when he said "Mister Hitler would not dare!" So no Sacred Heart for you tonight, Scragg.'

'Blessed Heart,' Floy corrected, 'not Sacred! *Blessed*,' he screamed.

Floy would stop when Carole Last appeared on our scene. Carole's father was in the Forces and the Lasts had been evacuated from London and the top floor of the house had been requisitioned, and Mrs Last had moved in with her shiny green lounge suite.

'How super!' we would go up and peer at it and exclaim, widening our eyes.

Mrs Last worked in a munitions factory and left at five every morning. Her daughter, a thin fair child of six with her hands always at her mouth, would stand on the top landing of Apslet tap-dancing softly to herself and singing 'You'd Be Far Better Off in a Home', till Cossey persuaded her to come down and play with us.

'Please sing and dance to us,' Vivian would beg in her lady-of-the-manor voice.

'I've only got that one song,' Carole confessed dubiously, 'and the one they learned us up at the Whip.'

'How super!' We widened our eyes with exaggerated enthusiasm: 'Will you sing the one you learned up at the Whip?'

So she began in her small toneless voice:

> On a Hill Far Away Stood an Old Rugged Cross,
> The Emble of Suffering and Shame.

'Please go on,' we begged, as she faltered and shifted from foot to foot. 'Please,' we pleaded in high theatrical voices. We took on Carole Last in a big way. '*Please* go on.'

> And I Love that Old Cross where the Dearest and Best
> For a World of Lost Sinners was Slain.

'Gosh! Wizard!' we Catholics cried, 'and do you really love that old ragged cross?'

'Rugged,' she fidgeted and corrected herself, 'only I got it wrong. It should of been "emblem" of suffering, and I said "emble".'

'Emblem of Suffering,' we swooned. 'Still, you do really love that old rugged cross?'

'Yes,' Carole laughed shyly.

'Honestly? Truthfully? Cross your heart?'

'Cross my heart!' She crossed her heart and spat on the ground. We giggled. Here at Apslet we were aristocrats before Mrs Rackham and her friends, in our clear piping accents with one eye and an ear on the top of the house where the Lasts lived.

'Oh you baddies!' Cossey had said when we had 'interrogated' Miss Lenege at Webbley Mansions. 'Oh you baddies!' she repeated now as we teased Carole Last.

'Do you really love that old ragged cross? Sorry, "rugged cross",' we would ask her in our sweetest voices. 'Rugged, but still, very nice.' Cossey egged us on with her laughter now that we had at last established ourselves as middle-class. Carole Last's small dogged voice would bring us back to her.

She opened her mouth and began shyly: 'I've got my Nanny coming,' she slipped her hand into Vivian's.

'Your Nanny? Why even the FizBootles of Bootles Hall don't have Nannies in wartime.'

'Well, but she's coming,' Carole pushed the toe of her shoe along a crack in the floorboards and smiled shyly.

She took us up proudly that evening to see her mother's mother.

'Oh how nice to meet you!' Vivian's voice was tuned down till the satire was almost gone. 'How *do* you *do*?' She held her hand graciously out. 'And how nice for Carole and Mrs Last to have you here.'

Mrs Last's mother was small and thin and birdlike. She lifted a slice of beetroot out of vinegar and laid it on bread and stirred her tea and waited for us to go. When we sat in the shed that we called our 'Residence' next day, her head came out of the dormer window at the top of the house: 'Carole. Carole. You come out of there. Back up here this instant or you'll know.'

Carole pulled at her skirt and stood there divided, till Vivian widened her eyes and called: 'Oh how lovely. Your Nanny is calling you. Quick. Lovely. Lucky you. Up you go.'

Carole flashed a tight smile and was gone. Floy did a Shirley Temple tap-dance after her and sang 'Animal Crackers in My Soup'. But Carole came back later. Her mother had her day off tomorrow, she said, and was going to take us down to the beach.

It was a two-mile walk across the marshes which had been mined and flooded except for a high causeway surrounded with singing barbed wire. Because the summer was so hot, the Army had cut an entrance through it down to the sea, and once a week they let you through to a patch of sea that wasn't mined. Samey slipped her hand into Mrs Last's as we walked down to the shingle.

'Will you swim with me first?'

'No! With me!' We clung round Mrs Last watching her undress.

'All white and wobbly,' we pronounced on the way home. 'How would you like to have bags of white meat hanging down in front of you and wobbling when you try to run?'

'The Kingdom of this World,' Floy sang and tried to make his chest wobble.

'You are revolting children,' Cossey said that night. 'Do try to be nice to Carole. She's been badly treated.' But we could see that Cossey was amused, and we went on about Mrs Last's 'pom-poms', 'bunches', 'milk-things', as though these were class attributes of people who smoked Woodbines and wore headscarves and sat on green shiny three-piece suites drinking sweet tea while the radio played 'Blue Skies Around The Corner'.

One day at breakfast Vivian announced that our 'Residence' was to become a School of Art. We were all told to paint works of modern art. But Floy and I escaped. Ever since Mrs Last had taken us swimming, the sound of the sea had remained in my ears rising and falling between the pebbles and making them rock and cry as it forced its way through. We wandered restlessly back towards the beach. There were 'beach people' living in railway carriages at the end nearest the village, old carriages propped on bricks and creosote drums, with 'Ladies' and 'Smokers' still written in the frosted glass along their windows. The children often slept underneath, and as we were walking along three beach boys came from behind a carriage that had been tarred black. They stood there watching us.

The beach children had their own row of desks at the side of the five 'standards' in our school classroom. The beach girls wore plimsolls and faded cotton dresses with coats over in the winter and sat in a row along the playground railings at break when the village girls were playing Chains or skipping to 'Jam Jam, Strawberry Jam'. The beach girls huddled together away from the boys and holding their skirts down.

The beach boys wore their fathers' trousers and jerseys cut-down, and their hands smelt of pee and mice when they opened their fingers to pick up a pencil or be caned. Sometimes they came to school with impetigo and purple gentian stains round their mouths; sometimes Miss Hadland would stand the beach girls up and hand them lengths of string to tie back their hair, and when the school nurse called, would send them into the small ante-room where books and paper were stored, and they knelt on newspaper to have the nits combed out of their hair or killed in the oil that made the school reek when they came back to their desks with moist cloths wrapped round their heads.

The village women rode bicycles and cleaned in the big houses round about. The beach women pulled potatoes and cut sprouts, and, before the sea was barbed-wired off, their husbands used to stand at the end of the beach road with buckets of the fish they caught from small boats they dragged up on to the shore at night. But now the sea and the men had gone. In the summer when the children got time off from school to pick blackcurrants as war-work, the beach women could be seen hoeing on the lower fields, and in the autumn, when the village women came up to Mrs Rackham's with big baskets and the wells taken out of their prams to pick Victorias and Coxes and carry their own perks home abundantly every night, the beach women were pulling peas that were slimy even when the weather was dry, and made them smell foul and put the village women off their Victorias at tea that night.

Floy and I stood by the corrugated iron mission-hut. It reeked of creosote and darkaline in the sun and the smell of the Elsans that stood in a row in a ruined fisherman's house further along the beach. The wind's lips were hissing in the long hair grass and sand was singing through the barbed wire and hitting the corrugated iron and shingle where only sorrel and black-dock and sea-peas would grow. As we stood there hearing the sea against the pebbles, we saw one of the beach girls, Betty Hubb, standing with a bucket in the wind. Her legs were very thin and dropped into her plimsolls leaving a gap at the heel as though she could step out of them. She had a twin sister who was as thin and frightened and staring as herself. They both had red hair and spectacles so thick that you couldn't see their eyes behind. Betty stood there with her bucket as impassively and as dutifully as though she were about to roll up her sleeves or put her arms across her chest to be thumped by Miss Hadland.

One of the Hubbs would come to school without her glasses again and sit staring blindly round her desk till Miss Hadland saw. Or the other was still unable to grasp how to 'carry one' when she was adding tens in arithmetic. We would be working silently when the sound of a contest would make us look up – the sound of Miss Hadland's leather shoes struggling against Betty Hubb's rubber ones: the squeak of rubber shoes being kicked over the desk-frame then dragged up the room to the teacher's desk. Then there was a pause as the child slowly took her glasses off and laid them carefully on Miss Hadland's pen-stand; rolled up her sleeve and placed her thin freckled arms round her head and chest. We took in this obscene moment's cries. Then the glasses were put back on, and the twin went back to her seat. There were no tears, and Miss Hadland never spoke as she caned. But if it was one of the beach boys, she took him into the ante-room and the silence as they prepared themselves for encounter was a longer one; he cantered back out with his head ducked afterwards, and they were both flushed. As we saw Betty Hubb standing there with her bucket, while Vivian was organizing an Art School, the sea rose and sang in my ears. The tide pushed the shingle and made it rock and cry.

'Was it nice at school on Friday?' I asked in my best Apslet voice. 'Do you like Miss Hadland? Is she nice?' Betty nodded blankly and held her bucket. She was, without her glasses, lost on the miles of shingle as though she might accidentally wander into the sea. We went back home to see how the School of Art was progressing. But when we got to the end of the road three of the beach boys came out of the drainage ditch that separated them from the village, and blocked our path.

We'd always managed to avoid Trevor Helps in school. 'Dear Lord of Thee Three Things We Pray,' we would chant in our 'standards' at the end of the afternoon, shuffling backwards with our arms out in front of us and our fingers on the shoulders of the pupil in front; 'To Know Thee More Clearly,' we would sing, planning how to get our coats off the pegs and get across the playground before Trevor came running out; 'To Love Thee More Dearly,' and we would be back in our safe, knowing middle-class world while he was cantering his way towards the beach.

But he had talked and answered back – or he had forgotten to stand and put his first two fingers by his right eye when the Vicar came in that morning to read the day's lesson. Or he still couldn't read, and was danced into the ante-room. And now Trevor stood here with his friends in our path; three big boys with long willow switches that were still green with leaves and sharp with snappy fingers. They whipped us down into the ditch and laid us carefully and methodically on the black bandaged drain-pipe that ran at the bottom. One of them dug his thin knees into Floy's arms and muscled him; one whipped my legs, and Trevor banged my head up and down on the joint of the pipe.

'Bring your sister down – you mid – and we'll let you gid up. Bring the "Scattie" down. The big one with the bomps. Promid! Promid you mid!'

We promised, and they let us go.

The words 'Art Gallery' had been written across both sides of the shed when we got back, and handbills had been pinned all round the village:

WORKS OF ART, TRANSITAL AND PREDILECTIC etc
for sale.

Inspection invited. You may buy at any reasonable price.

Carole and Samey were working feverishly to produce the art works that Vivian demanded on sheets and pillowcases she had stripped from the beds.

'Connoisseurs and art-buyers may start arriving at any moment,' she reproached me. 'So buck up.' Floy shook his head and said through clenched teeth: 'Bugger-bugger. I must visit ye olde thatched crappe box.'

'Go against the wall,' Vivian directed, protesting, 'we're working against time.'

'But my posterior bags are in full voice,' he held his stomach, 'and I must flee the land . . . The Gates of Hell are opening,' he doubled up, 'but they shall not prevail.'

'Go on the compost heap,' Vivian dictated. But he rushed away.

'Vivian, shall we go down the beach road?' His head appeared at the first floor window. He wailed pitifully: 'I want to show you something down there.'

111

'This is chronic scandal,' Vivian shouted back. 'Connoisseurs are arriving . . .'

But Floy's head appeared at the second floor window. 'I want to show you something funny down on the beach road.' He lowered spit down. The children sighed and put their brushes down and Vivian took the opportunity to scrutinize their work. Floy's was a laughing butcher; Samey's was the bottom of the sea; Carole had done a Walt Disney bambi, with big eyelashes.

Vivian paused in front of it and bit her lip: 'Incidentally, Carole,' she said slowly, but her voice expressed something far from incidental. 'Incidentally, Carole,' she repeated after some reflection on the bambi in front of her, 'there's a play called "Macbeth".'

'I know,' Carole pressed her lips together and went on painting.

'You don't know. You've never been to the theatre in your life.'

'I have. I've been to the Odeon up at the Whip and maybe I'm going to be a film-star when I grow up.'

'The theatre. The living theatre.' Vivian's satirical lady-of-the-manor voice merged into her real one. 'The theatre with a proper stage and live people and a velvet curtain with jewels on. Not just a screen and sloppy love-stories and music like "Blue Skies Around the Corner".'

'I know.'

'You don't know,' Vivian shouted. 'You've never been to a theatre in your life. You can't even imagine the curtain trembling before it goes up, and the actors – *not* film-stars – incidentally – cutting little holes in the thick ancient velvet so that they can see out.' She was almost screaming as though Carole were about to rob us of everything we possessed.

But Carole just hummed and repeated: 'I know, because one day . . .'

'What?'

'I may be a film-star.' Vivian tore up Carole's work. Carole stared and bit her lip and took more paper and began again.

'Carole,' I whispered, 'why don't you come out with me

instead? I've got something nice to show you down the beach road. There's a cinema behind the tin chapel, and something special.'

Floy was still in the bathroom. I could hear his mannered choirboy voice echoing round the bath:

> Not forever by still waters
> Would we idly rest and stay.

He was still sitting there listening to his own voice:

> But would strike the living fountains . . .

The house was old and the water-system simple. When you pulled a chain in one lavatory you sent a flood of water up all three pans in the rest of the house. I would creep up to the Lasts' floor and pull their chain and stop his 'Living Fountains' below. But when I got up to their floor I saw Carole's mother and grandmother sitting at their table by the window, eating beetroot.

'I think he only done it to spite me,' Mrs Last was saying.

'Well, it's a man's world.' Her mother ate grimly. She took a bite of scotch pancake and a sip of tea. Each time her throat moved it made a crackling noise like cardboard being bent. 'Still, an eel gets used to skinning, they say.'

Mrs Last said something angry and went over to the sink. There were bluish lines under her eyes and her face was thin and white. Her arms and legs were thin as well, but her stomach stuck out almost to her chin. She propelled herself across the room behind this great hump and stuck it between herself and the sink.

'Hey,' I called to Floy, 'Mrs Last's going to have another baby.'

Floy came running out with his braces trailing along the floor: 'I've suspected that for months.' He lowered some more spit on to the creeper outside the window.

'Months, don't be silly. But still, her milk-things have been looking pretty bulgy for a long time.' Floy did some judicious shadow-boxing against a watercolour of some daffodils that hung on the wall and went back to the bathroom and his hymn. Then

Vivian came up to inspect the working-class scene. Then Cossey came.

We all knew what husbands and wives did when they wanted another baby. But Mrs Last's husband was away fighting in North Africa. And anyway, the expression on his wife's face was hardly one of the joyful achievement our mother talked of. Quite the reverse. We called the others one by one to come and look. Vivian, though, was surprisingly subdued. 'You only have a baby when you want one,' she kept repeating, till Floy came in with a bra our mother had tactfully bought and put in Vivian's drawer. He had draped it round his head like Bacchus crowned in leaves. 'You only have a baby if you want one,' Vivian repeated firmly.

'Oh no you don't,' he contradicted her, dancing round drunkenly. 'There are wounded birds in your drawer. Someone's been wounding birds and they've gone to her drawer to bleed and die. Samey rushed out to see.

Vivian started to weep: 'Connoisseurs and buyers may be arriving at any moment and all you can think of is Mrs Last making her smelly baby.'

I clasped Carole Last's hand. 'There's a cinema down the beach road you've never seen,' Floy told her. 'An Odeon like the one up at the Whip only this one's full of film stars and Snow White and . . .'

We could hear the sea singing at the end of the beach road as it broke against the barbed wire and the shingle. Carole clasped my hand and hummed happily to herself as we went on.

'Would you like me to take you there? You don't even have to pay to get in, and everyone is very nice to you . . .' The sea called louder and louder as we went down the beach road, Carole skipping beside me past 'Snice'ere' and 'Vanmee' and the railway carriages with their respectable markings, 'Ladies', 'Smoking', 'Third Class'. 'And there's the Seven Dwarfs too,' we went on. Carole hummed happily. The sea seemed to swell up on to the shingle and take the pebbles one by one. 'And ice-cream afterwards and lollypops.'

The sea sang in my head, as we led her into the mission chapel where the beach boys were standing and lifted her on to the communion table and started to undress her: 'But first we're going to play hospitals,' Floy said.

The beach boys made her 'show sites', but they really wanted the big one, Vivian, 'the scattie with the dids who'll put up a fight'.

Floy stood there smiling. Then he grew angry and put on an Apslet House voice and cried: 'Rubbish. You swines. I don't even know what you're talking about, except that you're all filthy beach shit.'

I'd never heard him talk like that before. We started back home leaving Carole 'at her Odeon' on the beach road. I looked back once or twice to see if she were following us, but she wasn't. I couldn't get rid of the look on her face, so happy and trusting, as she had clasped my hand and skipped down the beach road to see real film stars.

Samey was still painting in our art gallery and Vivian was still supervising when we got back.

'Where's Carole?' she asked. Then, 'Ah well, her art works are all rather mucky and film-starish.' Carole came back later that day, but she never let on to her mother, just pursed her lips together and endured the thumping she got.

'So Mrs Last's making another baby.' Floy laughed. 'Like making pastry on a table. She doesn't want it any more than you do,' he looked at Vivian. 'It's all just your filth.'

'I'm not making a baby,' Vivian exclaimed angrily. 'And in any case, you only make a baby when you want to. If-and-when,' she pursed her lips firmly and appealed to Cossey, 'if-and-when you want one. Don't you Cossey?'

Cossey didn't reply, but it was then that I sensed some signalling between her and Floy as Vivian cried: 'I'm never going to marry. I'm going to be a Little Sister of Ara Coeli. Haven't you ever heard of them? And anyway, you have as many children as you want.' She shouted up almost as a command at Mrs Last upstairs who just rubbed her nose with the side of her hand and joined in the hard laughter, then called down: 'You keep out of here. The lot of you. And Carole, this is what I've got for you . . .'

Above Carole's soft and regular crying I could hear Vivian still repeating in a shrill voice: 'Not true. Simply not true. Ignore Floy.'

Mrs Last slammed her door shut muttering about children who didn't get enough hidings, and big girls who should be out at work by now. 'I'll warm their backsides for them, I will,' Mrs Last would add. We could still hear Carole weeping faintly.

'Look at you two snoggling over there,' Vivian shouted at Cossey and Floy. She tried to sound her old haughty self, but her voice trembled as she saw how old allegiances had been split up by the beach road. She withdrew more and more into herself. We noticed she smelt of warm stale blood and scruffy upholstery. Floy screwed up his nose and looked at Cossey again, as if there had been a complicity, and gave that funny smile again that seemed to distance him from us girls. Vivian saw and seized the bread knife and chased him round the table till Cossey intervened. Floy became our leader now. All our lives we had been dominated by Vivian. Even when Cossey and Dad had gone away and we played only 'dear' games, as we now called them, it was Vivian who had organized them and changed the rules and invented new ones. But now it was Floy who set us our tasks in the new art gallery while Vivian went out alone picking gooseberries for Cossey's jam.

'Was it nice down the beach road?' I asked Carole as she came creeping down the stairs, peering at us through the banisters. 'Was it lovely down there?'

She smiled shyly and nodded.

'Cross your heart?'

'Cross my heart,' she crossed it and spat.

I could hear Samey still painting in the art gallery, humming to herself as Carole had hummed once, innocently drawing Snow White and film-stars. After that Carole never came down to play. The Battle of Britain had started and there were daily dogfights in the sky. France had fallen and the Battle of Britain had begun. We would watch the fighters doing sword-dances overhead, silver in the blue air as the *tank-tank* of anti-aircraft guns came from the school playground where the guns had been installed. It sounded more like an animal's cry of pain than of machinery, and we took shelter when shrapnel started falling and never went down the beach road. Floy took over the running of the art gallery and Samey and Carole played there alone.

When silence came in late September I saw Floy going down the beach road again. He had given instructions for a new kind of art and wandered down to the beach road dragging his arm casually in the dense topiaried hedge while we still only played 'dear' games up here at Apslet, collecting shrapnel or swapping beach shells, or playing Feet-off-ground, or Bouncing-Go or French cricket. 'Foul talk' was punished by expulsion, and Vivian spent her time hanging round Cossey in the kitchen, helping her make jam and begging her for riding lessons. The art gallery was turned into a bedroom for her and me. She no longer wanted to sleep in the same room as Floy, and Cossey insisted that I share with her now. We never bathed together again, either. Cossey talked of a boarding school for Floy up in the north. He said he wanted to be a priest and I gaped at him and burst out laughing:

> Laddie-boy as priesty-ho
> Holy wine and brandy-oh.

Vivian grew even more silent and uncommunicative. She sat alone reading soppy *Girls' Crystal* stories and withdrew to her bedroom and barred the door and listened to the radio she kept under her bed.

'Time you started looking for a job, Vivian,' Cossey would say. 'But you'll never get one if you don't pull your shoulders back and stand better.' Then Floy would look at Vivian and then at Cossey and again there still seemed to be an understanding. 'Pull your tummy in, Vivian, and try to speak properly. You're not a beach girl.'

I climbed to the top of the house, to the Lasts' floor, and peered in at the kitchen watching Mrs Last's heavy movement. By standing on the tenth stair up I could see her propelling herself grimly round the kitchen. 'He only done it to spite me,' I could hear her saying bitterly.

'Ah well, it's a man's world,' her mother would reply with a grunt. 'An eel gets used to skinning, don't it, eh?'

Vivian usually fell asleep before me in bed at nights and it seemed as though she had dropped away from us for good. I lay there alone, hearing a great tide of water in my head. It was coming up and taking her like a bride back to the soft but massive bed of the sea, and leaving Floy and Samey and me behind. Floy would go down the beach road alone now, and I would cycle in to Winchester on Saturday afternoons and wander round Woolworth's studying sanitary belts and pads and bandages and all the other white female equipment that Vivian now seemed to belong to. Until now I had always associated sex with class, but now my sister too was being fed and reared and educated for the wind to sing and for someone to take her down the beach road. Then she would trundle herself round grudgingly like Mrs Last, carrying what she didn't want and had no use for, under big tits bursting in a springtime that wasn't hers. Cossey had always hinted that women were cursed. They smiled and bled and watched it and acquiesced in the slow and steady seepage of themselves.

'Just been to inspect the working-class scene?' Vivian would ask sourly when Floy came back from the beach. She would fold her arms over her chest and Cossey would cry at Floy: 'Oh you baddy!' Floy was smiling. Floy and Cossey were still smiling together.

I went with him once down to the beach road. 'Let's get away from these women,' he had whispered to me. We walked along the rough unmade road. The landscape was dry and bleak as though no one had ever loved it or said anything about it or given it anything. There were no more dogfights now and the sky was grey and flat and only the rush and rest of the sea remained, the lips of the sea and Floy's smiling mouth.

'Are you really going to be a priest?' I asked him.

He smiled more. 'You can do anything to girls,' he replied obliquely.

'Why is that beetle only a beetle?' Samey was asking Cossey when we got back, lying on the steps.

'Because it *likes* being a beetle,' Cossey replied.

'Would you like to be a . . . a seaside?' Samey asked. 'Which would you rather be, a seaside or a leg?'

Floy and I were relieved. 'Which would you rather be, a ping-pong ball or wipe Samey's nose?' We grabbed at the chance of more 'dear' games. Only they were acceptable now.

Cossey was packing again. Mrs Rackham had arranged for Floy to go away to school. The rest of us were going back to London.

'We Gerbers never were country bumpkins,' Cossey explained to Mrs Last. 'We're city people and always will be. Aren't we all lucky going back to London!'

'And aren't you all lucky that an eel gets used to skinning,' Floy grinned and danced round us with Vivian's new bra on his head.

'Bacchus crowned in vine leaves,' Cossey laughed. We were glad that Floy was going. But it wasn't to be for long.

'My cousin . . . a doctor . . .' Cossey explained to Mrs Rackham in her county voice, 'being a doctor he's allowed petrol and a car, and he's coming down to pick us up. The country is lovely in summer but we all want to go back and fight Jerry. The country seems so sleepy . . . and complacent, now that Europe is engulfed in war.'

Cousin Jim arrived next day. 'Too Bad For You – I Love Another,' we sang in the dicky of his car as we drove back to London. But Cossey and Jim in front were silent. Perhaps it was just the strong wind that blew from the beach road and in at the open-air car that made them unable to talk.

Chapter XIII

Dad worked in Baker Street now, and lived in service flats alone. He had disappeared as we go away in sleep and without any noise or excuse. Cossey got a job interpreting information from aircraft returning from bombing missions over Europe. Sometimes she had to take down messages from crashing aircraft and pass them on to wives and lovers. More often she was directing the fighter pilots up above how to climb directly over the German aircraft in the night sky in order to shoot them down. Vivian looked after Webbley Mansions now. Floy was at school, Samey had been evacuated to Scotland and I went to the South London Emergency School. There was no sign of Miss Lenege's return and Cossey said she had been interned on the Isle of Man along with a lot of other aliens. We protested again that she was a refugee from Hitler, but Cossey shrugged. That was war. We wandered round Ransome's Fields feeling guilty again. The leaves clicked and blew along the paths. Two pasty-looking men were standing there gloomily, playing Bach's Air on a G string on flat bass trumpets by the bandstand while a third sang and banged a drum with his foot and swore to himself under his breath. Cossey was laughing silently at a letter from Floy.

'When this wicked war is over . . .,' she looked up and sighed. But she loved her war-work and loved coming home on leave and telling us about how awful it was for women before there was proper work for them. She would sit at the window of the Mansions looking out over the bombed streets and tell us how it had been in 1916 when she was expected to stay at home and knit comforters for the boys in the trenches and sing pious hymns at the piano.

But Cossey's stories weren't for us anymore and she would just give our carpet-sweeper a great kick and say: 'Because of my determination to be free, you and your generation will be grateful. You'll never have to stay at home and high-dust and swab down the mouldings on the ceilings with glycerine water. For the first time in my life I've got real work. How ashamed I am of all those stories I used to write with my tongue in my cheek. How ashamed I am of smarming up to Mrs Rackham.'

'What do you tell the pilots up there when you know they're going to crash?' I asked, but Vivian interrupted contemptuously: 'Cossey doesn't really have to take down their last messages. She just sits at a sort of typewriter-thing taking down numbers like 13857.3 over, and 84985.273 over.'

Cossey said nothing except: 'I hope you two girls are going to Mass on Sundays.' Then she gave the carpet-sweeper another kick and went back to her bomber station in East Anglia. We would sit and stare at the big posters of Churchill and Stalin that my school had told me to pin on the walls to raise money for guns. Vivian would go out early each night and come home late and sit by the Imperial Boiler tearing up bits of cloth to make rugs for bombed-out people.

We were alone now in Webbley Mansions. The Rattrays and Uncle Neary had gone away and the flats echoed and wobbled during a raid. We would gaze out on our street side at the gutted houses and wonder why the people who lived on either side of them suddenly seemed pinned there so bright and clean and house-proud with polished saucepans and newly washed linen hanging across the bomb-space just to prove. There was a permanent smell of rats and damp now as we walked through the back-doubles to the shops. Bits of grey sky hung in the spaces where roofs should have been, and a gas cooker would stand tilted towards the ground with one leg poised to fall through and on to the street below. The gutted houses were like saucepans of stale stew being stirred, and we kept thinking of Miss Lenege and how it must all seem to her and other 'enemy aliens'. We ate cake made with soya, and scrambled eggs made of thick yellow powder, and potatoes fried in cod liver oil. We felt sick and couldn't get the reek of fish oil out of the flat.

The air-raid noises echoed round. The flat seemed even emptier and noisier now that the Red Cross had taken Miss Lenege's furniture away and we had lost our windows. We went to shelter in the dugout that had been made in Ransome's Fields. The guns somehow seemed worse than the bombs. They sounded so much like a human's voice and so full of pain and rage. Or sometimes just pattering out as gently as a pencil being tapped against a table, or soft voices pattering reproach in a bus. When the all-clear had gone, the sounds of the city would start slowly reviving like things slowly stirring in a room, one by one. Then the sound of the trams came, telling us that everything was OK and the blood was circulating once more. Sometimes, when there was no raid, great gangs of girls would come roaring down the streets arm-in-arm in long chains singing about their boys overseas. They sang in melancholy thirds as they went round and round chanting 'Please Don't Take My Sunshine Away'.

Vivian worked in the cash-and-carry on Kennington Green and wore a hard, green overall far too big for her and a green cap. She peeled vegetables all morning and tipped scoops of mince and greens into basins and handed them out with spotted dick and stiff, bright yellow custard, and came home reeking of cabbage. Sometimes when she got in Cossey was there in her uniform: 'You do look a couple of frumpies,' she would exclaim. 'Do you really want to be a nun, Vivian? Cousin Jim will knock the nonsense out of you wanting to be a Little Sister of Ara Coeli. I'll give Jim a ring. He's working at Lambeth Hospital and I'm sure he'd love to see us again. He was asking after you when I went there for an overhaul.'

It was in late 1941 after a bad air raid that we met Cousin Jim again. Cossey had been for the day and she had been telling us about the times when her father was on Cemetery Duty on Sunday afternoons and how at four o'clock sharp they buried the paupers. 'I can still hear the sidesman at the back of the church,' she said, 'and how he pronounced the word "sharp" and pressed his lips flat. The paupers all went in one big grave in a row. Up and down and sideways. One big grave for the eight or ten white pinewood coffins.' Cossey shuddered and went.

It was a Sunday evening and after she had gone there was a raid and the Baptist Chapel over the Fields had a direct hit while they were at prayer, and Cousin Jim had been summoned from the Lambeth Hospital and we sat there in the silence hearing the cries and remembering how Cossey had told us that at four o'clock 'sharp' the paupers were all buried in one grave side-by-side. 'Sharp', the flats re-echoed.

Jim tried to cheer us up. He played the piano and we sang. He had decided to stay the night with us and we cooked him an omelette of dried eggs and Vivian smiled and watched him eat. Next day he said he had time off and took us out to the country. We understood what Cossey meant about the Welsh harpist as Jim stood there. We still felt very stupid about the Chapel, and kept crying when we dropped things. It was as though we had come out of a cinema into broad daylight and didn't know what it was all about. Vivian would still sit there by the Imperial Boiler tearing up bits of rags to make children's blankets and I would do my homework in silence till the siren went. Or Jim would come again and take us round his hospital at night and give us a bar of chocolate or take a hot knife and divide a Mars Bar in three.

Or he would come to the flat again and take us out at weekends and sit there on the hillside just a little in front of us, with a gentle breeze blowing over one cheek, and white clouds unfolding beside the other. The bleating of sheep followed us here and there, and Jim still sat a bit ahead and with his back to us. We could see he was smiling by the shape of his right cheek and ear. I couldn't see his face, but his hands were pressed on the ground as though he knew a secret joy. Vivian looked very beautiful too, I noticed, with her dark hair wrapped round her face by the wind. Jim came again in the summer and took us to the Downs, and we stared into the wind. The sun lay on the hills above us, and the trees sent down long shadows. Jim said that perhaps the humpier shadow was a pre-Roman burial place. A barrow. Its shadow spread down the hillside. The barrow began to stir as though it had a pulse. There wasn't the slightest breath of wind on the hill or in the valley below, and yet the leaves on the trees seemed to be waving and fidgeting.

Jim said the worst of the war was still to come. The Russians were fighting well but us not well enough. It seemed funny, the way he said 'fighting well', as though we were adults. He was saying now that the Allies were eventually going to invade Europe while Germany was still stuck into the bleeding wound of Russia. That would only be the beginning but he would look after us.

After this Vivian started buying women's magazines and going to evening classes at big LCC schools with 'Evening Institute' written in blue blackout paper over the school playgrounds. She went to Morley College as well, she told me, and she came back smelling of coffee and tobacco and I knew she met Jim there. She always had a snug and curled-up look these days, rather like Cousin Jim's. She just stared when Cossey came home, as a sleek cat might stare out at the world it has nothing much to do with, then settle back on its comfortable sill. I knew she met Jim nearly every night.

Cossey must have grown anxious because she came home one weekend in a smart green utility suit with her bare knees showing and said with cool interest, her voice very bright and calm, that there was a lovely convent in Wales where we could both do war-work – real proper war-work – till the war was over. She said it carefully, as though she were doing a calculation, that we'd have all the chances she never had living in the heart of a war-ravaged city. London wasn't safe. It was beautiful as well as safe at Bwlch, she pronounced carefully.

'There's pottery and archery,' she began with excited eyes. 'I always wanted my children to have a modern progressive education. Bwlch is a marvellous place for girls to run wild in. And it will lick you both into shape and give you both a bit of polish. And they do domestic science and mothercraft as well,' she added laughing. Vivian was angry. 'And for Alma there's plenty of music and speech-training.' Cossey had put on a pair of black celluloid spectacles she had won in a raffle and added: 'I've given you all your freedom.'

'I'm very grateful to you,' Vivian replied, 'letting me borrow the clothes that really belong to you. But this has got nothing to do with you, really.'

'Yes, it has,' Cossey declared emphatically, 'because it was I who gave you your freedom. Right from the moment you were born. And I gave Dad his freedom too.'

'And I suppose you gave Miss Lenege her freedom too, to go off and be interned.'

'She had TB like the awful family in Ondels Grove,' Cossey said without much conviction. 'That's why she had to go.'

'Jim and I are going to get married,' Vivian said.

'Yes, I gave Jim my consent. I gave him his freedom to marry you.' But then Cossey started to cry and lay on her bed in her celluloid glasses, and we carefully eased them off her nose and fed her with porridge which she took up in little spoonfuls between her sobs: 'Thank you. Thank you,' she choked.

We remembered how Dad had found his mother weeping when he was a child of five because she had been to hear Madame Patti. But this was different, and Cossey cheered up and went to the window and looked down over Ransome's Fields and the hole where the chapel had been and said: 'It's this terrible war that's upset me. For days now I've been talking on my radar screen to the airmen up there in the sky and wishing them good luck and telling them they'll soon be home. A lot of them are so afraid. They're only a bit older than Floy . . .'

We went to Battersea Park and rowed on the lake with Jim after Cossey had gone back to East Anglia.

We went to Lyons Corner House in the Strand and had baked beans on toast. Then they left me in a News Cinema at Piccadilly. They left me there every night, or we went to tea-dances and I danced with a serviceman who had very big jutting out ears and swore that we would meet again.

When we got in Cossey was there. She had a letter from Floy's school in her hand. It said they were sending Floy home. Not an expulsion but a suspension. Cossey didn't tell us why, but I was afraid of the look in her eye as she asked me to make up his bed. I had pushed the beach road carefully out of my mind when we got back to Webbley Mansions, and now here it was again, but Vivian was glistening with happiness now, not hurt and anger.

Floy came home laughing. He seemed much taller now and his

voice had broken. Cossey said he'd have to go to the Emergency School too. Or come back to East Anglia with her.

Vivian locked herself in the bathroom. She said the thought of Floy made her sick. Or she had put too much sugar in her tea and that had made her sick. Cossey stared straight ahead every time Vivian went into the bathroom. 'It must have been that fish-oil I fried the potatoes in last night.'

'Yes,' Cossey stared straight ahead. Floy had fractured his arm and spent a lot of time gazing on the innocent white of the plaster. He was angry with me for touching it. He guarded it like a precious white jewel, or something holy like the Sacrament.

Floy and Cossey seemed conspirators again now that Floy had been sent home from his school, but Vivian and I never knew what they were talking about or planning. It must be about girls and marriage and eels that get used to skinning I thought, as Floy stared in at us from the door of our room, or they both sat together in the big basket chair that had once been ours.

'You two lovers,' I shouted. 'Floy wants Cossey to have another baby. This time another beautiful boy.' The basket chair creaked and uncoiled itself in the fire's heat after they had left it. I began to see why Cossey loved going up in the fairground Chairoplanes so much. She and Floy were both as excited as if they had both just got off one. Vivian stood by the sink peeling potatoes for our supper; she reminded me of Mrs Last as she leaned over at the sink, leaning over her stomach. I looked at her shocked. Then Floy said in his new baying and unreliable voice, chasing Vivian round the table with a wet drying-up cloth and flicking it against her stomach: 'You filthy track. You foul smelly mess of wet flesh.'

'It's all right, Floy,' Cossey tried to stop him. She imprisoned him at last in the big basket chair by the fire. 'Isn't it exciting. Vivian's making a baby. That's women's form of creativity. Making babies.'

'She's not making it,' Floy jeered. 'It's being made *on* her. Like those funguses on the trees in the Fields. You can do anything to a woman,' he suddenly started to cackle in a husky voice. He turned to Cossey: 'She can't stay here with that squishy mess growing inside her.'

'It's an odd period in a boy's life,' Cossey explained to Vivian and me, but it seemed to be as much in Cossey's life as in Floy's. 'He'll grow up and sort things out,' she added.

'What a pity I can't,' Vivian retorted. 'And what a pity you can't give Floy *his* freedom too, to go back to that school and stay there.'

'You have as many children as you want,' I could hear Vivian maintaining at Apslet the time we spied Mrs Last at her sink and her mother sighing about the eel. I gazed at Vivian staring grimly at the sink and dabbing at the potatoes again. Her stomach seemed so high up in her stiff cash-and-carry overall disguise, as though it had only been pinned there. I was shocked at what had been dumped on her as though she were a vacant lot, or a cupboard where you stored things you didn't want. She was only three years older than I was, and we still sometimes got out our dolls when no one was about and played swap-exchanges with their clothes. She seemed too perilously near myself to be a construction site. We could hear the hooters on the river warning us, and Vivian seemed to have obeyed and to be as dutifully passive as the children of Nanton Road School waiting for a world to be erected on them. Any little cry of protest would come from some other corner of the room, like a ventriloquist's puppet: 'If you want to scream, scream into the pillow.'

I could see us all back at Apslet House and the sea flooding through the barbed wire along the beach, and Floy's lips as active as the lips of the sea. He stood in the kitchen of Webbley Mansions now, as though he were going to do another of his 'turns' for Mrs Rackham's guests, or inspect the working-class scene.

But Cossey intervened: 'I've got it all planned out,' she said in an excited voice. 'After all, *I* ran away on the *Percy Warrior* with Dad because I knew the alternative was dust and ashes and rows of little houses with net curtains tightly pinned over the windows to keep life out. In Wales you two will be able to have all the freedom that I never had at Ondels Grove. And I shall be there with you in your hour of need. I'll get time off like a good mum. How lovely it will be for me to have a grandchild. What marvellous stories I'll be able to tell him about my theories of freedom and how I fought for them in horrible Edwardian London. It will be beautiful in Wales away from all this blitz. I gave you all your freedom, didn't I?' But we weren't sure whether Vivian was pregnant because we'd had our freedom or because we had refused it. Cossey seemed to be saying: 'You must be like me but you can't be.'

'I'd rather go to the Home for Fallen Girls opposite the Bedlam,' Vivian retorted.

Floy wouldn't eat with us now, or sit with us. He would lie on his bed all day in disgust, reading, and Cossey would take him his meals. 'It's a funny period in a boy's life. Baddy Floy! Feet on the bedspread!' Whenever Floy happened to come across Vivian he would make funny movements and blink his eyelids and he kept washing his hands, as he used to down at Apslet.

'It's all right, Floy. Nothing bad has happened,' Cossey would reassure him while we stood there, Vivian and I feeling equally guilty and alone, now that life had changed so much.

Cossey was busy writing letters and going across the Fields to the phone. She came back smiling: 'When is he due?' she asked Vivian. 'We must go to a doctor and find out. How lovely it will be. I always wanted you all to marry younger than I did. It's a pity though that you didn't mention it before to me . . .' Her voice came in a torrent. 'You'll have lovely fun at Bwlch. The Sisters want you both to help a bit in the convent kitchens, and', Vivian just stared all the time with her slight smile, 'in return for riding lessons and piano and all the other things, you're both going to help with some of the children there who aren't all that strong. War-work for both of you two lovies! Some war-work at last.'

She took Vivian and me to Paddington, Floy staring after us as we went. As we crossed the Fields we pictured Dad being dropped into occupied Holland where women like his mother sheltered him and sent him home with secret messages. But Dad didn't come and as our train steamed out of the station Vivian pressed her lips together and gave a slight obstinate smile just as Carole Last had done instead of answering back. Vivian looked as though she were going to fall right through the seat. Then she leaned out of the window and was sick again and again.

Jim hadn't come to see us off either, and everything on the journey down to Wales seemed bare and cold. We sat side-by-side in silence as the blank grey fields went padding past. We didn't even feel like eating the sweets Cossey had secured for us from the NAAFI shop on her airbase. An old lady sat opposite us telling us about her life and how angry she was with her hairdresser for chopping off her curls. She patted her hair then fumbled in her suitcase and brought out two china doves and a ball of wool, and asked us which was the girl dove. We didn't know and didn't want to know, but she kept on asking us as the train sped towards Wales. Finally she pointed at the dove that was nearest the ball of wool and said: '*That* is the girl dove because she is standing beside her egg.' Vivian was sick again. 'You two do look poor sad little doves. I'm not boring you am I? Let me see if I can cheer you up a bit . . .', and she began again: 'Now can you tell me which is the girl dove . . .?' To stop Vivian being sick again I invented a game where one of you had to try and make the other say a certain forbidden word. But even that didn't make the journey go any faster, and it was almost dark when huge mountains started to clamber nearer and nearer to the train, and there was a smell of pine forests and clear cold water, and the people in the next compartment were all talking Welsh.

Chapter XIV

It was November when Cossey came down to see us at Bwlch. We were standing round the school-room rehearsing our Nativity play. Christmas was drawing near and we felt cheerful again, as though we were back in Ransome's Fields, as the piano in the corner twanged and the greenish-black stage curtains were jerked back. There was the Angel of the Lord running forward in her callipers to salute the Virgin Mary. Someone's crutch clapped down against the wooden platform and the cotton curtains shivered in the draught, but everyone was cheerful as the angel swung forward again on her crutches singing: 'Fear not, Mary, for I bring you news of great joy.' Vivian's baby started to hiccup.

Vivian would throw her daughter, Thomasa, into the air and catch her. She would make her walk along the refectory table tops singing 'It's a Hap-Hap-Happy Day'. The Sisters didn't like her playing with her baby. 'In case I contaminate her,' Vivian would laugh and swing her higher and higher, then stow her away in her cot for the night at the end of the dormitory behind a black cotton curtain.

We had arrived at Bwlch late at night and were driven in a trap up to the convent which stood black against the damp black rock-face of the mountain as though it had slithered a few feet out of place and might be swallowed back inside. The stars were in a crystal bowl above but it was dark and cold inside the house and as damp as the dripping water we heard coming down the rock-face behind. We had been given soup with fatty globes on its surface, then taken down the long dormitory and told we could lie in tomorrow. When we woke in the morning the iron beds round us were all empty and stripped and the rock outside the window was still dripping and the invalid children sat in rows in the kitchen in their wheel chairs peeling potatoes slowly and clumsily with heavy blunt knives, and one elderly girl with fair hair falling over her squinting eyes kept stealing raw potatoes and pushing them up her knicker legs or stuffing them in her mouth till the Sister grew angry and cried, 'Paula.'

The girl clasped her chin in her fist and shook it and cried to herself: 'Paula, in a minute I'm going to get very angry with you.' She would beat on her head and cry again and again: 'Naughty Paula,' as water dripped down the rock-face behind the school. That was the most constant sound of our lives at the convent. After the regular chime of bells for the Offices, this dripping was the sound that determined our days like a clock that never stopped. This tick-tocking of the rock on the mountainside was the nearest we would ever get to an outside world.

If our mother saw this when she at last came down to Bwlch, she never said so. She would gaze at the invalid children and exclaim leaning over their chairs: 'What a marvellous place for fun.' Then she would gaze at her grand-daughter. Thomasa seemed to lie to attention and gaze back as though this were how she interpreted Cossey's command to have fun. 'Do you have fun?' Cossey repeated as Vivian stood there in her 'trainee' uniform with a brush in one hand and a bucket of damp tea-leaves in the other.

We wore maids' clothes and washed up after meals and wiped the bottoms of the invalids in the freezing courtyard lavatories, and got them to bed and got them up again next day and helped them across the frozen cobbles to the stable that had been turned into a chapel for daily Mass. Cossey had bought an anthology of poetry and inscribed it: 'To Vivian to celebrate the first year of her war-work.' She had promised to be with Vivian in her 'hour of need', but in fact she said she'd been on emergency duty at her airbase, so the Sisters had taken Vivian to a shepherd's hut on the hillside because she had screamed so much in labour.

'I see now why Cossey despises girls so much,' Vivian said when she came back from the hut to be churched in the chapel and restored to the kitchen and the invalids. 'Stupid cows we are,' she looked down at her swollen breasts. 'It would be nice to be a weed that no one ever wants to take anywhere.'

'I think it's lovely fun being a woman,' Cossey said when she and Floy came down. Floy curled up his lips and smiled and went on repairing a battered suitcase with glue and string. We all stared at the baby who stared back at us.

Then we were all sitting in the school-room rehearsing our Nativity play. The priest stood there nodding in his black skirt, clutching his black silk biretta, and the Sister's cracked leather shoe creaked against the worn pedal of the piano as she played. We sang and the shepherds sat round a torch with red paper wrapped round it warming themselves at their fire and chanting: 'The world is old tonight. The stars do show . . . how old the fold . . . as it was told . . . so cold . . .'

'The Messiah really did come, you know,' the priest turned to Gertrud, a Jewish pupil, then to Ernst, her younger brother. 'But he came like one of us, a poor child, like this baby here, lying in his cradle.' Gertrud gave a whimper of a laugh. We banged our frozen hands together. Our teeth chattered and the crowns and cloaks and angels' wings all came loose and thick yellow smoke came out of the grate. We had decorated the invalid children's wheelchairs with holly and crepe-bows and bits of red ribbon.

'What's wrong with us?' Ernst asked his older sister, staring at Clive who was swinging his calipered legs in the air.

'Man over. Man overboard,' Clive cried as the leather burst out of the padding along his crutch's top. He swung the censer at Mass and was teaching Floy how to do it, using a dressing gown cord with an old shoe tied on its end. More straw burst out of the leather of his crutch like a big 'Oh – Oh what a surprise.'

'What's wrong with us?' Ernst would repeat, gazing at Paula who was still beating at her face.

'There's nothing wrong with you,' Sister Thelia would reply, holding her hood away from her face in the draught. She looked as though the person who had made her face had grown tired and gone away leaving one eye without any colour and one side of her mouth slack and undone.

'Well, why are we all here then?' Ernst started to cry. 'Is it a joke or what?'

The Sister would clasp his two hot hands in hers and swing them and cry:

> The Red Cross Will Come
> And we shall have fun . . .

'Didn't we have lovely fun though, at Ransome's Fields,' Cossey hugged us and kissed us and the baby. 'Goodbye to all that. Still, you can keep up your piano lessons here, can't you Alma?' she asked me.

But Vivian and I were 'Volunteers' and paid no school fees, and dressed in green gingham with starched white overalls and caps like the girls at Nanton Road School that Cossey had tried to write all those angry articles about. Most of the invalids weren't strong enough to dress themselves or walk, so there wasn't much time for playing the piano, I told Cossey, but she just nodded and went on: 'Do you do science and hockey and archery? It says in the prospectus that you can do any of these things. You must ask the Sisters . . . When I was your age there was nothing like this. My father was pastor of St Egbert's Mission and once we were taken to see a dead child with forget-me-nots on her chest . . .' Cossey started up but a bell rang and we unfolded our starched caps and put them on to wash the children and take them into chapel.

Gertrud, the Jewish girl, who had been cast as Mary in our play, was a Volunteer as well. She had been sent over from Vienna with her brother Ernst in 1936 and they were still waiting for their parents to follow them as they had promised they would. In the meantime Gertrud would give a little patient laugh as we swept the unplastered corridors where the saints looked remote in their niches in the high window sills. We would follow a Sister who had an arm with a hook at the end that brought down dust and dead leaves and empty fish-paste jars and dead chrysanthemums. We followed her arm with dusters and I told Vivian I didn't like the 'I-told-you-so' look in the Virgin's superior smile, and Vivian said she'd accidentally smashed St Joseph's beard and showed me the piece she had knocked off, then tied it on a string to dangle over her baby. We got up at six each morning to get the children washed and dressed and into their callipers. I was supposed to help Paula each day, but she was older and much heavier than me, and I would stare at her when I had helped her across the courtyard, or helped her mount her huge tricycle that she struggled like Sisyphus to cycle up to the path that led down to Bwlch, the nearest village.

'Was it lovely cycling round and round?' I would lean over her and ask with exaggerated interest, widening my eyes as we used to do with Carole Last at Apslet, or down on the beach road, where the lips of the sea rushed at the barbed wire.

'Was it lovely cycling round and round on your sports model and away and away and a ho-ho-ho?' Floy added leaning over her as well. Paula chuckled and clasped her lanky hair and giggled as Floy went on: 'What shall we do for you, oh beautiful one? Blessed art thou amongst women.'

'We only play "dear" games here,' I protested smugly to Floy.

He replied as though he had a cold in his nose: 'Dear Gabes, how are you? Today I shot dowd ted swads.'

Vivian would frown angrily and Cossey would laugh: 'Oh you two baddies. Try not to tease.'

Some of the invalids were even heavier than Paula, and one was a lady of over sixty who taught us French. We had to help her downstairs from her bedroom at the top of the house where we were forbidden to go. The wall of the corridor outside was always warm and Vivian said there was a fire in there where the very old and frail nuns lived. Sometimes we would hear coughing from inside and sometimes see one or other of the kitchen Sisters carrying up trays of food and lifting back the prie-dieu which we were forbidden to pass. The Sister would clear her throat as she passed into the consecrated part of the house and Gertrud would give her small whimpering laugh.

Vivian always had to wake her baby for her feeds. Thomasa never seemed hungry and she very rarely cried. We would both get up at three and stand there leaning against the warm patch on the wall where the Sisters' quarters started and the harsh electric lighting stopped. We would stand there listening to the tick-tock of the water dripping down the rock-face, and Vivian would write to Jim, leaning against the warm wall, and he would send postcards back: 'I loved your description of the mountains. Do you paint?' Or 'Give Thomasa my love and hugs. I'm longing to see her. When this war is over, maybe we'll find ourselves in Australia or somewhere fresh.' Sometimes Jim would send a bar of chocolate from the NAAFI, and Sister Thelia would cut it into six squares and distribute them to children who had been good.

But the children were seldom naughty. Most of them were too frail or too defeated for mischief or quarrels. Some of them saw that we were all in the same boat. The refugee children, like Gertrud and Ernst, were constantly being reminded that they were mere guests in this country, and the rest of us were warned repeatedly that Mr Hitler was very near as it was, and he would get even nearer if we slacked or teased or wasted the food on our plates.

As we stood in chapel doing the Stations of the Cross, I remembered how a lady had once given us a Union Jack at Ransome's Fields for doing the Stations so nicely. We had sewn the sides of the flag together and poured milk into it to make a patriotic cheese for supper. But now a great ocean seemed to be set between us and those days. I could hear the lips of the sea against the pebbles on the beach at Apslet.

'We don't play beach games any more now,' I told Floy as he watched Paula or whispered with Clive.

So we tried to play nothing but 'dear' games, though when Floy came down it was hard not to feel back at Apslet House with Carole Last: 'So you're the Queen of the May when you go cycling round and round.'

Sister Thelia would frown and call me away. We would leave Paula and creep up to the silent quarters of the convent beyond the harsh electric lighting of the children's part of the house.

Vivian would wake Thomasa for her early morning feed and we would stand at the window looking out at the forests. They stirred all night like animals turning for ever in their sleep. The stars licked the blue silk sky clean as a sword. We loved the nude blue night.

'Do you think the Hoppes' parents will ever come?' I would ask when Gertrud cried out in her sleep. Then she would be standing there beside us: 'The Red Cross has all the names and addresses,' she would recite, then give her whimpering laugh. Daylight would come like something bright placed suddenly there. We could hear the stream running and the lambs' cry on the mountains where we were never allowed to go. We hung our heads sleepily at breakfast over the boiled swedes and turnips that the Sisters grew on terraces down the mountain's face. Then Vivian and Gertrud would disappear to the kitchens and I would help get the children to the school-room where we did arithmetic all morning till the Angelus bell went and we sang: 'And the angel of the Lord brought tidings to Mary.'

We went back to the refectory for great tins of steaming mutton soaked in black jelly, and the invalids would stare patiently in a silence broken only by their heavy breathing as they dragged heavy spoons to their mouths and the Sisters murmured behind the screen where they sat hidden from us.

'Often have they fought against me from my youth upwards,' they would chant.

'I don't believe it,' Cossey would put down her spoon in protest. 'The only person who ever fought against me from my youth upwards was that awful gas-cooker we all shared in Baston Square. These swedes are making me burp.'

We tried to shush Cossey up. We weren't supposed to speak during meals and she ate in thoughtful silence making up little rhymes which she recited to us afterwards as we took her round the convent. It was decorated for Christmas and she grew excited at its beauty.

'I always wanted you to be Catholics,' she said. 'Everyone in Ondels Grove believed that Catholics were so wicked. We were never allowed to speak to them as children. But once when I had to do a scholarship exam, I had to go to a convent school to write the papers. It was out at Clapham near the Common, and a kind nun, not looking at all wicked, gave me a glass of lemonade and told me to go out into the gardens with the other girls and play. The garden was full of leafy trees and under the leaves and branches there were smiling statues of the Virgin and St Joseph and St Aloysius. The girls all looked so happy and smiling, and pleased to be alive. They were all chasing each other round the statues and they didn't look at all wicked either. They laughed and danced and rode bicycles just like normal girls and the saints on their tall stands all seemed pleased to see us children running around them. How lucky you are, both of you, to be here when Floy and I are battling against foul Jerry in poor old London.'

'It's a pity they can't keep the war going for ever for you,' Vivian pressed her lips together.

Cossey just laughed: 'What a good thing it was that I was able to give you both your freedom away from it all.'

Floy smiled and looked at his shoes. Vivian looked at Cossey. Her baby lay there as though she too were listening to Cossey's patter, then she gave a little frown as though the only reason she didn't stand upright with the rest of us and join in the squabble was that she prized her independence too much. All the same, Cossey seemed delighted by her grandchild. We stood there in our green-and-white gingham dresses and starched caps.

'I gave you all the freedom that I never had,' Cossey repeated almost reproachfully.

'You make it sound like a donation to charity,' Vivian picked at her nose then wiped her fingers on her starched cap. Then she excused herself. She had to go and feed Thomasa behind a screen in the bathroom.

Cossey beamed, then sighed. She still couldn't decide whether we were at Bwlch as a punishment or as a reward. 'How lovely it is here,' she kept exclaiming. 'And how lovely it is having a grandchild. But what a pity it is that things didn't work out for everyone.'

'What things?'

I thought she meant the invalids. We had gone into the school-room and they were all sitting in their wheel chairs round the piano singing 'How Far Is It To Bethlehem?'. When they reached the line 'For All Weary Children, Mary Must Weep' they nodded carefully towards the Sister who sat at the piano giving them their beat. They nodded and sang as though they didn't think that Mary might be weeping for them any more than Verity Cruffts at Nanton Road School had done. The maximum assertion the children could make was to increase the volume of their sing-song and to make their accompanying gestures a shade more pronounced.

Then Pat, whose wheelchair I was in charge of, lowered his huge head slowly on to his shoulders and snapped his fingers slowly at me and called: 'Woman, come over here. Come and be my woman.' He grinned and made socking gestures at the statue of the Madonna on the mantlepiece and then at me. The Madonna seemed to smile back at him in pallid sympathy. I glared at Pat.

'Be my woman,' he said, 'and we'll live in a green creep and eat elderberry tarts.'

We sat round the fire with Cossey in the little guest parlour, with Gertrud and Ernst. 'Won't it be lovely,' Cossey sighed, 'when Thomasa's old enough to climb all these mountains of yours.'

She looked at the randomly-stacked invalid chairs outside. Sometimes a wheel would shift a little of its own accord like something trying to get back into the sun that had abandoned it.

'Won't it be lovely for Thomasa,' Cossey repeated. 'Oh dear, I shall miss you all when I get back to my airbase. Just rows of women. All just sitting by their radars! I've always hated women,' she exclaimed, staring at us in our long woollen skirts and cardigans. Our grandmother had recently died, and Cossey had posted most of her clothes on to us in a big parcel. 'I always hated women. They smell of stagnation and old clothes. I think that's why I hated Miss Lenege so.'

The visit ended in silence. Floy hardly spoke the whole time. Cossey said he wanted to be a priest and would soon be going to a special school for training up in the north.

Thomasa lay at attention in her pram. It was as though Cossey had shocked her to attention, and in fact kept all our thoughts focussed on her as she repeated: 'How I hate women. How I hate their smell.'

Christmas was over and Cossey and Floy had gone. The

mountains stood over us sheathed in snow, and we put on coats that hung all winter in rows in the damp stables where the chairs were kept. We shivered with the cold and turned down on to the path to Bwlch and into the icy mouth that had been suddenly opened. We gasped and held our breath and beat our tortured fingers against the handles of the chairs. We raced the invalids in their chairs down the side of the hill. Then it snowed more and we made snow pianos for them to play at while we danced, and they sat there beating their frozen hands and singing:

> Half-past three
> You and We,
> Sitting by the
> Icy sea.

We pushed them down to the place in the stream that was deep and green and had frozen over so that ghostly people seemed to live and move below.

Spring came and thaw. We made a port there and the shadowy people below went and the birds came back and started to sing, and we turned the pool into a naval station and launched ships there all the summer, by the stream that ran down to Bwlch, and Gertrud tied old bits of the Sisters' discarded habits on to the soles of our shoes and bees-waxed them so that we could shunt up and down the tiled convent floors, singing as we polished, chasing each other and pushing the invalids in their chairs and playing 'He' with them. We played by the stream all summer with Vivian's baby, and in the autumn we collected chestnuts and roasted them on a bonfire. Snow came early, fell suddenly, and we could hear the sounds of the village two miles away, the sounds of its forge; the chink of the hammer, the whoof of a blacksmith's bellows and the horses' stamping and breathing above the tinkle of his irons. We were not supposed to take the children near Bwlch, so we crept out at night and climbed the mountain behind the convent, and told Ernst Hoppe as he stood there next day in the red jersey that was too small for him, that we had been up there to find the Red Cross and that they had said they would come, and Ernst nodded and cried. Tears ran on to the inside of his wrists which he always held out at you as though it were just this small problem of his wet wrists that needed your attention. Then the bell would go and the Sisters digging below in the valley would raise themselves from their crops for the Angelus, and come slowly back to the convent holding their flapping hoods against the mountain winds. Snow fell again and we crept out at nights and brought it in bucketsfull for the children to plunge their feet and fingers in to scotch their raving chilblains, and they cried in relief as the hot burrowing worms were crushed, and sang out: 'Don't let it ever stop.'

After we had put them to bed, we would go upstairs to the box-room at the top of the house where the warm wall was, and where trunks and suitcases and raffia baskets and wicker boxes were stored. There was a violin on a shelf in a black wooden case, and a tailor's dummy and an old eiderdown and a tall circular typewriter and some Jewish plates and candles. Vivian would look at the piles of manuscript neatly tied together with pink ribbon and marked: 'For the attention of the Red Cross.' We looked at pages and pages of poetry written in script that Gertrud said was Gothic. We would sit there with her on a huge trunk, eating hot bread we had stolen from the bakery and hearing the Sisters sighing on the other side of the warm wall, and trying to keep warm. Vivian would write to Jim, and sometimes we would be caught and sent downstairs to sit by the playroom fire. It was blocked up with bricks for economy and a Sister with red eyebrows kept feeding the poor flame with potato peelings and wet tea-leaves to damp it down. It was spring, and someone threw a book at the smoking coal and a flame burst through but the Sister with red eyebrows came back with two pieces of cardboard and crushed the single lip of flame.

Frau Wallisch whom we would help to get dressed in the mornings in the private part of the convent was sitting with us. She taught us French and started, half-asleep, to drone: 'When you wish to say that an action was being done for a long time, you must use the imperfect . . . *Quand je chantais.*' She sat there in her black woollen dress: '*Quand je . . .*' Then the Rabbi came in and she laughed and half-bowed, sat there sweating and pressing her hands together. But when she tried to stand up to take his hand, she fell forward on to the settee and sat there beside her glasses, smiling at no one. With the Rabbi's help we carried her upstairs towards the forbidden room beyond ours. The kneeling frame was lifted back and we helped carry her inside the forbidden room with the warm wall.

There was a fire burning just where we pictured it would be, and, in a bed beside it, with a chair on its side for support, lay Miss Lenege from Ransome's Fields. She lay there smiling as though she wasn't at all surprised to see us here. We had sent her here after all. But she didn't seem accusing. She just told us she had been shipped to Australia with other alien internees, but the ship had been torpedoed and she had been several days in an open boat with frostbite and had never recovered the use of her legs. She would cough too, much more than she had done at Webbley Mansions, and lean over the flat counterpane and spit into a cup covered with a piece of folded newspaper.

We were ashamed of having thought so little of Miss Lenege since we left Ransome's Fields. We didn't know what to say to her except: 'Do you like it in Wales?' Or: 'How is your cough today?' We were afraid of saying anything that might remind her of us at Ransome's Fields. We looked at her thin white face and rosy cheeks. We were ashamed of having teased her. But we didn't know what to say to her now except, 'Do you like it in Wales?' or, 'Have you got everything you want?' It was as though we had done it.

We crept away in case Sister Thelia should find us in the forbidden part of the house. But we couldn't help thinking of Miss Lenege still up there at the top of the convent coughing and looking down on us as we wheeled the chairs down to the deep pool in the stream or raced them over the courtyard. Maybe other people were hidden away up there as well? The Lasts? The Rattrays, Gertrud and Ernst Hoppe's parents? And invalids too badly deformed to be brought downstairs to where we were playing guessing games with Sister Thelia. The convent's 'other' people seemed to be stowed away upstairs at the top of the house and looking down reproachfully.

'Does Cossey mean us to stay here for ever?' I asked Vivian. We decided to run away and stole bread and hid it in Thomasa's pram, and together with Ernst and Gertrud we crept out at night and walked in the dark down to Bwlch and the railway station to wait for the night train. But the village women saw us and rang the police and the Sisters told them that Vivian and Gertrud were 'Directed Labour' and we were brought back and spent a day in the gun room where the Sisters stored hoes and scythes and hip-baths and the decorations for their Easter Passion.

After that, Vivian and I often climbed up the mountainside behind the house. We scrambled over the scree and once found a disused quarry with workmen's abandoned tools still lying outside it rusting by their billy-cans. We sat down and Vivian tore at some bread she had stolen. Then we tried to go inside, but a great owl sailed heavily out and put us off.

'How *old* are the invalids?' I asked, staring at the abandoned tools.

For a moment it seemed that we might all be transferred up here to the quarry. I could see us all tucked away up here with Miss Lenege and Ernst and Gertrud Hoppe's parents and Pat and Clive, all of them sitting up here. All of them old and bearded. And Thomasa was here too, and even she was old and grey as she sat there with them chanting: 'How Far Is It to Bethlehem?'

'How *old* are the invalids?' I asked Vivian again, picturing us all as upstairs people sitting for ever up here singing while one of the Sisters conducted. All of us sitting here with such patience and duty over the candles they were lighting to set off into the dark with.

I tried to think of London and Webbley Mansions and Ransome's Fields, but I could only hear the tugs hooting and the trams whining and the wind banging monotonously on the abandoned billy-cans outside the quarry: 'Lie Low. Take cover. Try to be without corners or hopes or promises.' The upstairs people had an ageless monotony written across their wrinkled faces. The night would follow the day; the day follow night. But like clockwork. The seasons would switch on, then off, too, but not like the seasons we had known till now, sporadic, moody but with surprise. Now they would come with regularity like a door opened abruptly then shut; or a machine switched on, then off, and all of us with them. Tick-tock. Tick-tock, as the water dripped outside, and the wind knocked monotonously against the quarrymen's tools rocking them. Cossey seemed to be the only youthful, hopeful one. The only child among us, it seemed, as I pictured her dancing along with her bare legs and spiky dandelion coloured hair.

'I'll write and tell her about Miss L,' Vivian said judiciously as we clambered down the scree. But a mist had come down and we tripped and fell over dead sheep. I fell on the stomach of one and it burst open and I was covered in the bright green slime that ran out. My hands and face and grey lisle stockings seemed stuck together by this gaudy glue. We thought Sister Thelia would send us to the gun room again to spend the night, but she just smiled and said she had a surprise for us. We were to have a visitor. It was over a year since Cossey had been down and we planned to tell her about Miss Lenege.

'She'll feel so guilty that she'll have to let us all come home,' Vivian said. 'Ernst and Gertrud as well.'

Summer had come, and the stream leaped down the valley to Bwlch again. The Allies had invaded Europe and Dad had gone with them. He had never written to us at Bwlch except for an occasional postcard that said: 'Sweet daughters two, how do you do?' Or 'If you can't be good behave.' Now he had been parachuted into Holland, and Cossey had written that she was coming down to see us again, and that she had shot down two flying-bombs last night, and soon this wicked war would be over and give her special love to Thomasa.

She enclosed a stamp and a shampoo which we tried to divide into three as we rehearsed the accusations we were going to deliver when she came. The shampoo was a green powder in a sachet, and as we tried to divide it the wind blew it away, and our indignation seemed as hopeless.

Chapter XV

'Which would you rather have,' Vivian and I asked each other as we waited at the station for Cossey's train, 'which would you rather have, a Daisy Headache Powder or one of those turnips?'

We were far too early for the train so we had wandered round the empty streets of Bwlch and stood outside its one shop. Skeins of wool, muddy turnips, babies' pink bootees and burdock-and-dandelion wine were evenly spread across the sun-bleached paper of the shop window.

Vivian said it reminded her rather of Ransome's Fields, the way everything was just stuck there randomly round the shelves. The sun opened its eyes weakly on us. The stream had followed us from the convent right down the valley and the sound of its trickling had gradually become the sound of Cossey's train hissing round the bend. We stood there with the push-chair.

It had been a cruel winter again, but the snow had at last melted. A creaking sound had come one day from above us in the hills, like a signal for us Volunteers to break ranks. It was the sound of thaw. The stream was released, and curtseyed down into the deep blue pool.

The river was full, and then overflowing. It sounded as though a doorway into the woods had been opened, and into the mountains and the pale blue sky as the water rushed out and flooded the valley. We stood at the railway station feeling a wind from afar on our faces. We could smell the trees' young leaf and bark and the world's energy.

The train steamed in, but it was not our mother who came dancing out of the compartment with bare legs and yellow hair bouncing as she waved cheerfully: 'Hullo, lovies. Aren't you two lucky having this beautiful place to live in while we're battling away with Jerry in poor old London, having its guts torn out.'

Even if it had been her, Miss Lenege would have appeared there too, but the train moved out and Cousin Jim stood there on the platform, smiling slightly in the sun and putting his hand to the side of his face as though the sun were too strong. He was wearing an army uniform and when he came up and embraced us both, his tunic was rough on our cheeks. He dabbed awkwardly at his daughter's cheeks and poked her ribs and smiled. We could hear his train steaming away again down the valley. A church bell chimed once. The convent bell gave out one toll. A woman beating a carpet out in front of her cottage door stopped and smiled to see a man in uniform, and a woman raddling her step stopped and smiled as well.

Jim told us Cossey couldn't come. He'd come instead. Everyone went on smiling at us as they never smiled when we were here with the disabled children; the women standing by the milkman also seemed to understand and smile as they held their jugs up to the float, slung between the shafts of the pony's trap. They all seemed to have stopped still in the mild air as they watched Vivian and Jim and their baby. By the railway track a woman in a blue pinafore was plucking a goose over a kitchen chair. She too stopped to watch us as though we had brought something good with us like a charm to the valley. White feathers blew out round her and stuck in her hair and decorated the marigolds in her garden. Rain came bouncing down lightly on the new flashy green leaves. Everything danced up and down in the rhythm set by Jim and Thomasa jogging along ahead of us. Jim said he couldn't stay long. He only had forty-eight hours' leave. He was in the Royal Army Medical Corps and was being posted abroad now that Germany had been invaded.

We felt proud and important as we swung along together beside him. It was just a fit of the blues that Vivian and I had had up in the quarry. Now Jim was smiling at us both and at his daughter, and the village women gave us back smiles and flowers as we passed their gardens on our way back.

Sister Thelia had watched us coming up from the station with our cousin and beamed as though she didn't know the relationship were closer than that.

'Dr Allicot?' she smiled and consulted something written on her starched sleeve. 'Your mother said he might visit you. Perhaps you would like to take him out for a walk and show him our lovely mountains in which we take such great delight now that this lovely warm weather is about to break upon us grateful mortals.'

Jim grinned and imitated her with his lips as we pushed the pram down to the deep pool in the stream.

'Cossey wanted us to have higher education,' we told him. 'That's why she sent us here.' Jim nodded and grinned and nodded.

We paddled in the stream and Vivian with wet thighs laughed at Cossey's failures. We undressed Thomasa and tried to teach her to swim. When you lifted her up, she always held her legs and arms straight down as though she were preparing for soldiering, and she didn't give a murmur when we lowered her into the water that was always so cold. We all jumped in and splashed water at each other and tried to pick up coloured stones from the bottom of the pool but it was too deep and too cold, so we chased each other round the little beach of shingle to get warm again. I was almost as happy as Vivian that day. The war would soon be over, Jim seemed to be saying, and the convent gone. Jim gazed round him at the woods that clambered up the sides of the mountain, and the great oak trees and rhododendrons rocking in the slight mild wind. And one heavy buzzard hanging high over, like Jim waiting to take us.

'Have you got a dog?' he asked suddenly and we were puzzled. 'Would you like one, eh? What say you?' We laughed again and Vivian splashed water at him, embarrassed as he went on: 'Do you paint?' We stood still with surprise as he went on, turning to me: 'Do you like music?' He smiled and corrected himself: 'Do you *still* like music?'

'We wheel the chairs out and we sweep wet tea-leaves up off the carpet. We make the frozen lavatories work again and we peel the swedes. Cossey always was fond of war-work.' We all laughed. 'And we mix slag and water with potato peelings and drag it round to feed the fires in case they grow too big and enjoy themselves too much. It's a pity Cossey is such a great believer in freedom.'

Jim smiled, but he only replied: 'I've been in touch with your esteemed mother about Thomasa. Clothes and school fees and all the etceteras. It's very beautiful here.'

A swallow swooped over and we ran down the road to a mill and climbed a stile and were in some woods with the silence Jim had just given us shining like snow all round. This was a kinder place than Cossey had ever told us of. It had crept up stealthily and taken Vivian unawares. Jim had given it to us. The Welsh harpist was no longer anything to do with Cossey.

I left them alone together sitting by the water and wandered towards some meadows. Jim seemed shorter and stockier in his RAMC khaki. He sat there wrinkling his scalp and suddenly making his forehead seem huge and elastic under his thick black hair. His hands were long and thin and seemed to hang much too far down his body like rudders. His smile had that licked and concise look, as he sat there with Vivian, that same cat-look and smile that Cossey had loved six years ago when he sat by our fire at Webbley Mansions and told us about Clarice, and Cossey had threatened to fry her wedding dress, and we had wondered how it was possible for this slender and muslin-dressed woman doctor to cut off people's legs and demolish men with their own instruments of torture.

We walked on in a silence that shaped itself all round us from the peace we had. Our stream had other deep pools in it we discovered; other places where it paused and stopped and the only noise was a slight shudder from underneath. It grew another pool and then another. Jim seemed to be able to summon them up as we walked along the banks carrying Thomasa. Then the stream became a river, wide and deep, and kingfishers skimmed it with flashes of blue. It made a different sound now, almost a tread-tread, as it grew. Fish hung below in its heaviness and trees made a green twilight we were walking through, and a deep lulling sound came as though the war had never been. The silence and the twilight seemed to grow bigger and bigger, and the occasional click of the fishes was the only sound, and the click of Jim's lips.

It wasn't until we turned back at the end of the afternoon that the silence was broken. Jim had his daughter on his shoulders and he turned to us and asked rather awkwardly again whether we liked all the sheep and the cattle here after London. He gazed up at the mountains and said: 'I expect you have some scrambles and some scrapes.'

Again we were slightly puzzled. When we were at Webbley Mansions during the blitz he and Vivian went to Morley College and Russian films and we all three went to dances. Now he was asking us about sheep. Next day we went into Llangarrach, the nearest town. We'd never been there. Neither of us had been to the other side of the mountain that the convent leaned against. So we pushed our skivvies' cuffs and caps into our pockets and put coats over our green-and-white gingham uniforms and went back to the railway-station with him, and followed the river again, this time by train, and soon after the stream became a river we reached Llangarrach and had our photos taken, two sisters standing side-by-side laughing against a cardboard palm tree.

'We'll send it to Cossey,' Jim said as we sat in a tea-room above a baker's shop eating Chelsea buns.

Thomasa opened her mouth. It was round like a piece of tubing. Vivian put some bun into it, but it dropped out again as though she had not inserted it far enough, and Thomasa stared at us as though she were old again and in thick spectacles. Vivian made her do a little dance on the glass table top and knocked the milk jug off as she sang 'Run, Rabbit, Run'.

'Can you say "Dad"?' Vivian asked her. 'No, she says she doesn't want to.' She wiped her face on a piece of newspaper. 'Not until the war's over and we've got rid of here.'

'It's very lovely here,' Jim said.

'We ought to have had a photo taken of Thomasa too,' I said.

Thomasa stood there taking no offence. We went back to the

photographer's shop, but it was shut so Jim pretended to take a photo of her: 'Smile please,' as Vivian bounced her on a bench in the municipal park.

'I'm going to emigrate too,' I said. Jim laughed and we set off for the station. On our way up to the convent from the railway we passed the deserted mill where the Sisters had once baked their bread. It had the air of failure; its emptiness was not one that we liked so we walked quickly away. Its silence was like the silence of goings away.

When we got back to the convent gardens, Sister Thelia was clapping her hands together and crying, 'Beware. Beware the Danes,' so we seized the handles of the invalid chairs and pushed them away into the bushes where the 'Danes' couldn't find them. Jim stood there beside Pat in his wheelchair in the bushes, both of them hiding. Pat was playing with a shoe-scraper laid across his chair-arms. He lifted his huge head up and then dropped over it and let his heavy fingers rise and fall slowly between the scraper's rungs. 'The birds all sit along its bars,' he sang. 'The birds all have their separate residences. They have to sing before they fly away to Africa.'

'We're going to emigrate too,' said Vivian, 'so we'll probably meet you birds at the top left-hand corner of Australia, wondering what to do next.'

'Yes,' Jim laughed. 'That's right. We'll be off, all of us, down-under.' He grinned in the way Cossey loved. 'Down under.'

We thought this was a very amusing name for Australia, and laughed even more when Jim said: 'To the land where the birds fly backwards.'

We all laughed even louder and waited for him to say something more. Pat lifted his huge head up and laughed with a jerk. Jim had brought me a pair of cutting-out scissors and for Vivian a cape-thing that you put round your shoulders when you comb your hair so that loose hair and dandruff don't get on to your collar. Vivian put it on and the invalids laughed more. Jim had brought with him a sense of the unexpected, and we accepted the odd presents just as we had done the new blue pools he seemed to have created.

Pat made his birds sing again in the rungs of the shoe-scraper across his knees. Jim leaned over him and Pat smiled as he felt the rough cloth of his officer's jacket. Jim stroked the fingers that were the migrating birds. He leaned over and looked intently into Pat's face: 'What's the name of that bird? That end one? And the green one beside him? And the yellow one? . . .'

The invalids all held out their arms, and tried to grab at Jim. Some of them had never seen a man before. Pat was clinging on to Jim's epaulettes now. Jim didn't seem to want to stop talking about the birds in Pat's shoe-scraper. Vivian stood there, but Cousin Jim went on as though there were too much to say to Pat before the train came. He looked at his watch and then he looked for Thomasa. Vivian was up a tree in her cape. Her baby had gone. We all started looking for Thomasa. Perhaps she had hidden herself in the game of 'Danes'. I found her in the stables tied into one of the big invalid's chairs, hanging out of it. Cousin Jim hugged Vivian and then tried to hug his child. But Thomasa hung stiffly down and Pat made socking gestures with his fist at her from his wheel chair.

'Emigrate,' he chanted. 'Emigrate. Emi . . . grate.'

Jim laughed and looked away from his daughter. He gave Vivian and me a kiss on our foreheads.

'Keep your peckers up,' he laughed again, 'and this war will soon be over.' We walked in silence back to the station.

'Will you really emigrate to Africa?' I asked to break the silence.

'Rather,' said Jim in a keen voice. 'Only too gladly. What?' Then he clapped his hands together and cried: 'Beware the Danes.'

We saw him into his train and watched it disappear, waving till Jim's white handkerchief had gone. The train seemed like a tide that had gone out. But it would come back. It was just a fit of the blues we had had on the mountainside up by the quarry, when we thought that the seasons would just go on switching themselves off and on like a machine, up to two or three thousand. And hadn't Cossey had that same feeling of stuckness before she ran away from Ondels Grove? And from us?

Early in 1945, Miss Lenege died. We stood in the chapel while the Sisters sang her Requiem Mass. We prayed for the souls departed as her coffin came squeaking back from where it had been laid among flowers and lighted candles. The coffin was yellow and small – and almost oblong. Miss Lenege, it dawned on us, had lost both her legs from frostbite in the small boat on the November Atlantic. The coffin came squeaking down the tiles of the aisle on cheap tin wheels twisting this way and that, uncertain of their direction. We'd never associated Miss Lenege with such cheap furniture. The coffin seemed so wrong, as though we had given this finishing touch to her life.

She was buried in the Sisters' small graveyard down in the valley where the soil was deep enough for interments. She was laid in a corner a little apart from the Community graves with their rusty iron crosses. The invalids sat round her in their wheel chairs and we stood behind them holding the chair-handles as we sang:

> Days and Moments Quickly Flying
> Blend the Living and the Dead;
> Soon Our Bodies Will Be Lying
> Each Within its Narrow bed.

We decided not to say anything about the funeral to Cossey. The quarry was a thing of the past. We stood in the box-room at the top of the stairs in the warm forbidden part of the convent. We could see Miss Lenege's heavy trunk and books and spinning wheel stacked above us on shelves. They all seemed very still too, so dead and ended that we decided again that it would be pointless to say anything to Cossey if she did ever come again. We never went near the box-room now. The thought of Jim made us forget that box-room's stillness.

May came and the war was almost over. We pushed the wheel chairs out into the hot fields and among the poppies and loosestrife and picked great bunches of meadowsweet and snapdragon and decorated the chairs with them and made more great bunches that we took down to Bwlch singing:

> A May garland we've brought you.
> Before your doors we stand.
> It's only a bit but it smells very sweet
> And it comes from Our Lady's hand.

But this time, the village women scowled at Papists, and only gave us cotton reels. We pushed the invalids back past the places where Jim had made the deep green pools.

'Maybe Ernst and Gertrud Hoppe will come back to Ransome's Fields with us when this war is over,' I said as victory came nearer.

'Maybe,' Vivian replied doubtfully. She was looking for Thomasa. The child was always toddling off on her own now. 'Cossey's coming down again,' Vivian went on. 'So you can ask her.' Vivian went to look for her child. We had decided to forgive Cossey. After all, wasn't it just the war that had put us all here? Nothing more. We were not Pat or Paula or Clive or any of the children who sat in their wheelchairs with heavy fingers slowly trying to shell peas and calling laboriously: 'Someone. Anyone. My buttons. My crutch has fallen.'

The voices were not ours any more than the birds' voices were, or the Sisters chanting in the chapel: 'Behold from my youth upwards . . .' We didn't belong here any more than we belonged with the beach children at Apslet. The voices of the upstairs people had stopped.

Soon Cossey came dancing up the path that led to the convent and Floy was with her again smiling as though he had won a game. He was on holiday from his seminary school and wore a black suit with an Eton collar outside his jacket collar. He stared at Thomasa who was wearing a hat Jim had bought for her. It was too big for her and fell over her eyes, and in any case was made of fur which was too hot for summer.

'Fur,' Floy stared at her. 'My most unfavourite stuff. And anyway it says it's too hot.'

'*She*,' Vivian hissed at him. '*She*, please,' she shouted as he stood there as he used to do at Apslet House when we went upstairs to inspect the working-class scene. Floy stared at the children in wheelchairs.

'We only play "dear" games now? Eh?' He joggled Thomasa up and down. 'We only play "dear" games don't we? It's wet. Vivian take it. It's wet.'

Chapter XVI

—— · ——

'I shot down the last two buzz-bombs of the war,' Cossey told us proudly when we were settled in the little guest-room that looked out over the cobbled courtyard. 'And then a rocket got me. V2's we call them.' She looked out of the window. A tree tapped on it. The place was full of lightness and young leaves. 'Isn't this a marvellous place for Thomasa to grow up in? Among the leaves so green-oh. And soon this terrible war will be over-oh.'

Floy was standing outside talking to Clive in his chair. The two of them were tinkering with the wheelchairs and gazing at the invalids at the other side of the courtyard where the chapel was. The children were dipping bread into mugs of watery cocoa, and supping it up. Floy's face kept bobbing up and down besides Clive's chair. They were hunting for adders, they told us. But the two of them stopped whispering as soon as we leaned out or anyone came near. Then Floy would put on his Apslet voice and lean over Paula who sat in the middle of the courtyard by the pump, astride her big tricycle.

'Fee-fo-fy-fum. I smell the blood of an English woman,' he smiled at her and she laughed back shyly and tugged at her hair and spilt her cocoa. The rest of us went back to the table in the guest-room with Ernst and Gertrud Hoppe. Floy came back in, and then Sister Thelia with the slag to put on the fire.

Cossey turned to her: 'Won't it be lovely when this war is over?'

'It will indeed.'

'In London there's a rocket every half-hour or so, and I think nothing of getting the splinters of shrapnel out of my thighs and my behind every night when I get in. I take a needle and some scissors, but of course I can't reach . . .' Sister Thelia simply went on mending the fire, so Cossey went on: 'Still. I've grown used to it now. What's a bit of pain when one is defeating old Jerry? I hop down to the hospital standing on the tram because I daren't sit down till my Cousin Jim at Lambeth Hospital has whipped the splinters out for me on his couch. He lies me down . . .' Floy laughed but Sister Thelia just went on poking the fire. Then she turned and went. 'Oh dear,' said Cossey, 'I hope I haven't shocked her.' Floy laughed again.

'I expect,' Vivian said slowly and disdainfully, 'she was wondering why you never got any shrapnel or bits of rocket in your hands and feet. What a lot you would have missed if it had only fallen in your shoes or your handbag.'

Floy gave a braying laugh and came back in: 'You can do anything to a woman,' he said and Cossey laughed.

'That's right. We women are tough.' She spelt it out: 'T.U.F.'

'And I suppose,' Vivian went on, 'you got so many bits of rocket in your bottom that the chief surgeon at Lambeth Hospital had to come himself and help Cousin Jim hoik them all out.'

Cossey laughed again.

'Did I tell you? I've left my body after my death to Lambeth Hospital, to be cut up by the students, so that they can find out what made me the woman I am.'

Floy laughed again, another husky braying laugh, full of delight: 'You can do anything to a woman.'

'That's right. We are T.U.F.' said Cossey. 'Knock us down and we'll come bobbing up again for more. Isn't that right, Vivian?' Floy laughed in a way that made us feel they had had this conversation before. Many times.

'They can cut up my brain,' Cossey went on, 'and find out what it was that made me into a busy journalist with five children first landing all those aircraft safely, and then shooting down all those buzz-bombs.'

'And then,' said Vivian, widening her eyes, 'giving your children all that freedom. Thank goodness Lambeth Hospital will never be interested in *our* bodies. I don't suppose they contain nearly enough freedom and rebellion and . . .'

'We could offer them a little child,' Floy grinned.

I pictured Cossey still being dissected by medical students.

'Where's Dad now?' I asked.

'He's gone abroad. To Europe. I told you I'd given him his freedom, when I gave you yours.'

'You didn't leave Hitler much to do then, did you?' Vivian sneered. 'I'm surprised there's any freedom left over for anyone else.' She bit her lip. On her lap, Thomasa seemed to shake her head and stare at us as if to say in her elderly way: 'I have always been free so don't worry about me.' Vivian took her out to the courtyard and then came back in.

'Still, what a lovely life I've had,' Cossey kicked off her shoes. 'First being an emancipated woman in the Great War and standing on a soap-box demanding the vote. What a pity none of you took after me. A pity none of you have had the secret of happiness. A pity none of you ever heard the Welsh harpist.'

'How do you know we haven't?' we asked her.

She stared at us in our grandmother's grey knitted skirts and cardigans. When she had sent them to us she put a bar of chocolate in one of the pockets and a note saying 'Sweets for the sweet. Think of me when you eat.'

'Did you get the sweets?' she asked us.

We nodded: 'And we heard the Welsh harpist too.'

Cossey frowned: 'I don't think your kind of person,' she looked at us appraisingly, 'hears him. And any way, there's no Ondels Grove any more. No terrible secret streets round here that you want to fold up and throw away. You children have never had any challenges in your lives. Perhaps that's why you're so . . .' She paused.

'So what?' we pressed her.

'Well,' said Cossey, 'perhaps it's my fault. My fault all along.'

'*What* is your fault?'

Cossey shook her head. All she would say was: 'I apologize.'

'What for?' we asked, enraged. 'Exactly what for?'

Cossey didn't look apologetic; on the contrary, she looked angry. We decided to change the subject.

'Did you know that Miss Lenege was here?' Vivian asked abruptly.

'Oh dear,' Cossey laughed. 'I shall have to mind my p's and q's.' She put her hand over her mouth. 'I shall have to reform, won't I? What subject does she teach? German? Ach so. Wo ist die mouthen waschen brusche?' she imitated Miss Lenege. 'Und wo ist die Frauen whichen gobblen up alle dem fungishes in dem fields?'

I started to laugh but Vivian interrupted: 'She doesn't teach anything because she's dead. She was in bed upstairs and we weren't supposed to go into that part of the house. But I expect we could get permission to go down to the graveyard.'

'I'd better not get into any more trouble,' Cossey said. 'Let's be goodly now.' Cossey had just been told off by one of the Sisters for helping Paula peel potatoes in the kitchen. 'Safer not to meddle,' she said. 'I'm in the Sisters' bad books already. Poor Miss Lenege. We *did* rub her up the wrong way all the time. And she would insist on paying the rent and the school fees.'

'Why did you hate her so much? Why do you hate women so?'

Cossey was silent for a moment; then she sighed: 'It's true. I do dislike women. I hate our smell, and I hate the way we just accept everything. And I hated the way Miss Lenege used to cross Ransome's Fields every morning to the TB clinic at the other side as though she were setting the Fields in order. I hated her methodicalness and I hated the way she breathed out and I hated the smell of her . . . that awful sinister pink-and-white TB look. And her smile that was so superior and long-suffering. The same "God's will" smile that the Grippe family had in Ondels Grove. Miss Lenege was dragging us back to Victorian England. But I didn't mean to send her away for good. Dad and I both knew she wasn't a spy and that she was only translating some German stuff. A leaflet about the Stations of the Cross. Or something.'

Cossey stopped, then went on: 'In any case, Miss Lenege would have had to go even if I hadn't spoken to the police. It was the war. The . . . what was it? The police explained to us . . . The 18B regulations. I'm sorry she's dead. But I can't say more than that. It's always as though I'm several storeys up. Higher up even than Webbley Mansions. I'm in a balloon attached by just one thread and I'm seeing poor Miss Lenege and poor everyone else from right up here. You'll never reform me because I can see that there might not be anything down there at all except the thud of cold mud and the cold plod of silence forever. Not even winds of ash or bits of clinker and quicklime.' Cossey paused again. 'Nothing much matters. Very few things do.'

We looked at Gertrud and Ernst Hoppe who were with us that day in the guest-room. We waited for them to adjudicate.

'I was always having to remind my mother,' Cossey went on, staring at us in our granny clothes, 'that *sub specie aeternitatis* nothing matters all that much. Dad and I had run away on the *Percy Warrior* and she insisted on us doing the conventional thing and getting marrried. Fortunately those days are over when men and women had to get married just because she'd slipped up. Now, thank God, women are free. I had to point that out to Jim when he told me he was getting engaged . . .'

Vivian smiled. 'What did you have to tell him?'

'That we Gerbers aren't really marrying people.' Vivian opened her lips and looked puzzled. 'But perhaps,' Cossey looked at her sadly, 'my ideas didn't work. I take the entire blame.'

Again we were enraged and shouted: 'What for?'

Cossey was silent. Floy went back out again into the courtyard where Clive was sitting. They were mending the wheels of the chairs. A wheel had come off one of them on a steep mountain path and the Sisters were angry.

'Show scars,' we could hear Floy outside as he leaned over Clive's chair. 'Try and open mine if you can.'

'Marriage is the oldest bondage in the world,' Cossey sighed. 'I had to tell Jim that.' A great storm blew between us and when it had died down Cossey was saying: 'I suppose what it *is* is that you children never had any shadows in your lives. Never any great challenges that there were in mine. No Ondels Grove. That's why . . .'

'Why *what?*' we begged her, but Cossey just looked mysteriously beyond her and we couldn't decide whether Vivian's crime was to be pleased about Jim and Thomasa or to be ashamed.

'That's why,' Cossey went on dreamily, 'I had to tell him . . .'

'Tell him what?'

'Jim and I were just good friends,' Cossey said firmly. 'We always agreed he'd do best by marrying another doctor. Doctors usually marry other doctors,' Cossey was patiently explaining. 'So keep your pecker up. It'll be lovely for Thomasa growing up among all these beautiful mountains.'

'She's not my child,' Vivian said quietly but firmly. 'That's why she stares so and never talks. And looks so wary.'

'Whose child is she then?' Cossey laughed. 'Give me three guesses.'

'Floy got full marks for boydom down on the beach road, so he should know.'

'I see,' said Cossey, still as though Vivian were being amusing. 'Or maybe after the war we'll rent one of those big houses on the other side of Ransome's Fields. And Alma,' she turned to me, 'you'll be able to have piano lessons again.' Cossey was still smiling and we still weren't sure whether she was blaming or congratulating Vivian for her child.

There was another silence, then another storm stood between us again and Cossey seemed to shout over it: 'The wedding is to be in August. Isn't it exciting?'

'Whose wedding?'

'Didn't he tell you? Cousin Jim? He's marrying Clarice as soon as she's qualified. He told me he had been down to tell you all about it. So what went wrong?'

The storm between us was too big for us to hope that any reply would reach Cossey. She sat there grinning and swinging Thomasa's shoes up and down between her bare feet.

Finally when the storm had died down Vivian put a few words together like a jig-saw: 'Jim . . . getting . . . married . . . to Clarice?'

Cossey nodded. 'Isn't it exciting? Clarice,' she repeated. 'And I hated her so much at Webbley Mansions and wanted to cut up her wedding dress and fry it. Ransome's Fields . . .'

But Ransome's Fields seemed suddenly like a leg that has gone to sleep. Cossey stared at our dull faces, then at our rough hands. 'I admit it was my fault. My ideas were all wrong . . . wanting to give my children their freedom when they were really too young for it. I should have been the conventional mother and done my dreary duty and not let you run wild and run your own lives and learn by experience . . . So, Viv, you mustn't for one moment think it's your fault.'

Another great storm stood between us. Then there was silence – just a gong ringing which became the high whine of the trams running past Webbley Mansions, and the Air Raid Warden's bark: 'Put out that light.'

'You've never had to be afraid,' Cossey was saying sadly, 'so what went wrong?' Vivian seemed to be in a cage. She opened her mouth but nothing came.

Cossey hugged us and said goodbye. 'The world will soon be free now. Where's Thomasa? Well, say goodbye to her from both of us.'

But after Cossey and Floy had gone, we realized Thomasa had been away for most of the day. Vivian thought she was out with the Sisters on the terraces helping them weed. But she wasn't out there and she wasn't in the courtyard. We searched the gardens and rushed down to the stream that limped into the deep blue pool. The Sisters came out of chapel and joined in the search. It turned out that none of them had seen the child all day.

The children in the wheel chairs joined the search calling like flocks of birds: 'Thomasa. Thomasa. Come back.' Then Vivian disappeared too and I set off up the mountain to the disused quarry where we had once pictured all the upstairs people, but she wasn't there.

We found Vivian at last making peppermint fudge with dried milk in a secret corner of the kitchen.

'Where's Thomasa?' we asked her.

'She didn't want to miss her train,' Vivian replied, smiling slightly and shaping the white blobs daintily into fudge lumps. 'So I'm making her some assorted sweets for the journey. Sweets for the sweet. Think of me when you eat.'

Vivian's eyes were bright and I went back to the quarry calling, and Vivian came after me calling too, then saying: 'Shhhhh.' She put her finger to her lips when we reached the place where the quarrymen had abandoned their tools. 'You mustn't disturb their tools. There might be a bad scene.'

I ran inside calling, but the owl flew out and Vivian called me back: 'Don't for goodness' sake disturb them. This is the palace for when they are old and dishevelled and too heavy for normal every-day duty.'

I was frightened of Vivian's grin as she repeated: 'Don't disturb them in their picture-palace.' I was afraid of her sudden radiance. We clambered down the hillside together slipping on the scree and colliding. When we got back, the Sisters had organized a search party and we set off again up the mountain with a few of the local shepherds and with torches.

Vivian was still smiling when we came back several hours later. They kept asking her again and again where Thomasa was, and she kept crossing her fingers and saying: 'Fains not it.' Then: 'She was far older than any of us all along.' She kept singing it out: 'They only stored her away with me as their deputy.' Vivian kept singing this out to the police too when they came. Thomasa had had to be stored away like the invalids and Miss Lenege.

When Vivian had repeated 'stored away' for about the twentieth time, I went up to the box-room with the warm wall where we often met and where Vivian had written to Jim as we tore at stolen bread with Gertrud Hoppe on cold nights, among the stored-away possessions of the refugees. The heavy leather trunk still stood there in reproachful silence along with the other redundant things and a pile of Miss Lenege's poems and translations tied up in pink ribbon and noted in one of the Sisters' neat handwriting: 'For the attention of the Red Cross.'

I tried the lid of the trunk but it was locked. The key was still in the lock though and I turned it and lifted the lid. Thomasa lay inside curled up on her face. All I could see at first in the dark room was the tartan of her kilt that had been pushed over her head.

The Sisters came running up to their part of the house. Men weren't allowed into the consecrated part, they hinted as the police followed them.

'The child must have come up here on her own. The wall was always so warm.'

She must have climbed into the trunk and let the lid fall on her. The Sisters spent so much time in the chapel and out in the gardens digging that they had not noticed Thomasa climbing their secret stairs. We had lost the child so many times before and had gone round the gardens calling: 'Thomasa, where are you?' And she would call back: 'I'm not Thomasa.'

'What are you then?'

'I'm a something else. I'm me.'

Or the Sisters would find her upstairs in the forbidden part of the house and shoo her gently down to the yard where the invalids were threading cotton-reels as part of their war-work.

'Was the trunk locked?' they asked me again and again. 'Did you have to turn the key to open it?'

'Oh no,' I lied again and again. 'It wasn't locked. I just lifted the lid up.'

Vivian had a satisfied smile on her face. She was suffering from shock, they all suggested, but she just shook her head and said it was normal practice among women who were T.U.F.

'And anyway,' she went on slightly petulantly, 'she was always touching my things. As I see it,' she said with a laugh, 'she's been fingering the Sisters' toys and things and thinks a finger lingers. So it was perfectly above board and proper. And now please may I go and restore order up there? You know the stuff is all above board and correct. Corr-ect,' she nodded. She was careful over her syllables. 'We had to give her back her freedom,' she laughed. 'Poor old ladies.'

The police came again and again and asked me whether I was sure the key to the trunk hadn't been turned and I lied again and again and repeated: 'I just lifted the lid.'

I started following Vivian everywhere, afraid she might give herself away by a slip of the tongue. I lied again and again till the hand I had unlocked the trunk with seemed huge and separate like a ventriloquist's dummy that might suddenly throb out of its own accord: 'Someone locked the trunk with the child inside.' It was as though a sword had been hung over our heads by one thread that might snap at any moment unless I stood there. Vivian was taken away to hospital. She was suffering from the terrible shock, we were told.

Chapter XVII

——— . ———

They took Vivian away and I stayed behind at the convent helping with the children, and on my free afternoons, I used to take the train down the valley to Pentre where the hospital was.

The admission ward was a low brick building like a factory with nissen huts all round it marked 'No Refuse Here', 'Please Sign for Admission', and 'Condemned Garments Only'. By the 'Condemned Garments' there was a patch of grass Vivian called the 'Condemned Garden' or the Mount of Olives.

It was a little court surrounded by a high wall and had a tree at one end. Visitors would cross it on their way to the wards and iron bedsteads were stacked here and clocking-on machines, rows of lockers, and the dustbins where people shuffled and delved.

We visitors would queue up in front of a stout woman in a faded tartan dress who was selling threepenny tickets for cups of tea. Then we queued again outside Bluebell Ward till the clock had struck two. Some of the visitors would start to grumble: 'It's all the way from Pandy I've come and if I miss the three o'clock bus, there's no knowing . . . no knowing . . .', the voices would echo down the corridor.

Then suddenly the huge woman in the tartan dress would pull away the chair where she had been sitting and allow us to walk into the ward. They were such broken people, the visitors, all sitting side-by-side, then leaning against the sides of the iron beds, whispering and rummaging furtively in bags and spreading out the newspapers they had brought over the beds, then all of them staring in silence down the ward to the ticking clock. They seemed such pale and beaten people, and their eyes seemed glued open like the eyes of the fishes in the aquarium on the windowsill.

Some of the visitors had been coming here for years, they told me, to sit in a silence broken only by the ticking of the clock, the rustle of paper bags, or a chair being dragged over the board floors, and the low whispers: 'Mrs Dai Evans has made you the dry-pudding again, Vanbach, she was asking . . .' The voices would trail away and then come again like a feeble tide trying to get up a stony beach: 'Is it the dry-pudding you'll have then? Shall I put it in your locker?'

Vivian never seemed particularly surprised to see me, and sometimes she would wander off to the wash-stands at the end of the room as I sat there and wash her hair. Sometimes she was sitting by the window smiling and talking about the state of the birds as though she would soon be off on a shooting party. Once she was immaculately dressed in white except for the bloody sanitary towel hung round her neck as a final decorative touch.

'This is the condemned garden,' she said to Cossey who was visiting her this particular day.

Cossey laughed at the gesture and said: 'Lovey, you must try not to feel so guilty. I take the entire blame. You weren't old enough to be given what I gave you. I should have left well alone and played the conventional mother and brought you all up without any fun or laughter. Then there'd be no condemned garden.'

It was then that Vivian tied the sanitary towel round her mother's mouth like a gag.

Cossey was heartbroken since the death of Thomasa, but Vivian never said anything about her child except: 'You have as many children as you want. I have it on the highest authority and I won't be gainsaid even in a rainstead. So don't tell me what authority to work from.'

They put Vivian in a special ward with blackouts at the windows and gave her insulin injections which sent her into a coma every day for months. She grew very fat and hairy and went round giggling with a bottle of glucose water tied round her neck. She still said nothing about Thomasa except: 'The Lord giveth and the Lord taketh a holiday. And anyway, how can anything beginning with a TH, or any capital-letter come out – O.U.T. – of a milk bottle?'

After about a year, when she still denied the child was hers, she was moved up to a huge ward, three storeys up. It was an oblong room with an aquarium in the middle, and rows of seats round the walls where women sat and smoked and dropped ash on the board floors, or gazed at the goldfish in the tank in the middle, or sat on each other's knees and masturbated. The ward had diamond-paned windows like a cottage and I pictured thatched roofs and beehives and spinning wheels. For smocks, the women all wore the identical faded tartan dresses that Madge wore, and smelt of piss and retex.

Vivian sat there alone by a photograph of herself: 'What did I say?' she would smile vaguely, 'we were always meant to live at the tops of mountains and such like advances and adversions and mansions, with or without the boot black.'

'I've brought you some sweets.' I put them in Vivian's locker and the huge woman patient who sold the tea-tickets at the ward doors heaved herself up and down the ward dishing out the food and checking everything that went in and out of the lockers. She would watch me give things to Vivian and then take half of them away. Muzak seeped from a green box in the wall and Madge kicked it on and off at intervals with a huge ladle.

An elderly lady with a cracked but aristocratic voice struggled down the ward plunging her greasy hands into a linen shoulder-bag and pulling out scraps of stale greasy meat to feed her cats and calling them: 'Come Emma. Come Fifi. Come my lovely ones.' The sour smell of dustbins and stale dripping encased her and she clapped her greasy hands together, wiped her rouged cheeks and cried: 'Yesterday was my mother's birthday.' She stroked Vivian's hair, 'and the week before we brought her a beautiful pink nightdress and a red ribbon for her lovely golden hair. Do you remember how the doctor brought his students to see her beautiful body at rest? She's very beautiful, my mother is. Doctor, I'm in a running-away mood.'

'If you don't behave and serve out these teas,' Madge shouted at Vivian and me, 'they'll put you on a ward where they're not half so nice to you. Do you want them to have another go at you?'

But sometimes Madge herself had bad attacks and screamed down the ward for her money and clothes till they gave her electric shocks. Then there was no food on Bluebell Ward, and when Madge had recovered she stared at Vivian: 'Are they going to do you too? Your turn next, eh? You all have to have it in the end. To rub the corners off. They don't want the corners on you.' The patients all gazed at Vivian. 'They had me last time,' Madge went on: 'What I haven't done for England. So now it's your turn.' She pointed at Vivian with her soup ladle. A smell of sweat and onions, soup and loose skin came down the ward. And the smell of confinement and vaginal discharge.

Vivian had grown very thin now. Her nose was always red and snubbed and you could see the sockets her eyes were fixed in. She didn't eat, and she breathed through her mouth all the time. Her mouth was always open as though the flesh around it had retreated so far that it could no longer hold together her teeth and jaws, and lips. Her speech was slurred, and her eyes smiled at me, the only thing that still reminded me of her as she said: 'I'm Janet from another planet. So don't rub me in.'

The nurses would put coloured rubber tubes down her nostrils till they jabbed at her stomach and she cried out and water poured from her eyes. They fed her raw egg and glucose. But as soon as the tubes were out, she would vomit it all up: 'Here goes. In the throes. First time lucky one. Lucky winner.'

'If they done me once,' Madge stared at Vivian, then went through her locker, 'they've done me a thousand times, and if you don't behave, Vivy Vi, they'll have a go at you.'

She used to stand in front of Vivian leaning on her ladle and staring at her, then calling to the man who came to wind the ward clocks, a small white-faced man in crumpled trousers whose big nose seemed soft in his putty face, and whose eyes were different sizes.

'I can remember,' he would smile slowly, 'when the patients were given electric shocks till their eyes rolled up.' He smiled at Vivian. 'Then the doctor's knife went in and under. Got them under the eyelids, they did then, and when they came out of the operating theatre there was two lovely black eyes for you and no more noise, eh Madge? And when the relatives come they says: "Have you been in a quarrel with the doctors and the nurses, eh? To get them two eyes? You need a nice piece of raw meat on those two."'

The clock-winder stared at Vivian and went on: 'They cried something when they told them they got to have it done, but afterwards they just sits there and squits in a dump hugging their p's and q's in their heads.'

Madge and the clock-winder would both stare at Vivian but she would only laugh: 'There's someone here whose name doesn't begin with a G and she's the keeper of the cupboard with the key, key, key. There should be a convent with a box-room for disposables on every ward,' Vivian went on. 'And a crib. The only crib in the world. I asked the Father to come and bless my rosary, but he said "Come back on Tuesday" and I have my doubts about Tuesdays because someone keeps praying for me at three in the mornings and I wish they wouldn't. Will you tell them from me just to cut it right out? Right out!' she repeated in a shout. 'What was it that held Webbley Mansions up above Ransome's Fields? Was it you? And what holds this place up, this condemned garden that has no giraffes even, or the water-thingy, or the gas-thingy, I'd like to know? And in the interests of all I'd like to know how in fact does Bluebell stay up now that they've taken my suspender belt away? They said I got it all wrong about T. Or is it TH she prefers? The TH thing? They did say, but dash it all, who wants to be involved in a bigamy suit these days? So I must take all the blame. Shame eh?'

That was the closest I ever got to Vivian then, in her condemned garden.

'They come down the ward with clippers,' the clock-winder would nod. 'And they shaved them first. All over they did,' he smiled excitedly, 'and they put them in white night-caps to show they was to be done. Then the Justice in Lunacy,' he would drop his voice, 'he had that little tobacconist and sweet shop down the road, and he come in his little car and says: "Do you come from this part of the world? And are you quite happy here?" No, they didn't know, even then, what they was in for.' The clock-winder would smile slightly and touch his head and look at Vivian. 'There'll be no more "condemned garden" when they've had her. Because there's no more nonsense from any of them after. And I've been winding clocks here fifty years, so I've seen the lot.'

'What are they going to do to Vivian?' I asked in alarm.

Vivian had been certified so her consent was no longer needed for any treatment the doctors thought was necessary. But Cossey had been consulted and she said more cheerfully than she had for a long time: 'It's all right. The surgeon is just going to balance her up. It was all my mistake all along, I must confess to you all. I tried to give you all the freedom I never had when I was your age. But that was just *my* big mistake . . . To think you weren't just rather ordinary children like that pedestrian little girl at Apslet House who was so keen on film-stars and all that kind of stuff.'

Cossey gazed out of the high-up windows: 'What a lovely view you've got here. I can see right over to Bwlch almost. What a fine time you must have in these grounds.' We could see a line of patients clinging to each other like the gassed in the First World War being led blindly across a battlefield.

'Do you play tennis?' Cossey asked. 'And go swimming? And climb those huge trees? The trees remind me of Ransome's Fields and how I used to go out with bare feet at night and hug them. It was so lovely at Webbley Mansions after the two rooms we had at the top of that house in Baston Square that always smelt of pickles. I never wanted you to have the awful shadows that there were in my childhood . . . the shadows of people just going on and on till they stepped into the river of death. I thought . . . but I apologize . . .'

She paused and Vivian interrupted her, chanting: 'There might have been nothing at all, but instead there are six of me with six birds and six brains but only one to be dealt with *this* time. Four or six times a week according to the weather.'

'Soon I shall be getting a persecution complex,' Cossey protested with a laugh, 'if you go on like this. But the world was meant to be such a beautiful place, so now,' Cossey suddenly sounded triumphant, 'I shall just have to treat you all like rather humdrum people. Like those children at Nanton Road School and that little sparrow, Carole, was that her name? The one Floy was so fond of and taught to paint in that funny art gallery you ran, and used to take for nature walks down the beach road. I don't suppose there was much nature down on the beach road. It was all pebbles and shingle and sea-peas . . . How lovely it would be to be back at Apslet House. Only Dad never liked it there. He said it wasn't the place for the hoi polloi.

'That's why I want you to have the op, Vivian. So that there'll be no more about the "condemned garden". Instead you'll think of Ransome's Fields and come back to us again, and we'll be the rather unusual people we were in London. When we went to Mass at St Anne's that first Sunday, they all said: "Who are those interesting looking children?" And Father Piggot said: "Those are the Gerbers from Ransome's Fields" . . .

'That's why I want you to have the op, Vivian. So that you'll see the world in the cheerful way you used to when we sat round the fire on winter evenings telling each other stories . . . Happiness is so important. So they're just going to tidy you up a bit. Neaten up a bit of the grey matter in your top storey, and ease away a few of the difficult corners in your upstairs. Isn't it lovely up here in this upstairs part of the hospital? You've got such lovely views. You can almost see the mountains at Bwlch . . .'

'Why can't they just leave her alone?' I protested.

'It's a new and revolutionary form of treatment,' Cossey explained. 'Vivian, you'll be helping to pioneer a new world.'

Madge stood there watching us and winking at Vivian: 'You and I together,' she sang, then 'Tip-Toe Through the Tulips with me.'

'Why can't they just leave her alone?' I cried again.

'Vivian was never a happy child,' Cossey explained. 'She was always questioning everything and always arguing. Even as a child she was nervy and edgy and worrying. We sent her away to Wales to see what good fresh air and practical work would do for her. But she was still a hostile young person. So now I want her to have the benefits of modern science and modern surgery so that she'll have the more normal kinds of happiness that young people should.'

It seemed as though we were on a ship that was drifting further and further away from the shore where Cossey stood, or rather where the real world and Ransome's Fields were. I seemed to call, and shout even, but the wind took my voice and an even greater space settled itself between us and our mother. Cossey seemed much further away than Vivian did, and I tried bringing jig-saw puzzles that Vivian could do to prove she was all right; I tried making up poems for her to finish to show too that there was nothing wrong. I brought a big piece of cloth and tried to get her to stitch it with me, one at each side, to prove . . .

But Cossey and the doctor seemed not to notice as I sat there asking Vivian what she had done today, and was it nice in the sunshine. Instead Madge stood at the end of the ward with her huge soup-ladle, nodding and counting the minutes, and counting the patients and their visitors, till the clock's hands could move round to three and she could lift the big hand-bell that stood beside her and ring it to evacuate the ward.

'Time, ladies,' she shouted to sever us. 'Out you scram. And Buster and Mrs Keating and all the rest of the rag-bag of trouble lawyers. Time now.' She watched Cossey and me leaving the ward.

'They really are going to balance Vivian up,' Cossey said to me with excitement in her eyes. 'I've seen her doctor and we hit it off so well. Marvellously, as I knew we should. I wonder why it is that all Vivian's friends and yours are women, and all mine are men.'

I tried writing to Dad in Germany, but he only replied in his archaic way: 'Children all, great and small, never argue with your parents.'

It was the kind of day people die on, the day Vivian was carried away to the Cardiff hospital for neuro-surgery. After they had washed her and shaved her on Bluebell Ward, the psychologist came to test her intelligence and personality, assessing her with ticks and crosses put in boxes down his long sheet. Before the ambulance came though, she ran naked and shaved down the ward singing: 'Too Bad for You – I Love Another.' Then they gave her an injection and she lay low and didn't resist any more. All that day the sun barely lifted itself from the horizon and then at three or so the clouds closed over the day with big eyelids as if in fear or guilt.

So Vivian was leucotomized as a lot of women were then in 1947, and Cossey at last had her revenge on her sex.

Vivian was much gentler to Cossey when she came back from Cardiff and surgery. She was less reticent too, with the other patients on the ward, and would call down the rows of beds, standing there in her white cap to keep her naked head warm and snug: 'I've got the trots, doc. Got the trots and a v. sore trot bot.'

'Viv dear,' Cossey called as she stood at the top of the flight of stairs up to the ward. She had rung the ward bell and Madge had let her in with a laugh. Cossey looked down the ranks of beds, side-by-side and end-to-end, then at last she saw Vivian by her locker rearranging photographs of herself on its top and on the wall behind.

'Come and see my pin-ups,' she called to us. 'There's a whole world here.' There was a picture of herself naked: 'But it isn't good enough,' she declared. 'The clock-winder came yesterday and he said he wanted several of me. A dozen pin-ups, in my birthday suit, so watch out, all of you. Look sharp. Here we come.'

Cossey sat down by the locker with her cup of tea. Madge was still hovering and asking: 'Vivy, when you had the knife, when they did you, which doctor was it you had? The little dark one with the devil eyes? He got me where it hurt. It's a man's world, eh?'

Vivian laughed, a real guffaw, and Cossey said quickly: 'How lovely it is, Vivian, that you've come back to us at last.' Vivian gave another guffaw.

'They got me where it hurts most,' she pointed at her forehead. 'Do you want to see my scars certificate?' She held up a piece of paper. 'This is to certify that Vivian Gerber Murder has had three pounds of grey matter removed from her well-head and is now ready for a bloke.'

Madge guffawed as well. They were companions now.

'You devil,' Madge said in a deep voice, 'now we know what you got up to when they did you.'

'Well, at least you're real again,' Cossey interrupted, giving Vivian a kiss. Vivian stood up and saluted, then linked arms with Madge and they marched up and down the ward chanting and kissing the world at large:

> Hey there Mister
> You better mind your sister . . .

'Oh you baddy,' Cossey tried to laugh.

Vivian went on: 'Got anything for me? You and I,' she pointed at Cossey, 'need lots of little goodies.' She rummaged in Cossey's bag: 'You and me, we boxed and coxed together, didn't we? With Cousin Jim, eh? You and me, we both coxed with the same oke bloke. No end. And then the Angel of the Lord brought the baby to Vivy, but like the Virgin Mary's little one, it wasn't for keeps. They nailed her to a rhubarb tree.'

It wasn't for a long time that it dawned on Cossey that the new Vivian was here for good. The doctors kept saying: 'Give her time. We'll soon get her resocialized again.' I wanted to cry at the word 'resocialize her'. It sounded as though it had nothing to do with going back to Ransome's Fields.

At first Cossey would stare at her daughter as though it was within Vivian's power to take off the mask and fancy dress and hug her mother and say: 'Tomorrow we're opening a School of Translectic Art. So hurry up! Connoisseurs may be arriving at any moment. Come on Alma and Floy. Come on Samey and Carole. Or shall we all see if we can get to the end of the road without touching the ground?'

But Cossey left Pentre Hospital without Vivian and sadly. She went back to Ransome's Fields to wait in vain for Vivian and Dad to come back. She had to remind herself that her grandchild would never play as her children had played around the green bandstand, in the middle of Ransome's Fields.

Chapter XVIII

The war ended and the seasons turned themselves on and off at Bwlch as we had thought they might when we discovered the quarry in the mountainside. The months went by like blank pages of paper coming out of a machine as the children's voices called: 'Someone, my crutch.' Or: 'Someone, my buttons.'

I used to dream I was looking through a huge telephone directory for Jim's wife, but every entry said simply: 'Dial here tomorrow.'

But tomorrow clicked on and off like a light switch: 'Someone, I've finished.' Or: 'Someone, my pencil's dropped.'

Or sometimes it seemed as though it was more like a lift going up and down and the only future for us was to be up or down.

I would go down the valley at Christmas to see Vivian at the hospital on her long-stay upstairs ward. The ward decorations would flap as the patients yawned, and the ward's Babe of Bethlehem would hang sketchily beside its Santa Claus and Wizard of Oz.

The nurses would put tinsel in their hair, and one of them dressed Vivian up as the Star over the stable. Or there was a party in the big reception room and the Matron was shaking hands with the long queue of patients that shuffled forward to receive a pink parcel if they were female or a blue one if they were men. Vivian got a jar of Nivea Creme and dipped her fingers in it and ate and dipped and licked till the nurse told her to put it on her face, and she sat there all afternoon in a white mask like Coco the Clown, among the paper bows and crepe bells and dirty cotton wool sheep that had been launched along the windowsills.

'The history of my feet,' Vivian would laugh as she watched

the decorations' rhythmic flapping on the walls. 'The history of my feet is likewise: Born in a cabin in Idaho and came to fruition in Ransome's Deals. Feet say yes, but other members say no advance in progress. Feet say stop all relocomotion.'

The patients would shift restlessly and unmoor the baby's crib from the wall, and dirty stardust would fall like dandruff on their shoulders. The recreation hall smelt of warm beef and over-boiled sprouts, fart and gardenia, and the chief male nurse would adjust the loudspeaker as a torn Father Christmas on his sledge was hauled backwards over his head and a terrible scream came from the loudspeaker as he called down the room: 'Hullo. Can you hear me? Now ladies and gentlemen, take your partners for the Paul Jones.'

Cossey would stare with huge dead eyes as her daughter repeated: 'The history of my feet is likewise . . . Madge, how many feet are there in the Salvation Army? And how many inches?' Vivian would gaze out of the window and giggle: 'Do you remember how I used to go on so about the "Condemned Garden"? What a drip I must have been then. I mustn't let my past catch up on me, eh Madge?'

'Take your partners for an excuse-me waltz,' the voice came through the loudspeaker attached to the wall.

Madge would light a cigarette and let Vivian have a puff: 'Who's my little pin-up, eh?'

'I didn't know it would be like this,' Cossey would repeat, staring at her daughter. 'Vivian, would you like to go back to Bwlch? Or would you like to come home to Ransome's Fields?'

Then, after Christmas, winter would be cut off and spring stuck there, and then summer instead, like a label, and I went down the valley again for the annual fancy-dress fete at the hospital, and heard the patients rehearsing their songs in the occupational therapy ward: 'And if *one* green bottle,' they sang, emphasizing the word 'one' and nodding their heads attentively at 'should accidentally *fall*' . . . A policeman took his trousers off and Bette Davis scratched her armpit and Winston Churchill blew up balloons till they burst and made the girl standing next to him in the chorus burst into tears. But the song went on relentlessly: 'There'd be *three* green bottles . . .'

This seemed the nearest they got to defining the future. Then the patients began to trail round the gardens dragging their fancy-dress behind them. Bette Davis was pulling at a bit of loose skin on her heel and three girls with sharks' fins and scales were watching a youth feeding punched cards into an old steam organ so that 'Down The Mall' changed to 'I Know That My Redeemer Liveth', and the papier-mâché girls on the organ's panelled side sprang to life and saluted and rattled their tambourines and jerked their star-spangled thighs up and down.

The aristocratic old lady with the rouged cheeks and greasy hands wearing a huge cardboard beak nose stared at them: 'Today's my mother's wedding day and the doctors all say they've never seen such a beautiful body.'

A nun in a black habit turned to the clock-winder dressed as the Loch Ness Monster and shouted angrily tucking into a plate of cream horns: 'Shoo. This garden is private. It's my own personal recreation ground. So please go away. Shoo,' she cried again as the patients began to move into a long straggling queue waiting for the signal to begin to celebrate. The royal princesses were there, and the Queen and Gypsy Lee and Hitler putting fudge into his mouth and a girl with orange hair and orange fur mittens having a nose-bleed beside Vivian as they stood waiting for the toffee-apple stall to open up.

Vivian dipped her fingers into the boiling hot toffee and burnt her hands and mouth, and a male nurse holding a bear's head under his arm was saying again and again to the girl with the orange hair: 'If you'd learn to conform, you'd get well.' And the girl replied: 'I'd rather take cyanide than become like her.'

She pointed at Vivian in a man's cap licking her burnt fingers. Vivian had a cigarette stuck at right angles to the middle of her mouth and kept calling again and again in a thick voice like a man's: 'A penny for the guy.'

She took to plodding round with an old colonel who was always pushing a bath-chair full of empty medicine bottles round the grounds. Vivian would light a cigarette and call out hoarsely again: 'Penny for the guy. Penny for the rag-tag guy.'

She had grown very heavy and was always eating. The nurses

tried to restrict her to a carrot an hour – sweets were still rationed – but Vivian would go to other people's lockers and steal biscuits, and sat in the lavatory tearing at them, or at bread and dripping she had dipped in the sugar bowl. Then she would wait behind the trees for the old colonel and his wheel-chair full of medicine bottles: 'Captain Borstall,' she would call over, 'want a fag? Me and you should join forces, you know.'

Sometimes when I went to see her she was playing cards and would look up for long enough to say: 'He was a wild card. Was Jim. Was Jim a wild card. A wild one. As ever was.'

Cossey started going to Mass every day because Vivian had been forbidden to go. When the priest at the altar in one of the hospital's sitting rooms read in the liturgy, 'And drink His most precious blood', Vivian would cry: 'If His blood is so precious then it should be sent to the Blood Transfusion Service. Someone might be glad of it.' And when the consecration bell rang, she would continue: 'Grubs up, ladies and gents, and no fighting for the heavenly food and no bitching about second helps.' It seemed as though she and Cossey were quits now.

Floy came down once to see his leucotomized sister and she showed him the picture gallery of pin-ups round her locker in the ward and suddenly said to him: 'Do you still take the little ones for sixpenny Fitzbootle rides down the beach road?'

Floy laughed and shook his head as though he didn't understand. He had an almost satisfied look on his face now that they had 'done' Vivian and put the woman back in the place where she was safe. Soon after this, Vivian was allowed out on extended leave and I met her and took her back to Bwlch.

Sometimes Cossey came down and said in a new and toneless way: 'I didn't know they could do this to anyone. I didn't know they would use her as a guinea-pig.'

'Early days yet,' the doctors would say. 'She may eventually socialize.'

'Socialize?' asked Cossey as though she didn't understand, or the doctor had used some obscure medical term.

So Vivian came back to Bwlch and sat with Paula peeling vegetables in the kitchens, and eating them raw and laughing as slippery wet potatoes shot out of their numbed fingers. The seasons clicked on and off, and the deep blue pool in the stream disappeared and reappeared lower down, but Vivian only giggled at the thought of Cousin Jim and said: 'I don't want all and sundry to go getting morbid and sorting out my baddy-baddy days.' Floy went on staring with his satisfied expression and moved over to where Clive was sitting playing chess.

I was playing the piano for the children to sing to and Floy and Clive were still playing board games at the other end of the playroom. They were whispering together as they played, then pausing and whispering more. I could hear Floy telling Clive about Miss Lenege, and Webbley Mansions and her love of fungi and carved heavy furniture. 'You should see it all in the box-room upstairs. Up there. It's creepy. Wizardly creepy.'

I wondered how Floy knew what was in the box-room with the warm wall. Males weren't allowed up in to that secret part of the house.

'How do you know about all her things up there?' I asked him.

He shrugged: 'I don't. I'm just imagining all those carved chairs and things all being stacked upside down. And anyway,' he added defensively, 'Clive and I were down at the stream the whole of that afternoon.'

'What afternoon?' I asked.

I stared at him in silence. Even the police hadn't been able to establish the exact time of day Thomasa had climbed into the old trunk. Vivian had left her child with the other children for all of that day as she was busy in the kitchens. I stared at Floy: 'I suppose it was only "dear" games you played with Thomasa,' I said.

Floy curled his lip and shrugged and went away. Miles away on one of the hillsides a bonfire was burning. It seemed such a melancholy place for a bonfire. After that, Floy went away to do his National Service. Dad had been posted to Germany. Vivian spent more and more of her time in the convent kitchens. She wasn't allowed near the children now.

One day when I was over eighteen, the Reverend Mother summoned me to her office. I put on a black lace veil to go to her room in the secret consecrated part of the house, at the end of a long whitewashed corridor with grids set into the green tiles. At the end was a room with a huge crucifix on the wall and rows of bookshelves. The Reverend Mother had only been a shadowy figure to us children, a shape behind a screen at the end of the refectory at meals, and a clear voice that called grace down the long room: 'The eyes of all them do wait upon thee.'

And we would chant back: 'For thou givest them their meat in due season.'

Now she sat there, a big woman with big shoulders and hips and tiny hot hands that clasped mine together. Her face was massive and white, so white you could barely see where the skin of her chin met the white of her starched white wimple. And her face was so huge, and spread out so far in each direction that it seemed to leave her eyes and nose and mouth in a small whirlpool in the middle of a waste. You waited to hear breathing and were surprised when she spoke in such a dainty voice.

'How long is it now that you have been with us, Alma?'

'Since 1941. Nearly eight years.'

'And you had a terrible trouble . . .', she looked at me questioningly, 'but you managed with God's grace to develop great strength through your loss? And Vivian? In time she too will be happy again with the help of God's healers. I can see you have been praying and trying to find a meaning in what happened to your small niece here. There was sin in us all . . . and neglect. We Sisters too were negligent. But good usually comes out of such misfortune and sin. Have you ever thought that all of this might have been "meant"? Meant by God. His way of telling you that He wants you to do His special work? You must have asked yourself what God has been doing . . . I mean about all our sick children here, and poor distressed Vivian. Has it ever occurred to you that you might have a vocation? For the religious life as it is followed here?'

'Vivian used to want to be one of the Little Sisters of Ara Coeli. In London,' I said as though this were enough.

'Ah yes. Quite so. And she will be able to follow our life in part. In a way modified to suit her weaknesses and her strengths.

She'll be able to share in some of our offices and perhaps be able to give us such good help with the little ones again later. But you? What about you?' She smiled and her starched wimple shifted: 'God has given you such gifts.'

'I used to want to play the piano,' I gulped to control the choking in my throat.

'That too is a great gift,' the Mother Superior nodded, 'even if it is rather a subsidiary gift compared with the direct call to know and love Christ Himself.' She took my hands gently and shook them both and swung them up and down several times. 'Mmmmm?' she looked at me enquiringly. 'Think it over. All our thoughts will be with you as they were in your troubles.'

So the Sisters thought that it was sanctity that kept me here and not just anxiety that Vivian would spill the beans about the locked-up trunk. I saw that there was no need to chaperone her. Or lie. In any case, now no one was ever likely to take Vivian seriously again in her life, now that she wandered round, huge and forlorn, looking for sweets she might have hidden behind statues, stealing bread from the kitchens, sitting forever in the refectory waiting for meals, or flipping through magazines for pin-ups.

Now nothing cheered Cossey up, not the mention of Ondels Grove or the Welsh harpist; not the mention of Cousin Jim or the *Percy Warrior* or the reminder of the time she had helped Miss Lenege conceal the stolen blouse. Instead we all kept thinking of Vivian as a child, pulling at her plaits and inventing new games; how she would make us get home from school feet-off-ground; how she would organize theatres on the park seats or hospitals on our fire escape; or the secret blindfold walks she would take us on, or the stories she would make up about the fare-stages printed down bus and tram tickets to places like Elmers End . . . Hilly Fields . . . or Shepherd's Bush. Or the time she tried to reform Cossey by making her wear granny clothes and eat her dinner with a pair of tweezers to show that Cossey wasn't always the nicest. Or we would think of Vivian at Apslet and her gallery of modern art.

But then we thought of the big Tudor house where we had

'interrogated' Carole Last; we thought of the beach boys and the beach road and Floy's secret walks down there to the sea at the end and the tide breaking its big lips at us as it crashed through the barbed wire, and Carole danced excitedly at the thought of real live film-stars. Then we thought of Paula at Bwlch as she sat on her high tricycle while Floy put tinsel in her greying hair and I called out: 'Would you love to be a fairy-oh, on a Christmas tree, Paula-oh?' I would widen my eyes, and perhaps it was because I felt almost as guilty that I never told Cossey about Floy's visit to the box-room at Bwlch with the warm wall. Or perhaps it was because it seemed normal that women should bear the guilt.

Cossey's stories back at Ransome's Fields when we were young seemed to confirm the fact that women were destined to be the victims and that they could only survive if they acquiesced, and were only free if they moved in the direction that everything else was going in. So when I thought of Floy asking Thomasa if she would like to see chocolate soldiers upstairs, and chocolate bees, I said nothing, and only wondered if my destiny too would be to live in an upstairs somewhere, saying nothing, doing nothing.

Cossey tried to cheer us up though. 'After all,' she would say, 'there might not have been anything at all, so we should be grateful that there is at least a world, even though . . .' But then she would see Gertrud and Ernst who were staying with us now, and become silent and subdued, as though they were the only two people who were entitled to declare the world was a lovely place. Cossey would look at them appealingly, waiting for their verdict.

Sometimes she would try to be her old self and when we spilt something or the potatoes boiled over or someone sneezed over the supper table, she would try again to cry: 'Not very *comme il faut*. Not very *faut*. Do you like *faut* people, Gertrud? I can't bear them. They have wobbly voices at Mass and they smell of talcum powder and stewed veal.' Or Cossey would write funny postcards purporting to come from Joss, our youngest sister who had been evacuated to Scotland with Samey, and had stayed there in her billet. 'How many hours are there in a mountain?', the cards would run. Or 'The eagles here have cross and scrawny faces.'

Gertrud would pretend to laugh, but the rest of us were silent. Even Cossey didn't laugh now at her stale jokes. It seemed that in silencing Vivian, she had silenced herself, and her cheerfulness became hard and repetitive and she would add in a complaining voice: 'I tried hard to make you children see that life could be fun. So what went wrong? What did go wrong?' she would ask again later. 'If only I could get you to see how accidental the world is, and how there might have been only stoats and newts and red flies with spikey feet and bad-tempered eyes . . . Or there might have been nothing at all, not even tape-worms. But instead, look! There is all of us living ten fathoms up a red brick chimney wondering whether the lemon-curd is going to set or whether Mrs Blackfeet knows that her shoes match the red geraniums in the garden of Number 37.'

But we didn't laugh now, and Cossey would go on monotonously as the sea: 'Just think of us all moored here by one thread and wondering what to have for lunch or lying in a hammock reading leaflets about the Resurrection . . .' But we were still silent and Ernst and Gertrud were there with their straight smiles that they put on and took off again at nights when they were alone and waiting to hear from the Red Cross. We all saw now that they were the only ones who could pass a verdict on happiness or tell us where the line was that separated what matters from what does not. But they were always silent about that.

Once on a walk we passed Baston Square and heard the tube trains rattling past Nanton Road School.

'Poor Verity,' Cossey reminded us of the Cruffts and Verity who had died. 'Verity never expected much, did she? She thought her dry scrubbing and her wet were quite normal. And when her father hit her about it. At least Vivian . . .', then Cossey stopped and went on: 'At least Dad is doing what he wants out in Germany.' She tried to sound more cheerful but tears choked her.

It was a grey winter's day with its teeth clenched as we walked round the wintry park with ducks frozen into the dirty lace of ice on its little geometric brown pond. It felt like Vivian's

'Condemned Garden'. Cossey would try to treat me as an adult and ask me, as though I were an authority on music or disabled children or Wales: 'Alma is it true that the longest place name in Wales . . . Alma is it true that most children with infantile paralysis . . .? Or perhaps Floy will come home again and take Vivian out and get her back into circulation with his Army friends. But Floy is so funny now. Ever since Vivian was ill. He has such a funny smile now. And he and I used to be such good friends and have such fun together. But now he seems to boycott us all. Perhaps he's working very hard for Sandhurst and is going to give us a big surprise.'

Spring came and green hung from the roofs and green velvet swags and drapes ran along the old walls and Ransome's Fields was full of bright haemorrhages, and the stars were soft. We stared at them at night and it seemed strange to think that they were the same stars that we had seen at Baston Square ten or twelve years before, and that they had hung as faithfully over Germany and stricken Russia, stars untouched by war, not smashed, nor yielded, not having to retreat one jot from the awful banquet they had witnessed.

Then summer came and the streets were hushed as though someone majestic were up there, and Cossey kept saying: 'We'll take Vivian to a specialist.' The Lido had opened again now that the war was over and the women in green council costumes and caps were climbing up to the diving board again and jumping off, then climbing again. Cossey went sadly on: 'I always thought it would be like that. The swimmers diving down then coming up again for more. I always thought life should be like that, and that we'd all come back for more. We'll take Vivian to a specialist, and she'll learn to dance and paint and weave. There's a marvellous place I've heard of . . . And you Alma,' she turned to me, 'you'll go to a marvellous music school I've heard of and become famous. I could have been famous. I could have gone anywhere and done anything and married a . . .'

I was working now in a little glass cage in the front of a shop in High Holborn mending ladders in women's nylon stockings. It was close work and hurt my eyes but I knew that as long as I stuck to something like this I'd never be able to show my husband and family the Houses of Parliament or the Albert Memorial and cry: 'Just look what I've made for you all. Aren't you lucky.' And I'd never be able to play beach games, either.

Cossey went on: 'I'll write to Cousin Jim in Australia and ask him if he knows of a very good specialist.'

We could see the patients crossing from the TB clinic, and we thought of Miss Lenege and Cossey said: 'I'm going to help Gertrud and Ernst with their fare to New York. But first we'll find a specialist for Viv. I'll write lots of stories and make some money first.'

Once a month Sister Thelia wrote from Bwlch to tell us Vivian was making good progress: 'Great strides indeed,' she would write. 'Last week we felt able to let her walk down to the village alone and obtain our weekly sweet ration for us, and she came home triumphantly and so proud that the bars of plain chocolate were all in order and quite intact! Next time we plan to entrust even larger purchases to her. Who knows? One day she may even be helping us with the children again . . .'

'We'll take her to a specialist,' Cossey would repeat.

Dad came once on a motor bike, but it broke down and he spent his whole visit in the hall, mending it, stooping over it and adjusting things with his back always to us. Then he banged a kiss on all our cheeks and gave us all a playful slap on our bottoms and went away again. He said he was still with the Army of Occupation on the Rhine.

Once though, Cossey said she was going to meet him somewhere for a meal, and put on her best green utility suit with the short wartime skirt. She said goodbye and went. But when I opened the front door of our flat an hour later to put an empty milk bottle out, I saw she was still standing there. She looked frightened and came back in, saying 'Oh. Oh dear,' as though I were a stranger. 'I'm looking for a specialist for my big girl.'

People were all talking about Hiroshima now, and Nagasaki, and it seemed now that we must all lie as close to the ground as possible lest we attract the notice of restless powers. And when Cossey said: 'If ever there were another war . . .', we only laughed ruefully. And when the trams' high whines came at night now, clanging out: 'Women beware!' and when the hooters on the foggy river went on at dawn: 'No good can come to you unless you lie low and make yourself as small and acquiescent as possible,' it didn't seem quite correct any more. Or rather, after Nagasaki and Hiroshima, it was not just us women who would have to lie so low and compliant. Perhaps it would be better if we all became like Vivian back there at Bwlch, walking down to the village once a month, entrusted with plain chocolate, then later being doled out bigger things to console her for what they had done. The message at dawn from the river seemed now to be for *all* of us.

'Take cover for ever,' it hooted out, 'among the good things we are creating to comfort you.'

We would wrap up parcels to send to Vivian and once one of them came back 'Return to Sender'. I often thought it might be everyone who would receive and unwrap gifts as though a whole population had to become upstairs people under the constant dry white stars.

Also by Jennifer Dawson

JUDASLAND

'This elegant and wicked comedy of Oxonian bad manners is a sort of *Porterhouse Blue* with the condoms banished ... a confident, well written novel, worth packing for your holiday reading'
– *Literary Review*

'A seething mass of poetic, hilarious and repellant images ... Dawson's unique blend of hilarity and doom, and the sheer originality of her vision, make this novel unforgettable'
– *Kate Saunders, Sunday Times*

'So individual a voice, the too-familiar Oxford frolics can never be quite the same again' – *Guardian*

Clare Bonnard is the 'treasure' of Sanctus Spiritus College, Oxford – amanuensis, sympathetic ear and laundress. But Clare's cosy sexless image is in reality a hedge against the terrors of emotions and sexuality. As the city prepares for its May Day celebrations, events in Judasland, the suburb where she lives, open an unexpected new world to Clare.

THE HA-HA

'I was struck dumb by it, so startlingly unusual, so original, so accomplished – the style disarmingly direct, the writing beautifully elegant and spare' – *Susan Hill, Good Housekeeping*

'Cool, clever, well-constructed . . . Miss Dawson writes very well indeed . . . *The Ha-Ha* has definite distinction'
– *Penelope Mortimer, Sunday Times*

'A remarkably talented first novel' – *Observer*

Josephine, clever, funny, solitary, with a tendency towards hysteria, is removed from Oxford college life when her private world of absurdity overcomes her public mask. Committed to a mental institution, she is carefully coaxed towards 'normal' life by a German refugee sister, gradually beginning to 'slip silently and secretly into the real world as though I had never been absent'. But everywhere are pitfalls for the sensitive Josephine. Her excursions among ordinary people continue to be painful until she encounters a fellow patient, Alasdair. They meet every day in the garden, by the ha-ha, and it is through Alasdair that she begins to discover the joys of human contact – and sex. But Josephine is still immeasurably fragile, and for her this new life can be even more perilous than the old . . .

Also of interest

BROKEN WORDS

Helen Hodgman

'Stylishly bizarre ... funny and poignant, a vivid evocation of the cruelty and beauty of life' – *Shena Mackay*

'It is all Tom Sharpe – or even Dean Swift – and it is loathsome. And fearless. And very funny' – *Evening Standard*

As the sun rises and sets on Clapham Common, Moss, her young son, and lover Hazel scrape by on the DHSS. Then Moss's ex-husband tips up and Buster and Beulah and baby (courtesy of the milkman's sperm donation). And finally, the Bogeyman with chipped junkie eyes.

Helen Hodgman lives in Australia. Virago also publishes *Blue Skies & Jack and Jill*: 'It's ferociously funny to the end. Immensely stimulating, like a small dose of strychnine' – *The Times*

other new paperback fiction

THE MIDDLEMAN AND OTHER STORIES
Bharati Mukherjee
CHARADES
Janette Turner Hospital
THE BEAN TREES and HOMELAND AND OTHER STORIES
Barbara Kingsolver
AND THEY DIDN'T DIE
Lauretta Ngcobo
A LITTLE RATTLE IN THE AIR
June Oldham
WOODPECKER POINT AND OTHER STORIES
Carmel Bird